By An Eldritch Sea

by
Carolee Joy

Published by Authorlink Press
An imprint of Authorlink
(http://www.authorlink.com)
3720 Millswood Dr.
Irving, Texas 75062, USA

First published by Authorlink Press
An imprint of Authorlink
First Printing, April 2000

Printed in the United States of America

ISBN 1 92870416 6

For Justin, Kirby and Russell

Your boundless energies and imaginations
continually amaze me.
I love you guys.

Author's Notes

This is a work of fiction. All the names, characters, organizations, and events portrayed in this book are either the product of the author's imagination or are used fictitiously for verisimilitude. Any other resemblance to any organization, event, or actual person, living or dead, is unintended and entirely coincidental.

The Orkney I was born into was a place
Where there was no great distinction between
the ordinary and the fabulous; the lives of
living men turned into legend.

Edwin Muir

Chapter One

You must never return to Orkney.

Haunted by her father's words, Kelsey MacKenzie stood on the rocky bluff overlooking the inn and shivered. Waves curled around the boulders in a rare display of deceptive calm. Twenty-five years ago her mother had died in the mystic waters of the North Sea far below. Tears stung her eyes, but she wiped them away and pulled her windbreaker closer.

Naturally, her father never wanted to visit the place where he'd loved and lost her mother, but that didn't mean she shouldn't. Here were the answers to the questions that had plagued her for most of her life. She'd find out how her mother had died. Maybe then she would understand why.

The distant glow of the midnight sun cast an eerie half-light over the sea and the privately chartered boat she had taken from Aberdeen to the remote island far off Scotland's northern coast. The schooner became a speck on the slate sea, then disappeared from sight.

Nearby sat Murdoch Castle Inn, a five-hundred-year old testimony to fifteenth century Norse glory and the only sign of habitation. Weariness enveloped her like a lead cloak. She should go inside, settle into her room, and get the rest her jet-lagged body craved, but the weathered stone building piled at the edge of the sea looked even more forbidding in the gray light than it had when she arrived.

Wind tangled through her hair and slid its cold fingers across her neck. Kelsey suppressed a shudder and picked her way down from the precipice to the beach, not bothering to hide her slight limp, worsened from the cold, damp air and fatigue. Here, as in the lab, no one would notice. No one would care.

Trying to shake off feelings of unease, she focused on her professional reason for being there. Doing post-doctoral research with several of the most renowned scientists in marine biology would make her father proud of her. Then whenever he deigned to visit her, he wouldn't find it as difficult to meet her eyes as he had the last time, as if the slight imperfection of her gait made it too painful for him to acknowledge her as Annabelle's daughter.

Emptiness and desolation surrounded her, stretching further than she could see. The wind whipped a froth along the surface ôf the ocean and sent a chill through her, but she lingered. In a few days she'd be accustomed to the solitude and the mid-summer night that never quite arrived. She'd be caught up in her work and wouldn't feel so strange and alone. So far from home and out of her depth, so full of grief for the mother she barely remembered. Perhaps she'd even feel a kinship to this land of sea and sky she and her mother had been born to. Maybe then the ominous feeling clinging to her like cobwebs would vanish.

The tang of fish hung in air heavy with moisture and the taste of salt. Ignoring her fatigue, she roamed the rocky beach, stepping over hunks of seaweed and crushed shells and nearly tripped over a dead seal sprawled among the gray boulders lining the shore. Her heartbeat quickened at finding her first specimen. She'd never seen a seal this color before. Its silvery coat was like the kiss of moonbeams on water.

She covered her nose against the fetid odor and bent to examine the animal. Poor creature. It must be a victim of the strange disease plaguing the sea mammals. She'd have to figure out a way to move it before scavengers or the tide claimed it if she wanted to do tissue samples. Crouching, Kelsey reached out to touch the shiny fur.

"Dqn't." A voice growled behind her, making the hair on the back of her neck rise.

Kelsey gasped and fell to her knees. From the shadow light a darker shape emerged. She stifled a cry of fear as the man cupped her elbow and pulled her to her feet.

"I said don't touch her."

His voice held only the faintest trace of a Scottish accent and something she couldn't quite place. Who was he and where had he come from? Shaggy silver-blond hair brushed the shirt collar visible under his fisherman knit sweater, black jeans defined powerful legs. But it was his eyes that held her, so gray they were the color of polished pewter. So piercing, Kelsey couldn't look away, couldn't shake the sense that he could see all the way to her soul. The man looked equally startled, and after several tense moments, she eased from his grip.

"You shouldn't be here."

Did he mean on the island or out on the beach at such a late hour? "I'm—"

"We all know who you are." His rich voice faltered, but his gaze never wavered.

Kelsey took a deep breath, wondering why she felt the need to explain herself when he was the intruder. "Then you know I'm with the research team. This seal may have been poisoned, but we'll need to do tests to determine the cause of death."

"No."

The soft vehemence in his voice sent a shiver of fear through her. Why was he interfering, and why was she overreacting? He was probably just a local fisherman, unhappy with the appearance of strangers on his island. "Don't worry. We won't do anything to spoil the fishing. We're here to—"

"I know why you're here." His voice cut through her like the icy wind that snapped the ties of her jacket against her jeans.

Kelsey stumbled back from his cold fury. She'd have to ignore him, no matter how intimidating he was. Although it was late, lights still shone from the inn. She'd recruit the other two scientists to help her remove the seal from the beach. The autopsy could wait until morning.

The man laid his hand on her shoulder, freezing her in place with his steely gaze. Although she flinched and wanted to move away from his overwhelming touch, she tingled from her shoulder to the tips of her toes, and her limbs refused to respond.

"You won't cut her. You won't tell the others. You'll find your answers another way."

Feeling as if she had the breath stolen from her, Kelsey squeezed her eyes shut to avoid the mesmerizing gaze and tried to block out the hypnotic sound of his voice. His presence surrounded her like fog, bewildering and overpowering. After several long moments, the pressure on her shoulder eased. She staggered, opened her eyes and watched the man walk away until his shadow merged with other twilight shapes further up the beach.

She bent to examine the seal, but it was gone.

Impossible. Could she have moved during her conversation with the stranger? Had he forced her away? But the only sensation she recalled was the warm pressure of his hand on her shoulder. No, she was certain she hadn't taken more than a step, maybe two. Searching the area yielded only rocks and seaweed.

Her head ached. Frustrated, she combed a wider area until the excruciating pain in her forehead felt like her brain was rubbing the inside of her skull. Her uneven stride worsened by fatigue and pain, she walked slowly to the inn, each step jarring the uncharacteristic migraine.

The other scientists had gathered in the large room overlooking the sea, but the undertone of voices barely pierced the headache. She couldn't deal with seeing anyone now. Shadows danced in the dim hall as she bypassed the great room and made her way up the staircase to the turret facing the sea.

Thoughts of the strange man receded as she searched her luggage for aspirin, then choked down several dry tablets. She never had headaches, it must be a reaction to the long trip. Exhausted, she sprawled across the white-painted brass bed, but sleep eluded her. His eyes. She'd never forget those eyes. They seemed to probe her each time a gust blew the lace curtains away from the window. She felt his hand on her shoulder when she rolled to her side.

Why had he called the seal her? The thought chased away her fatigue and bothered her long after the others at the inn had quieted. Finally, night sounds of sea birds mingled with the occasional bleating of sheep and played a counterpoint to the lonely wail of a seal until she finally slept.

The next morning, her headache reduced to a twinge, Kelsey joined the other scientists in the small facility her former professor had outfitted for their laboratory next to the inn. Marveling at the high-tech equipment Dr. Bracken had managed to acquire in such a remote place, Kelsey returned his friendly greeting with a warm smile.

"Ah, Kelsey. Welcome, welcome." His quick embrace was fatherly, his smile infectious as he made introductions. "My protege, Kelsey MacKenzie. Kelsey, meet Erik Norlund, from Fiskebackskil—Sweden."

"It's an honor. I've read your work." Somewhat awed, Kelsey shook hands with the other scientist. Kristeneberg, the oldest marine science institution in Sweden was purely a research center for established scientists, and Dr. Norlund was one of their most distinguished biologists. She glanced at Dr. Bracken. "I thought there would be four of us."

"So there are. Here's Dr. Douglas now." Dr. Bracken laid a hand on her shoulder as another man entered the room. "Kelsey, I'd like to introduce you to Cade Douglas. Cade's been at Dalhousie University in Nova Scotia, although he's a native to these islands. A welcome addition he is, too."

Kelsey choked on her coffee as the man from the beach

stepped forward. Feeling foolish for her hesitation, she clasped his extended hand, trying to suppress the shiver those strange silver eyes gave her. Words of recognition died in her throat at the almost imperceptible shake of his head and the silent appeal in his gaze.

"A pleasure, Miss MacKenzie." Giving no acknowledgment of meeting her the day before, Dr. Douglas lingeringly held her hand in his, and Kelsey shared his reluctance to let go although the warmth of his palm never reached his eyes.

"Please call me Kelsey," she said. If not for the pressure of his fingers, she would have thought she'd imagined last night, imagined him and chalked it up to jet lag and lack of sleep.

"You'll want to visit with Dr. Douglas, Kelsey. He knows every inch of these islands, and you did say you wanted a chance to discover all you could about your birthplace. He can tell you about every rock, every type of plant life, every creature. He's done some fascinating studies on seals." Dr. Bracken's expression became mischievous. "If anyone can tell you about the legendary selkies that fascinated your mother, it's he. Why I'd wager he could even find them."

What did myths have to do with her search for answers about her mother's death? When Dr. Douglas made no response, Kelsey turned to him for an explanation. "Selkies? I don't remember—"

Dr. Douglas laughed, but suppressed fury, evident in the darkening of his pewter eyes and the faint color staining his cheeks belied his short bark of amusement. "A child's fairy tale. Nothing more than a bit of Scottish folklore. I'm afraid Dr. Bracken has been here too long and is letting his imagination run wild."

Dr. Bracken chuckled and began an animated discussion with Dr. Norlund about the various species of seals inhabiting the islands from Orkney to Shetland and as far away as Iceland. Dr. Douglas eased her away, obviously determined to eliminate conversation about mythical creatures or the dead one she'd found last night.

As if he had any reason to worry, Kelsey thought grimly. Wanting to tell Dr. Bracken about the seal only after she had proof, she had returned to the beach earlier that morning and made an exhaustive search but again found only rocks and high water. The odd idea struck her the seal's disappearance had nothing to do with the tide.

His presence enveloped her while the others in the room became a mere murmur of voices, like wind settling in tall grass. She wanted to like him, wanted to establish a good working relationship with each of her colleagues and tamped down the flutter of uneasiness he gave her.

"I feel very fortunate to be called in on this project," she confided. "If Lana Reynolds hadn't left, I wouldn't be here."

His expression became assessing, as if he were examining her college transcript. "Really. Even though you're William Bouschour's daughter?"

Dismay flooded Kelsey at the mention of her famous oceanographer father. Dr. Bracken knew she preferred anonymity. How had Dr. Douglas found out? Did he think she was here on the basis of her father's credentials? Maybe that was why he'd said last night he knew who she was. She decided to ignore his remark. "Dr. Bracken was my professor at Texas A & M University. He assisted me in my dissertation."

"Then you must have known Lana rather well. Did Dr. Bracken tell you what happened?"

"No. Just that she left." Kelsey took a small step backwards from his compelling presence.

He shook his head. "Damned tragic."

She swallowed. "What do you mean?"

"I suppose he didn't want to alarm you. Amazing how superstitious scholars can be."

"Tell me what happened to Lana." When he didn't respond, Kelsey laid her hand on his arm and was instantly sorry. She jerked her fingers away as if from live current. She remembered Lana from graduate school, where they had both been students of Dr. Bracken's. Attractive and impetuous, Lana had been brilliant, but Kelsey wondered if perhaps the strange aura surrounding the islands hadn't compelled her to run off with a Nordic fisherman.

"The sea here is whimsical. Unforgiving to those unfamiliar with its ways. I was surprised he found a replacement so quickly."

She glanced over to where Dr. Bracken continued his conversation with Dr. Norlund and dropped her voice to a whisper. "I didn't tell him about last night, about you. But I think you should return the favor by telling me what happened."

His lips twisted in a grimace of sympathy. "I'm sorry, Miss MacKenzie. Dr. Bracken should have been the one to tell you. Lana is dead."

Chapter Two

Lana was dead. Too shocked to speak, Kelsey stared at Dr. Douglas for several moments, a thousand questions whirling in her mind. Why hadn't Dr. Bracken told her? A dark memory clouded her vision, but refused to take shape beyond a vague sense of remembered danger. What if—She pushed the thought away. Certainly Lana couldn't have died the way Kelsey's mother had.

Kelsey stifled a gasp when her former professor touched her arm. Casting a narrowed glance at Cade, Dr. Bracken led her away, all the while speaking soothingly. "I overheard. I hadn't wanted to upset you so soon after you arrived."

"You should have told me." Kelsey struggled to keep an even tone, recognizing that perhaps Dr. Bracken had been concerned she'd turn the project down if she had known.

"We can discuss it later. I'm going to have Erik bring you up to date. We've got a lot of work to do to catch up."

Kelsey ignored his brusqueness and managed a slight smile. Once the school teacher, always the teacher, and Dr. Bracken was noted for his total absorption in his work. He was also very well respected, pioneering several discoveries in the genetic properties of sea mammals. He could teach her many things that she could utilize when she returned to her regular position at the aquarium in Baltimore.

Blond and blue eyed, Erik Norlund was a polar bear of a man, his large hands incongruous with the delicate nature of his work. He politely reviewed the research to date.

"Whatever is creating havoc among the seal population doesn't seem to be affecting the fish, although the herring have all but disappeared from the islands. Obviously, that's a big problem for the fishermen here." His voice droned on.

Her senses tingling, Kelsey glanced over her shoulder, but Dr. Douglas quickly looked away. Silver-blond hair feathered across his forehead and brushed the collar of his shirt. He bent over his microscope, then glanced up. His eyes met hers, but the knowing look she expected wasn't there. Rather he looked perplexed, as if she should be analyzed, then cataloged, and he wasn't certain how.

A strange man, she decided, his detached air at odds with the intensity of his gaze, his awareness of everyone in the room. His awareness of her. Kelsey had the disconcerting feeling he knew every time she took a breath.

She pulled her attention back to Dr. Norlund, back to her microscope and back to the lab reports spread across the table.

Kelsey met Dr. Bracken for lunch in the small dining room of the inn. Ladder back chairs stood at oak tables covered with linen cloths. Sprigs of heather adorned pressed glass vases. From a table looking out over the water, she studied the sky. A line of black clouds swarmed above the horizon, promising a late afternoon storm.

Dr. Bracken sipped his tea. "I don't want you to feel you were second choice, Kelsey. Your qualifications are excellent, as were Lana's, but I felt you were settled better where you were. Lana was planning to take a position at the University of California when the project is over." He shook his head. "Such a waste."

Kelsey toyed with her biscuit. "How did—"

"Drowned." He leaned forward, his arms on the table. "Tragic really. But the sea can be capricious."

Dr. Douglas' words echoed in her mind. *The sea here is unforgiving.*

Dr. Bracken continued. "Lana didn't heed the most basic safety rule about swimming."

"Swimming!" Kelsey sat back. "But why would she even

consider it? The water's so cold. And the beaches aren't exactly inviting."

Dr. Bracken shrugged and spread his hands. "That was our Lana. Remember the scrapes she'd get into? I remember you found her quite exasperating sometimes. So did I." A fond smile crossed his face. "A free spirit. Nevertheless, she must have decided to go for an impromptu swim and got caught in an undertow. Her clothes washed ashore a few days before she did."

Kelsey stared at him for several moments in shocked silence. "How horrible." She shuddered. How like the Lana she remembered: outrageous, daring. But never foolish. Kelsey couldn't help wondering what had lured Lana into the water and stolen her life. Kelsey's mother had died in a similarly baffling drowning years ago although Kelsey's father had never offered details about what had happened. Not too surprising, since he'd apparently been so devastated by her death he hadn't even kept a picture of Annabelle.

Poor, poor Lana. The biscuit crumbled, dry and floury, in Kelsey's mouth. She pushed her plate away.

"I know it's a bit much to ask before you even get a chance to get settled in yourself, but I need you to box up Lana's personal things and arrange for shipping back to her parents in the States. What with the distance, no one was able to arrange to come here and do it themselves. And after all, you two were friends." Dr. Bracken smiled.

Strange how he remembered hers and Lana's friendship when he needed a favor, yet hadn't bothered to let her know himself that Lana had died. She wondered why he hadn't asked the housekeeper to handle it. "I'll take care of it, Dr. Bracken."

"Splendid." He began talking about the project, where they had been obtaining samples and the results of tests that had been completed. Kelsey focused on what he was saying, surprised he spoke at length about everything except Cade Douglas.

She squeezed lemon into her tea and added a bit of sugar. "What about Dr. Douglas?" She might have imagined it, but Dr. Bracken's eyes became calculating. He looked towards the sea and was silent for several moments.

"An interesting case himself. His grandfather owned a fishing fleet. Made enough to send Cade to the University in Canada. Other than that, he's lived in these islands all his life. You were born here which means you two have a great deal in common. I'd like to hear his opinions about the research you were doing with seals back in Baltimore."

Kelsey stirred her tea, unease settling in her stomach like a rock.

His eyes lit up. "I believe he even knows where to find the silver seals your father was at one time determined to verify, but never could." Excitement emanated from him, making his high forehead gleam with a faint sheen of perspiration.

Bracken's uncharacteristic zeal made her decide against telling him about the seal she thought she'd found the night before. She imagined him leaping up from the table and hustling everyone to the beach for a search of what she had decided was a figment of her imagination. She'd never heard of silver seals. She couldn't remember her father ever talking about them, either, although she'd read every article and book he'd published.

"Just think, Kelsey, you could be in on one of the greatest discoveries of this century." He leaned toward her and lowered his voice. "I meant it when I said Cade knows the sea here, I mean, really knows it. Not the textbook stuff you and I and the others are so fond of spouting. I believe it's in his blood."

A chill crawled over Kelsey's skin, though why Dr. Bracken's words felt ominous, she couldn't have said.

"Perhaps Cade would be agreeable to sharing some of his secrets with you. Talk to him, Kelsey," Dr. Bracken urged.

She wondered just what kind of secrets Dr. Bracken had in mind. "Yes, I'll have to do that." She planned to confer with him, eventually, but didn't share Dr. Bracken's apparent sense of urgency about it. In fact, the less contact she had with Dr. Cade Douglas, the easier it would be to ignore the foreboding she had about him.

Later that afternoon, Kelsey returned to her room to get her sweater. Although the storm she'd noticed brewing earlier hovered nearer, blotting out the late afternoon sun and casting a pall over the landscape, she needed to ease the kinks and eyestrain from hours spent working and the urge to explore the shore would not be denied.

Most of her clothes hung in the closet. The remainder she'd folded and put in the drawers of the huge mahogany armoire that took up most of one wall of the small bedroom. Her sweater was nowhere to be seen. Aggravated, Kelsey yanked out the drawers and dumped the contents on the bed.

She knew she'd packed it, but when she closed her eyes to visualize where she'd stored it, an image of Cade Douglas came to mind instead. Last night on the beach, Cade, gray eyes as stormy as the clouds rolling in from the west. Cade, his touch on her shoulder as charged as the lightning-streaked sky beyond her window.

Cade, wearing an ivory, fisherman knit sweater, just like hers. Maybe she'd left hers in the great room and Cade, believing it to be his, had picked it up by mistake. Or maybe someone else had. Thousands of sweaters just like the one she'd bought in Fair Isle were shipped to the States. Thousands more must be sold in the United Kingdom. Besides, although Cade wasn't much taller than her own 5'5", he was too broad of shoulder not to require a noticeably larger sweater. He'd have to be sleep walking not to notice the difference.

Kelsey lifted the edge of the lace curtain, watched the approaching storm and sighed. She thought of their morning conversation, the way his eyes didn't quite meet hers. Why couldn't he have told her Lana had drowned? *The sea here is unforgiving.*

She tried not to picture Lana's futile struggle against the currents and chill water, tried not to imagine her mother's shocking death. Perhaps this was why her father had refused to return to the islands after he'd whisked Kelsey away and lugged her from assignment to assignment until he'd found a housekeeper to dump her with while he traveled the world chasing personal fame. She wished she remembered more about her mother and about living in Orkney. Faint memories teased her mind, like pictures out of focus and dim with age, but all she could distinctly recall was her mother's soft voice and gentle touch.

She couldn't force it. If the memories were there, eventually she'd find them. If Cade Douglas had been involved in Lana's death, she'd find that out, too, if she was patient and observant. Suddenly, it was very important Cade be as mystified about Lana's death as Kelsey knew Dr. Bracken was.

Kelsey grabbed her windbreaker and left her room, hoping that the cool air outside would dispel the nagging suspicions and doubts crowding her mind that Cade knew more about Lana's death than he was willing to admit.

Cade dropped his pencil atop the stack of lab reports and stared out the window at Kelsey's slender form scrambling over the boulders that separated the rise of land the inn sat on from a narrow strip of sand leading to the ocean. Already the sea was exerting its magnetic pull on her, its mysterious beckoning.

Amidst all the other problems and risks he was taking, he'd have to watch her as well. She was too curious, too keenly intelligent, even more so than Lana had been.

And more beautiful, with her eyes the blue-gray of the North Sea. Hair darker than a shadow swirled around her shoulders in the stiff ocean breeze, then she disappeared behind the ▴barrier of rocks edging the shore. He felt a tightening in his chest and bent over his paperwork. No, he whispered to himself. She wasn't just a woman, she was William Bouschour's daughter. He couldn't afford the distraction. But Kelsey MacKenzie threatened his reason. With the smallest smile, the turn of her head, she enticed him in ways he did not understand. Too well, he remembered his grandfather's words. *It is forbidden.* Numbers blurred together on the page. He closed his eyes, but the breeze filtering through the curtains carried the imperceptible scent of perfume to his highly tuned senses. Kelsey's scent. Like sunshine on wildflowers. Summer breezes across the moors. The seductive fragrance of a woman. Cade threw down his pencil and strode from the room.

Kelsey stumbled backwards as she turned, taken off guard by Cade's sudden appearance beside her. Jagged threads of lightning streaked the sky, illuminating the tension on his face. He reached out, gripping her arm, saving her from landing on her backside.

"You shouldn't be here."

She tensed, apprehensive at his scowl, yet trying to understand the reason for his anger. "The storm is still quite a ways off."

He shook his head and the anger radiating from him dissipated. An odd look settled in his eyes. Still holding her, he reached up and touched her hair, letting the strands sift through his fingers. Kelsey drew in a breath, a wild thrill chasing up her spine.

"Like sable," he murmured. His gaze shifted to her mouth.

Her throat as dry as the sand, she wet her lips and took a step backward, shaking off his grip and an overwhelming desire to taste his kiss.

"You're right. We should go inside." What would Dr.

Bracken think if he saw her engaged in such unprofessional behavior? She'd be on the next ferry out, and her big chance would be lost. "Did you want me for something?" She winced inwardly at her choice of words, turned and began walking down the edge of the shore.

Cade fell in step beside her. "Dr. Bracken tells me you've done some interesting research back in Baltimore."

"Well, nothing like this." Her hand swept the air. "Still, I hated to leave it behind."

"Then perhaps you should go back." He gripped her arm again and turned her to face him. "This isn't the place for novices, Kelsey. There's much at stake here."

Outraged, she bit back a hasty retort. Nothing would be gained in further alienating this arrogant man. "I realize that." What was his problem? She narrowed her eyes. "My background is well-suited for the project. In fact, it's very similar to Lana Reynolds's."

Cade snorted. "Lana was a fool."

Kelsey shook her head. "Impulsive, maybe. But Lana never did anything without a reason." She rested her hands on her hips. "Do you know why she decided to take a swim, here, in this forbidding sea? Or is there more to the story?"

Cade's eyes revealed nothing but a miniature reflection of herself, frowning, hair storm-tossed. "There was an inquest. Why don't you inquire of the Constable? I'm sure he would be thrilled to have some American woman calling his investigation into question."

So that's what this was all about. Cade, despite his similar age and background, was nothing more than an old-fashioned chauvinist. "If my being here is such a problem for you, Dr. Douglas, then perhaps you should take it up with Dr. Bracken. Or do you let personal biases stand in the way of science?"

When he didn't answer, she turned her back on him and headed up the beach towards the inn, forcing herself to walk slowly and evenly. Icy drops of rain spattered her face and hair. Still feeling the imprint of his fingers on her arm, Kelsey zipped her jacket up and trudged across the boulders. Glancing up, she saw Dr. Bracken silhouetted in the window. She waved. He responded with a curt nod and turned away.

But not before she saw his lips curl upward in what looked to Kelsey like the smile of a very self-satisfied man.

Chapter Three

A few days later, Kelsey stood in the room Lana had used and surveyed the disorder. Dr. Bracken had told her to have Lana's belongings ready so he could take them to the mainland and arrange for shipping when he and Dr. Norlund left in the morning. She sighed. She didn't want to do this, but felt she had no choice. Better by her than a stranger, especially since Mrs. Devon, the housekeeper, had been adamant about not having time to handle the task herself.

Lana's room at the back of the castle faced the gentle slope of green hills and was more spacious, but Kelsey was glad she had a view of the sea instead. Something about the hillside, or the room, made her feel closed in, as if there were a shortage of air to breathe. She suppressed a shudder. Going through her friend's things, knowing Lana's life had ended all too abruptly reminded her too much of her mother's tragic death.

She started by emptying the contents of the burled oak armoire onto the bed, then carefully folded blouses, dresses and slacks before placing them in the sturdy cartons Mrs. Devon had provided. Clothes neatly packed, Kelsey turned her attention to Lana's cluttered desk. Apparently in the years since Kelsey had roomed with her, Lana hadn't picked up any organizational skills.

A small framed photo of her and Lana, decked out in wide brimmed hats and old fashioned clothes caught her eye. She sat and picked up the picture. They'd been at the fair and, on a lark, had gone to the old time photography booth and dressed in costumes. A lump rose in her throat. Poor Lana.

She set the picture aside and began sorting through the

piles of papers and notebooks littering the desktop. Her hair seemed to stand on end with the sudden awareness that she wasn't alone. Kelsey turned to find Dr. Norlund watching her, his large frame completely occupying the doorway.

"Find anything of interest?" His tone was friendly and conversational but somehow inappropriate.

She swept her hand towards the desk. "Just Lana's own unique system of filing."

Dr. Norlund chuckled. "Ah, yes. Order wasn't her strong suit." An odd spark lit his pale eyes but was gone as suddenly as it appeared. "Would you like some help?"

She would, but the thought of Dr. Norlund pawing through Lana's personal belongings made apprehension crawl across her skin. She pushed the feeling away. He was just being polite and had no intention of giving assistance. "I'm okay. It's just hard to think of her being gone."

"It is, at that. Well, happy hunting." He left, and she continued packing.

By late afternoon, Kelsey had emptied the drawers and placed what looked worth saving into the boxes. She bent to push the large file-sized drawer closed when it jammed. She pushed again, but the drawer refused to slide in.

Funny. It had been closed when she sat down. She got on her knees and wriggled the heavy drawer, then tried again. The drawer slid into place until it got to the last few inches, then bounced back out. Something must have fallen behind which, considering the haphazard way Lana had piled things, wasn't too surprising. She reached into the recess and groped around, finding nothing until her hand bumped something slick tucked on the side rail.

After much wriggling and tugging, Kelsey pulled out a worn soft-cover book. *William Bouschour's Underwater Adventures.* This was her book, one she'd loaned to Lana while they were in graduate school. No wonder she hadn't been able to find it. She opened the front cover, saw her name, then found the inscription her father had scrawled across the title page. "For Kelsey, with deep affection, W. R. Bouschour."

As always, her father's remote formality saddened her, so she focused on why Lana had stashed her book away. How odd. Why would she have hidden it?

The answer was that she wouldn't. It must have simply fallen out of one of the drawers and become wedged. She flipped through the book and found a crumpled sheet of stationery.

Curious, she unfolded it although she couldn't shake the sense of invading Lana's privacy until she saw the salutation and realized it was a letter Lana had started to her.

Dear Kelsey, I know it's been a while but I'll get right to the point. Don't come to Orkney. I overheard Dr. Bracken discussing adding to the staff and your name came up. Please believe me when I say it's not a matter of professional jealousy, although I still think you're a much better researcher than I am, but there are things going on here I don't understand.

Dr. Bracken is not the same kindly professor you and I both remember. As for the other two scientists, Norlund suffers from delusions of grandeur, says he's going to take the project away from Bracken—Over my dead body! Then there's Cade Douglas—just being in the same room with him makes my flesh creep. If I didn't know better, I'd think....

The letter ended, the last letters blurry, as if Lana had been interrupted. A chill spread through her. What did it mean? The bell for dinner resounded from downstairs and dispelled her dark thoughts. Kelsey smoothed out the crumpled letter, then refolded it. There was no date. She'd have to look at it again later and not let her imagination overrule logic.

She stuffed the paper in the pocket of her jeans. Why hadn't Lana finished and sent the letter? The question plagued her all through dinner.

Afterwards, Kelsey stood just outside the great hall,

stopping in mid-step when she heard her name mentioned. "You shouldn't have brought her here." Dr. Douglas' voice was intense, urgent. Dr. Bracken's well-modulated tones flowed around her with his response, but his words were indistinct. "Having to break in another person could set us back weeks. Weeks we don't have. She's a distraction to all of us." Cade's voice rose. Dr. Bracken chuckled, and Kelsey seized the moment to enter the room and put an end to the ridiculous discussion.

"Ah, Kelsey," Dr. Bracken stood and squeezed her shoulder. "Cade was just talking about you."

"Is that right?" Kelsey turned a calm face towards the Scottish scientist, although inwardly she was seething. What century had he stepped from, that he would rail about the idea of having a woman on the research team? Had he protested Lana's presence? Was that why she hadn't liked him?

From his chair opposite the stone fireplace dominating an entire wall, Cade rose and met her gaze. A muscle twitched at his jaw. Pewter eyes bored into her as if he could see every doubt, every question, every insecurity Kelsey had ever had.

"It's nothing personal. I was just telling Dr. Bracken how difficult it will be, bringing you up to date on what we've accomplished so far."

Kelsey raised an eyebrow. "Since you're not any closer to knowing what's harming the seals than when the project began, I don't see how you can say you don't need me. So far, you've made some interesting suggestions, but nothing's been corroborated."

She held out a folder. "Dr. Bracken asked me to bring copies of some of my published articles for you and Dr. Norlund. Maybe you'd like to take a look or perhaps you've already read them?"

Cade scowled but accepted the papers and set them on the

coffee table. "Research on animals in captivity hardly
equates with what goes on in the real world. Nature's
world."

Dr. Bracken rubbed his hands together. "I can see the two
of you have some issues to resolve. In the morning, I'm
taking Dr. Norlund to the mainland. I'm interviewing two
bright, young scientists we may want to add to the team.
We'll most likely be gone a couple of days." He clapped a
hand on Cade's shoulder. "I'm counting on you. Take Kelsey
over to a few of the other islands, perhaps Eday or the
Brough of Birsay. Maybe you'll get lucky and find where the
seals are gathering."

Then he turned to Kelsey. "Anything you need, just ask. If
we don't have it here, we can have it air-freighted in from
Glasgow." He said goodnight and left.

Kelsey and Cade remained standing, nearly eye to eye.
She shifted her weight uneasily. He wasn't much taller than
she. Maybe that's what made him bluster like a cornered
animal, made the breath he took sound ragged and angry. He
started to turn away so she laid a hand on his arm. "Dr.
Douglas—"

He jerked away as if her touch burned. "If you're going to
insist on working here, I think you should call me Cade."

She searched his face, hoping to find a glimmer of an
answer in his implacable expression. "Why are you so
determined to run me off?"

"We need to be totally focused here. You have other
things on your mind."

Heat stole up her face. She couldn't deny what he said,
but the layers of implications in his words stripped away her
pretense at cool indifference. Why did this man, with his
hostile attitude, make her so aware of him?

Because she did the same thing to him. The answer came
as if he had spoken and Kelsey caught a glimmer of
frustration and longing in his eyes before he abruptly looked
away.

Kelsey moved to the window and searched the vast, unrelenting sea. "I will admit to wanting to learn more about my mother while I'm in the islands, but I swear it won't interfere with work." When he didn't respond, she decided to offer further explanations. "My mother died when I was very young. I just want to see where she lived, the places she loved, and try to understand why she died. Since Dr. Bracken doesn't have a problem about this, I don't see why you should."

"Perhaps you should consider why he's so intent on having you here, instead of trying to persuade me." He jammed his hands in his pockets, hesitating as if he would say more. Instead he picked up her folder and moved to the door. "I have a bit of reading to do. I'll see you in the lab tomorrow. Early. Good night."

Kelsey dropped into the overstuffed chair Dr. Bracken had vacated. Lana was right. Something odd was going on here. Dr. Bracken simmered with barely suppressed excitement, Cade openly resented her despite their mutual attraction. Or maybe because of it. Dr. Norlund was distant but polite and stayed buried in his work each day. She'd be glad when she'd been around long enough to have established some credibility.

She poured herself a dram of whisky from the bottle sitting on the table and sipped the fiery liquid. Staring into the flames snapping and crackling in the great stone fireplace, she saw Cade and tried to rationalize his animosity. Maybe it didn't make any difference that she was a woman, that she was the youngest, least experienced member of the team. Some people just expected others to prove themselves, refusing to take anyone at face value. Some people disliked Americans.

But as the whisky burned its way down her throat, her face grew warm remembering the way he'd looked at her on the beach. The way he'd touched her hair, his eyes so full of yearning the memory made her heart hesitate, then soar.

Too long. She'd been alone too long if a man as abrasive as Cade Douglas was all it took to get her motor running. She supposed she should spend less time working if she really wanted a long-term relationship. But not many men seemed to be interested in a woman who was more graceful in the water than on land. Or one who spent most of her days doing water ballet with dolphins and seals. She'd often been accused of being too independent. Cade wasn't alone in resenting that.

Well, too bad. He could blame her Scottish ancestors, but she was not changing to suit him or anyone else.

Kelsey stood and walked over to the windows, cupping her hand over her eyes to see out into the dusky light. She sighed. She loved her work. The chance to work with Dr. Bracken was the opportunity of a lifetime, her chance to prove herself. But sometimes loneliness assailed her like the cold wind that battered this desolate coast.

Cade stood on the beach, the sea at his back. The inn loomed above on a rise of land, the great room windows rectangles of glowing light against smoky clouds billowing overhead in the darkening sky. The evening breeze ruffled his hair, cooled his face.

"Kelsey," he whispered.

As if in response, her silhouette darkened a corner of the window. One small hand shaded her eyes. He felt her sigh and involuntarily took a step back, although he knew she couldn't see him. He still felt the brand of her touch on his arm, still reeled from the intoxicating scent of her. It had taken every bit of will he had to keep from sliding his fingers into her dark hair, pulling her close and tasting the exotic crimson of her mouth.

His thoughts whirled as an image of him and Kelsey locked together on the sand filled his mind. A primitive urge raged through him, kept him standing on the beach, staring up at her until he no longer knew if what he saw was what must be, or merely what he wished.

"From what mystic place did you happen? And what am I going to do about you?"

With Cade and his silver eyes occupying a persistent place in her dreams, Kelsey slept fitfully. Again, she awoke early. Gray light filtered around the edges of the shades. She lay in bed listening to the haunting calls of birds, the faraway bark of seals. A rush of wind rubbed the shutters against the inn's rough stones, an eerie sound like a voice calling her name. Apprehension crawled up her spine.

She threw back the covers, dashed to the window, and peeked out. Fog hung heavy over the sea, blurring the lines of land, water and sky, chilling the air. She shivered and started to turn away when she heard the noise again. This old building must have plenty of creaky woods and metals, Kelsey consoled herself. The locals even believed spirits lingered there.

She left the lights off and eased the shade up. A misty shape broke away from the mounds of rocks huddled near the shore, walked away from the inn, his back to her. Kelsey drew in a sharp breath. Cade. Even from a distance, she recognized his stride, remembered the way his sweater hugged his shoulders, the way his jeans fit.

Her breathing quickened, and she pushed the thoughts away. She couldn't let her attraction to him cloud her judgment. What was he doing combing the beach at five in the morning? She'd seen him other mornings, examining rocks, sometimes looking as if he were returning from some strange mission. She wished she knew what he was looking for, but except for a few brief conversations, he avoided her, which annoyed her as much as it relieved her.

Turning away from the window, Kelsey scrambled to find

a sweat suit and socks, then shoved her feet into tennis shoes and left her room. If she hurried, she might be able to follow him. The mist would conceal her, so with luck, she'd be able to find out what he was up to. That would put an end to her early morning vigils.

When she stepped outside into the gray half-light, she thought she'd lost him. Not a breath of life stirred as far as she could see. She walked along the embankment, letting the soft grass quiet her footsteps. The fog thinned, like a gauzy curtain, allowing a glimpse of shape and movement. He was still ahead of her. Kelsey stepped down to the boulders, below the tide line, and cautiously made her way to the sand. Fog wrapped ghostly tentacles around her, dampened her hair, nipped at her face and muffled the slight squish of her shoes.

She walked quietly for several minutes, straining to hear a sound in the stillness, but even the birds had grown silent. A seal barked nearby. Another answered. Dr. Bracken had said most of the seals had migrated to a nearby island where for some reason the sea was more hospitable for them. Even so, she heard their distinctive noises during the night, occasionally during the day ever since she'd arrived.

If Cade was working on a theory about what was killing the marine life on this island, he owed it to the rest of the team to share his findings, allow them all to find a solution. She'd thought that part of the reason for the international group was to foster scientific relationships, but Cade seemed bent on remaining in his own bit of isolation. She didn't intend to let him, despite his reservations about her.

She dug her hands in her sweatshirt pockets and walked on, following the shoreline. She stumbled on the remains of a fish and bent to examine it. The eyes had the same slimy film as others she'd examined.

Chill bumps formed along her neck with the sense of something, someone, breathing close by. She rose and whirled, restraining the urge to call out. For several minutes she stood listening. Silence.

Kelsey continued walking. The beach became rockier. Her leg ached, and her footsteps crunched in the quiet. The fog pressed against her, stifling and ominous, and she stumbled.

She stopped, dismayed. She'd lost him. Apparently, she'd also lost her way. Water lapped the edges of the shore on her right. That was wrong. The sea should be on her left.

She took a few more steps forward, unable to see anything except the rocks two paces ahead. And water on both sides.

She must have ended up on a peninsula, and there was nothing to do but return the way she had come. Retracing her footsteps, she came to more water, stretching out in front of her for the few feet of visibility she had in the gloomy light.

How had she gotten so hopelessly turned around? She wasn't sure which way led back to the inn. Which way led further out towards the sea. She couldn't have hiked far, or been gone long, but without a watch, it was impossible to guess the time. The fog wrapped around her like a pearly blanket, distorting the morning light and her sense of direction.

Kelsey dropped down onto a large boulder and rested her chin in her hands. A fine example of logic and intelligence she was. Following a whim and wandering around in the pre-dawn light in this uncanny place.

Tongues of water lapped steadily closer to her feet. She stared. Good, God, the tide was coming in. In a few minutes, icy water would be over her feet, over the small pile of boulders where she sat. What was she going to do? Was this what had really happened to Lana?

She bit her knuckle to hold back a terrified cry. Fear unlike any she had ever known seized the last bit of calm she possessed, made her want to spring from the boulders and charge through the water in careless disregard for the cold depths.

Don't panic! She took a deep breath, but exhaled on a sob as a wave licked at the toes of her sneakers. A sharp breeze lifted her hair and stroked her neck with cold fingers.

She shivered and drew her legs up, resting her chin on her knees, trying to conserve her body heat. If the water didn't climb past the rocks, if the rising wind didn't signal a storm brewing, someone would come looking for her. Maybe even Cade. And she'd be sitting like an errant mermaid, perched on her rock, luring, beckoning. He'd be angry, and she'd look foolish.

Maybe Dr. Bracken, worried and scolding, would appear in the skiff. Those hopes slid away as she remembered their conversation of the night before.

Dr. Bracken was gone.

Kelsey sat up straighter, dread knifing into her stomach. So was Dr. Norlund. Cade would be waiting in the lab for her, growing impatient, but he wouldn't search for her until it was too late. No one would think to look for her. No one would notice she was not where she was supposed to be. Except Cade, and he'd merely surmise she was behaving irresponsibly.

He'd be right.

What had she been thinking, roaming a strange beach alone? Not paying enough attention to her surroundings, nor heeding the tide and the time.

Wind tugged at the fog, and she studied the line of water visible through swirls of mist. The sea around her on the peninsula would be about knee deep now. If she could hold out a little longer, the sun might break through and she'd be able to tell which way she needed to go.

Currents, strong enough to sweep a person along to the frozen floes of the North Sea lurked beneath the placid water here. She remembered Cade's words regarding Lana's accident. *The sea here is unforgiving. Lana was a fool.* Kelsey understood all too well what might have compelled her former classmate to act impulsively. But where had Cade gone?

"Cade," she said, her voice loud in the silence. "Did you

plan to trap me here? And if you did, why?"

A rustling sound, like ducks taking to flight from the water, broke the stillness. The sea rippled, radiating outward from a circular center, as if a rock was being spewed up from the ocean floor. Sunlight burst through the fog, shimmering off the water, blinding her.

Kelsey raised her arm, shielding her face, but the glare increased. Her eyes burned and watered from the harsh light. She squinted. Cold water swirled around her ankles. She glanced down for a moment as brief as the flicker of an eyelash and heard her name breathed on the wind.

"Kelsey."

From the ocean, Cade emerged, water streaming from his silver hair like star shine in a stormy sky. Droplets of water glistened like iridescent pearls on his skin. Kelsey's breath froze. She couldn't speak, couldn't move, couldn't stop staring, mesmerized by the beads of water traveling down his sleek muscled chest, lower, tangling in a thatch of hair, sliding down muscular thighs. Blood rose in her face, and she yanked her gaze upward to meet his.

"Take my hand." His voice swirled through her mind, yet at the same time she wasn't sure he had spoken.

"Cade," she whispered. "How—"

"Trust me."

Pewter eyes locked with hers, and she found herself unable to look away, as if a force beyond her control linked her to him. She extended her hand, letting him pull her off the boulder. She floated to her feet. Cade pulled her to him, never taking his gaze from hers, and the world spun away. Caught in the center of a storm force, she felt his body hard against hers through her clothes. But not cold or wet like she expected.

"Why are you here?" She said the words in her mind, and he held her closer.

"Because I can't let harm befall you."

Lightheaded and dizzy, Kelsey felt her head jerk back.

Her eyes fluttered shut. She felt Cade's hand on her shoulder, heard his voice.

He shook her and said her name again.

Kelsey opened her eyes, letting out a shriek as she realized she sat on a large outcropping of rock less than a hundred yards from the inn. Scrambling to her feet, she backed away from Cade. A fully dressed Cade, wearing a gray warm up suit and windbreaker.

"I'm sorry," he said. "I didn't mean to startle you."

Chapter Four

Dazed, Kelsey stared at him. "How did we get here?"
Cade frowned, his forehead furrowing in puzzlement.
"You were late. When you didn't show up in the lab, I asked
the housekeeper to check your room. I saw you sitting out
here and came to remind you we have work to do. Doesn't
look like a very cozy place for a nap, anyway."

"I wasn't asleep," she snapped, trying to read his
fathomless expression, trying to ignore the pain throbbing in
her forehead. Even her eyes ached. "I got caught by the tide.
You..." she hesitated, remembering his naked form
emerging from the sea like Neptune. It couldn't be. One
moment he had been holding her close against his bare skin.
The next he was fully clothed, complete with laced-up high
tops?

Kelsey shivered, suddenly so cold her bones felt brittle.
She'd always prided herself on her rational mind. What was
happening to her? "I had a very strange dream."

Cade turned and stared out to sea. A few gray clouds
scuttled across the horizon, but the fog had evaporated. A
muscle twitched in his jaw. "Well, since you seem to be so
well rested, we need to get to work. I've already wasted half
the morning waiting for you."

"I missed breakfast." Her stomach growled, telling her
that, at least, she remembered correctly.

"Ask Mrs. Devon to fix you a plate. When you've
finished, meet me in the lab. I'm not interested in taking a
holiday simply because the others are gone."

"Neither am I." Kelsey fell into step behind him, hurrying
to catch up despite the pain that shot through her head each

time she moved. "I don't work well on an empty stomach. Maybe you'd like to—"

He stopped walking so suddenly, the toes of her shoes scraped his heels. He turned, gripped her arms fiercely and leveled a look of hot intensity on her. She curled her fingers and held her breath. Desire, as red hot as live embers, flared inside, fanned by the yearning she saw on his face.

She knew he was going to kiss her an instant before his lips brushed hers. Soft, silky, his mouth caressed hers, teasing and entreating. She responded like a rosebud to sunlight, her limbs softening, her defenses crumbling. He murmured her name like a caress and abruptly released her. Kelsey staggered back, dazed, confused. And hurt.

"What is the matter with you?"

"That's why you're a distraction." He turned, but not before she glimpsed the desperation and bewilderment in his eyes. "My apologies, Miss MacKenzie. I'll see you in the lab."

He strode away. Kelsey brushed her hair back and touched her lips with shaky fingers. There was something weird about this island, something very strange about Cade Douglas. But nothing unusual about the chemistry between the two of them. He was attractive, intense. She was lonely. He sensed it, and if she wasn't careful might use that to his advantage, then confront Dr. Bracken with another reason for her to leave.

She wouldn't allow that to happen. Carefully picking her way across the rocks, she steeled her resolve, then stopped, rubbing her forehead in amazement. Whatever else Cade had done for her this morning, at least her headache was gone.

After eating a quick meal of biscuits, fruit and tea, Kelsey joined Cade in the lab. For the rest of the morning, they worked silently. Kelsey tried to ease the sense of isolation, but Cade resisted her attempts to draw him into a discussion about the tests he was performing on a small fish.

"Here." He thrust a folder at her, half an inch thick with lab reports. "Try reading up on the work we've done so far instead of firing hundreds of questions at me."

Stung, Kelsey took the papers and retreated to her own work space. Cade was rude, insensitive, selfish.

Mysterious and fascinating. Head bent over a microscope, he seemed oblivious to her presence. Kelsey studied his profile. Long lashes cast shadows on smooth skin. His lab coat hung open, camouflaging the sleek muscles she remembered.

Remembered? Kelsey shook her head, sloughing off her imaginings like an overcoat suddenly too hot for comfort. She'd imagined the whole thing. Dreamed it, just as she dreamed of him each night since her arrival.

"Get a grip, MacKenzie," she mumbled, snapping the folder shut. She placed a carefully prepared slide under the lens and adjusted the microscope. She had work to do, and if she worked hard enough, long enough, she'd be able to gather more than enough information to use when she returned to the United States. She focused on the specimen, pushing all thoughts of Cade Douglas to the furthermost recess of her mind. But still she felt his body hard against hers, saw the droplets of water shimmer on his smooth skin and wondered how she could ignore his presence until her mind convinced her body about what had really happened.

Cade ignored Kelsey's suggestion that they take a lunch break. By the end of the day, her eyes burned. She rubbed the back of her neck. She wondered if Cade would have kept such a frenetic pace if Dr. Bracken had been there. Somehow she doubted it and speculated that his total immersion in work had more to do with a desire to avoid her conversation and ignore her presence. He scrupulously avoided touching her, laying a slide or document on the table rather than handing it to her where their fingers might brush.

After dinner, Kelsey found Cade in the great room, nearly hidden in the shadows. Undraped, the enormous windows let in the eerie half-glow of the omnipresent sun.

She sank into a huge overstuffed chair opposite him. "What's on the agenda for tomorrow?"

He jerked his gaze to her, visibly startled at seeing her. For a moment, desire darkened his eyes and just as suddenly was hidden behind a scowl.

"More tests, examinations. Research results to be recorded and documented."

"We've already analyzed all the samples in the lab," Kelsey pointed out.

Cade's gaze faltered, as if searching for a rebuttal for her next remark. "Yes, well—"

"Dr. Bracken is expecting you to show me the other islands."

Cade stood, snatching his sweater from the back of the chair. His hands tightened around the garment. "And we mustn't disappoint you or the good doctor, then must we?" He staggered back and pressed a hand to his forehead.

Kelsey leapt to her feet and reached for his arm. "Are you all right?"

"Yes," he ground out his answer and brushed her hands away as if she were a troublesome wasp. "A slight case of vertigo, nothing more."

"Maybe you should ask Mrs. Devon for some cold medicine," Kelsey suggested, remembering the slight cough he'd had all afternoon.

"Thank you, Dr. MacKenzie. If you'll excuse me, I'm going to turn in."

"What about tomorrow?" Kelsey crossed her arms and waited for his answer.

Cade studied her for several moments. "Very well, then. If it's fine in the morning, we'll take the skiff to the outer islands. Good night." He turned and strode from the room.

Kelsey sat in the great room, watching the midnight glow in the sky beyond the windows and went through her morning ordeal, moment by moment. She hadn't fallen asleep just footsteps from the inn. She hadn't. But what had really happened? What possible reason would Cade have for lying to her?

Cade spent a restless night. Cotton sheets scraped over his skin, burned to the touch. How he hated the artificial smell of the blue liquid the housekeeping staff insisted on putting in the laundry. He yanked the blanket off the bed and lay down on the floor. Wadding up Kelsey's fisherman knit sweater, he fashioned a pillow and closed his eyes.

Kelsey. Her scent filled him till he thought he'd burst from wanting. He fingered the sweater and let the images play through his tortured mind. Kelsey, mouth soft and pliable against his. Kelsey, naked and ready beneath him.

He gulped in a breath and forced himself to exhale slowly. Kelsey, the look on her face if she should discover what he was. Play the images, over and over if that's what it took to rid himself of the damned desire.

Going out alone on the skiff would be a disastrous error. Resolving to find a third person to accompany them in the morning, he finally slid into sleep, but in his dreams he claimed her again and again.

Although he went to the village early the next morning, Cade was unable to locate another person to man the boat. He surveyed the horizon. A few misty clouds laced the perfect blue sky. A knot of uneasiness formed in his stomach as he tried to come up with a plausible reason to work in the lab for the rest of the day. But the truth was, they did need more specimens, and with the weather as changeable as it

had been for the past week, this might be the best
opportunity.

Bracken expected it. Cade scowled, wondering exactly
why the inestimable scientist seemed determined to link him
and Kelsey. Why he'd chosen the days immediately after her
arrival to drag Dr. Norlund back to the mainland.

Just like with Lana. Only Bracken had abandoned his
attempts at forced togetherness when he seemed to realize
that she and Cade were completely disinterested in each
other, on a personal as well as professional level.

But now there was Kelsey. He closed his eyes and saw her
again as she had been stranded on that desolate strip of
beach. An ethereal wind played with her hair, teasing strands
of it across her perfectly sculpted face. His fingers ached to
trace those delicate brows, the slightly upturned nose, the
line of her jaw, the curve of her throat.

He shook off his imaginings as his body responded to the
powerful images of Kelsey, warm with wanting, waiting for
him. What was he thinking? To take her would be to destroy
them both.

"Are we going to do it, or not?" As if conjured by his
need and imagination, Kelsey came up behind him, impatient
for an answer to what was obviously a repeated question.

Startled, Cade turned so abruptly he nearly hit her. He
swallowed, took a step back and tried to refocus his
attention. The trip. She was taking about the boat trip. Her
entire attention was focused on a tour of the islands. As it
should be.

But the longing to have her grew until it seemed to take
on a life of its own, consuming his thoughts, awakening his
body into a painful state of readiness for what he knew he
should not have. Why couldn't she see how she affected
him?

"We'll take the skiff out after breakfast," he said gruffly,
although it wasn't at all what he had intended to say. Every
ounce of rationality screamed at him to recall the words. The

trouble was, when it came to Kelsey MacKenzie, rationality was merely a word. The wisdom spoken from graying elders on the hazards of lusting, usually not easily ignored, faded into oblivion.

With Kelsey, his instincts could not be subdued.

Chapter Five

She smiled, the flawless morning absolute perfection with the prospect of the boat trip. At last, she would see something besides this tiny island. "Great. Mrs. Devon packed us some lunch and drinks. I'll get my jacket and supplies and meet you back here."

Half an hour later, tiny ripples drifted across a cobalt sea as the small boat skimmed away from the mooring at the inn. Kelsey tightened her fingers around the seat cushion and reveled in the feel of the wind through her hair. She closed her eyes and opened them in time to catch Cade gazing at her with a mixture of frustration and undisguised lust that made her heart slam against her side.

Heat curled through her, and with tremendous effort she dragged her gaze from his. She and Cade were truly alone. The sense of isolation filled her with nervous anticipation. What would she do if—? She forced the thoughts away and stood, turning her back on him and watching the gray mountains of the island fall further away.

"Are we going to the seal rookeries first?" She turned and repeated her question.

"There is no such place anymore." Cade's white knuckled fingers gripped the boat's wheel.

"But Dr. Bracken said—"

"For a scientist, Dr. Bracken harbors some interesting notions. There were seals on many of the islands here, as well as in the harbors of the mainland. But most of them have migrated to more hospitable shores. And as far as an island which harbors any particular breed of seal, he is mistaken."

Kelsey pondered his remarks against what she had been told by both of the other researchers. Although he wasn't in agreement with their findings, Cade was a native to the islands. Dr. Bracken and Dr. Norlund were not. "Then where are they?"

"Some of the seals have migrated as far as Iceland. After many seasons, they will return here. We may never be able to determine the reasons why."

Cade skirted the islands wide at some points. At others, he drew the boat in close to the shore. Although Kelsey expected him to beach the boat in order to allow them to collect samples, he seemed content to behave as if he were a tour director, and Kelsey was on holiday.

She hauled up one of the nets to see what they had been able to capture. Nothing. "If I didn't know better, Cade, I'd think you were a jinx. I've been on plenty of expeditions and we always capture something in the nets."

Cade was silent.

Exasperated, Kelsey turned back to island watching. "At some point, we're going to have to go in to shore, or there's no point to this whole trip."

"As you wish," he said, but continued ambling through the North Sound.

At a few of the smaller islands, emerald green fields leveled out to marshland dotted with white flowers, their honey scent drifting over the sunshine-warmed air. On others, sandy coastland rose to hills purpled with heather and Scottish primrose.

West of Sanday, a small island rose from the sea like a drifting sand dune anchored with large outcroppings of rocks. Open grassland sparkled with golden marigolds and stretched down to embrace a beach of clean white sand. Dark shapes peppered the shore. Kelsey stared. "Cade, look. I think we've found the seals." She snatched up the binoculars and adjusted the focus, but saw only shadows from the rocks scattered along the beach. She could have sworn... She tugged on his sleeve. "Did you see them?"

He shook his head and glanced at the sky. The earlier blue had deepened to a gunmetal gray. A stiff breeze chased whitecaps across the water. "We'd best be going back. A storm is brewing."

Kelsey followed his gaze. "You're kidding. There's not a cloud in the sky. Besides, we've been on the water for hours but don't seem to have traveled far."

She pulled her jacket tighter and turned to Cade, the wind snatching her voice away so that she had to repeat her question several times. "See the birds?" Red-throated divers skittered to a clumsy landing on the shore. Puffins, black and white plumage like miniature tuxedos, bills bright splotches of orange against the white washed rocks, squawked noisy threats to the approaching boat. "There's bound to be some shellfish here."

"Fine." He veered the boat towards a narrow strip of sand. "We'll explore the tide pools, try to find some mollusks." He eased back on the throttle, as if attempting to dodge something she couldn't see.

"Look out!" Kelsey grabbed his shirtsleeve and pointed to a submerged mass inches below the surface on the opposite side.

Cade yanked the wheel hard to the left. The boat shuddered. Something snapped, a loud cracking sound that popped Kelsey's ears. The wheel spun uselessly beneath his hands.

"Damn it!" He pulled back on the throttle, but the craft sputtered and died. The puffins cackle filled the resulting silence.

Kelsey ventured a look over the side. The boat appeared to be wedged on a sand bar just a few feet away from treacherous rocks. "What do we do now?"

Cade's expression was thunderous. "The steering cable broke, apparently. I'll see if I can repair it and radio for help if I can't."

"We won't be stranded here, will we?" The thought filled her with alarm as much from the isolation as from the idea of being alone for an indeterminate time with Cade.

He narrowed a glance on her. "Of course not. I'm sure I can fix the steering, and then we'll be on our way."

Kelsey sighed. She couldn't just sit here, watching him work. At least if she could collect a few mollusks or snails the trip wouldn't be a complete waste of time. As the boat rocked gently, she removed her shoes and socks and rolled her jeans past her knees. She grabbed a bucket and bounded into the water.

"What do you think you're doing, Kelsey?" Cade stood on the deck, arms crossed, scowling.

"I never claimed to be a mechanic. You take care of the boat, I'll do the exploring." She waded through the icy water, gritted her teeth and forced herself not to wince. She reached the beach, waved to Cade and wandered over the rocks. Crouching, she examined a small depression in the shore. Purple snails, mussels and starfish clung to the edges of a small pool. A giant owl limpet hung clamped to a small rock, and she carefully placed it in the bucket. These creatures would be just what they needed to see if something was different about this island than the others.

Absorbed, she roamed over outcroppings, let her toes sink into cold sand and shut Cade from view when she rounded a dark crag nearer the sloping hills. Squeezing between massive rocks, she found the entrance to a small cave.

Sunlight filtered through cracks in the rocks, casting the completely enclosed sandy bottom cave in a hazy illumination. She inched further inside. Acorn barnacles, limy sides attached to the rocks, glowed in the white light. Awed by the sensation of being inside a sanctuary, she let the quiet envelop her.

The sea lapped a muffled song. The hair on the back of her neck prickled. Kelsey whirled to find Cade close behind her. "Is the boat fixed?"

He shook his head and took another step towards her as if drawn against his own volition.

"Did you call for help?"

Again he shook his head, and the tremor of apprehension in the pit of her stomach exploded into desire when his fingers spiked into her hair, and his mouth took hers.

The bucket clattered to the ground. Twining her arms around his neck, she parted her lips, letting his tongue slide against hers, tangling, teasing, and answered his desperate call with her own. She nearly cried with dismay when he dragged his hot mouth from hers, until he pressed his lips against her throat and moaned her name. His hands slid down her back, cupped her buttocks and pressed her against his hardness.

His fingers fumbled with the buttons on her sweater, then the clasp on her jeans, and she was helpless to deny him, caught in a whirlpool of heat and mystery she could no more escape from than she could stop breathing. Something about this place overpowered rational thought, made her feel as if she'd been born for this moment, for him. She'd give in to it and put an end to the craving they had for each other before it created even more problems.

"Help me, Kelsey, help me." He mumbled against her skin, tugging her garments off until she stood, naked and trembling, her clothes in a pile around her feet.

He took a deep breath and touched her, slowly, his eyes warm and filled with wonder. His hands tentatively cupped her breasts, stroking the nipples with his thumbs. Gentle hands traced her throat, then the curve of her stomach down to the silky thatch of hair.

His other arm circled her waist, catching her to him. His fingers plucked at her, invading and tormenting. Kelsey moaned and leaned back against his arm. His mouth came down on her breast and gently tugged, the pleasure piercing her insides.

She pushed his jacket off his shoulders and down his arms

and began unbuttoning his shirt. Her shaky fingers outlined the contour of his chest, her palms rubbed smooth skin, satiny muscles. He was warm and taut and looked utterly driven, as if nothing could stop the conclusion her body screamed for.

He shed his jeans and urged her to the ground, then buried his mouth against her neck. A thousand flames roared inside her. Sand chafed her back, but she didn't care and locked her fingers behind his head, encouraging him as his mouth explored her throat, then her shoulders, tasting, nipping, licking.

She lay back, felt his breath against her stomach as his hands slid down her sides, cupped her buttocks and lifted her to him. His tongue sworled on her, stabbed inside. Kelsey arched her back and gasped as a river of liquid heat raged through her.

He lay over her, covering her with his body, probing, seeking entry. She stroked the length of him, felt him pulse against her hand, then raised her hips and guided him inside. His first thrust made her wince, but when he withdrew partway, she whimpered and wrapped her legs around his thighs.

Murmuring her name, he eased in, deeper this time, and began stroking her until she felt his touch everywhere, from the tips of her fingers and toes to the furthest recesses of her soul.

The sounds of the ocean penetrated his fevered mind. Awareness of what he was doing slammed into him, but Kelsey moaned softly, tightened around him, and he was once again lost. Lost in her heat, the beat of her heart, the taste of her mouth. She clenched around him like a hot, velvet fist until he could no longer stop himself from moving with her, taking and giving, joining with her rhythm until she sighed his name, and he flowed inside her.

He wanted more. He nibbled on her shoulder, watched her eyelashes flutter, then gently savored her breasts as if she were a precious elixir. He moved lower, stroking her sides, her legs with the palms of his hands.

"Cade," she whispered uncertainly, tensing and pushing on his shoulders.

Eyes hot as molten pewter bore into hers. "I could feast on you for days," he murmured against the sensitive skin of her inner thighs. "Don't deny me, Kelsey."

Reaching down, she touched his hair, letting the silver strands feather through her fingers. She let the madness take her and dug her fingers into his shoulders, crying his name as release shuddered through her again and again.

He kissed her, letting their lips cling softly before he claimed her mouth and body again, harder this time, thrusting deeper. He would take her a hundred times if he had to, to get this fever from his blood, his mind. He would take her until he had nothing left to give, until she begged him to stop.

But she didn't. Each time he took her, she greeted him with an eagerness that sent his blood past the boiling point, over and over.

Finally depleted, unable to contemplate the consequences of his actions, he lay on his back, Kelsey stretched out beside him. His hand cupped the back of her head, coaxing her closer until she curled against his side. Her kiss, gentle and uncertain, made his heart stand still, then flutter like a thousand sea birds taking flight

There would be no turning back. His hand drifted down her arm, over the curve of her hip. "May the gods help us, Kelsey," he murmured, thankful that she at least had drifted off into a peaceful slumber.

Kelsey stirred, a deep sense of contentment heating her blood like warm syrup. She smiled and stretched, reaching out for Cade beside her. Her fingers scraped over starched cotton, and she bolted upright.

Moonlight streamed in through the window of her room at the inn. Curtains puffed in with the evening breeze. She rubbed her hand down her flannel pajamas as desperate fear filled her stomach. She was alone.

She jumped from the bed and confronted her image in the mirror. Pulling off her garments, she examined herself. No signs of Cade's passionate kisses on her throat. She rubbed her hand over her stomach. She felt different, no longer an innocent, yet she looked the same.

Another dream, then? *No*, she moaned and dug her fingers through her hair. It was real, he was real, his hands on her skin, making love to her until she thought she'd melt. A tear rolled down her face, and she brushed it away. What was happening to her? Why was she here, in her room, instead of with Cade on the island?

Moving to the window, she stared out. The boat was moored to the dock, rocking gently in moon rippled water. Cade was nowhere in sight.

She tore through the room, hunting for the clothes she'd worn to the island. Her jeans and sweater hung neatly in the armoire. Her shoes stood against the wall, her socks stuffed down inside them.

She didn't remember leaving, coming back here. She remembered…. Images of Cade looming over her, thrusting into her, flared in her mind. She tasted the salty tang of his kiss, felt his mouth on her and stumbled, her knees suddenly too weak to support her.

"Nooo—" she cried, flinging herself across the bed. She wasn't crazy, it had happened. It wasn't a dream. Her hands clutched the bedclothes, rubbed over grit. She sat up.

Yanking the covers off the bed, she scooted her hands across the sheets. The almost imperceptible residue of the beach clung to her palms. What had happened? How did she get back here? Where was Cade? And why had he left her?

Chapter Six

Too restless to sleep, Kelsey put on her robe and stepped quietly out into the hall. The click of the doorknob sounded loud against the thick silence of midnight. Cade's room was at the opposite end of the hall. She made her way there first, guided only by small night-lights interspersed down the narrow expanse of hall. She knocked, but no one answered.

Pressing her ear to the door, she listened, hoping to hear the squeak of springs, the rustle of crisp sheets, but heard only her own breathing. Emptiness echoing through her soul, she knew he was gone. With the other scientists gone as well, the inn was eerie and ominous.

Her head ached, a low throbbing at the base of her skull, and she decided to go downstairs and fix some warm milk. Maybe with a shot of Mrs. Devon's famous whisky. As owners of the inn, the Devons were the only workers who lived on premises but their quarters were in a small cottage set some distance away from the main building.

She was completely alone.

Stairs creaked beneath her feet as she made her way carefully down the darkened staircase to the kitchen.

She found a pan, poured in the milk and waited for it to heat. The rustle of branches outside the window, the rattle of the door made her glance over her shoulder. The wind. It was only the wind.

Not wanting to stand with her back to the room, she heated the milk only enough to take the chill off, then poured it into a heavy mug. She positioned herself at the window so that she could view the room as well and forced herself to sip the whisky laced concoction. The kitchen, located on the back of the building, looked out over the hills. Moonlight combined with the eerie twilight, dappling the mountains like a faraway moonscape.

Her thoughts returned to the sea cave. What had possessed Cade? What had possessed her? She'd wanted him every bit as much as he'd wanted her, but she wondered if she would have been able to stop him if she hadn't.

Their lovemaking had been beautiful, perfect. Remembering his touch made shivers dance across her skin. How could he have engineered such an elaborate set up? Did he want her to think the afternoon had never happened? She could never have imagined being so coldly, so cruelly abandoned. "Cade," she whispered. "Why did you leave me?"

Cade groaned and tried to shut out the sight and sound of his grandfather, but found he didn't have the strength to move.

"You were with the woman." Meredith Douglas' voice seemed to come from a long way off. His weathered face filled Cade's vision as if he peered down a long tunnel.

"Wasting yourself, risking our lives. You could have just brought her back the same way you got there." Meredith continued grumbling as he spooned chowder into his grandson's mouth. "Modern women are used to that. They do what they like and take the consequences."

Somewhat restored, Cade sat, holding his head in his hands against a fresh wave of dizziness. "I panicked."

His grandfather snorted. "Obviously." He laid a cool cloth against Cade's neck, then stepped back and surveyed him through narrowed eyes topped by gray bushy brows. "You did have her then? Despite all my warnings?" Flinty eyes pierced through Cade's soul.

"Yes." Cade flushed and looked away from his grandfather's knowing gaze.

"So why did you come here? Do you expect me to pat your shoulder and tell you everything will be all right? That everything I taught you doesn't matter?"

"Of course not. It's just—" his voice trailed off and he buried his face in his hands. "I find myself doing things I don't understand, wanting what I know is wrong."

"I see. And what of Shayla? Have you forgotten her so soon?"

Guilt sliced through him, but Cade raised his eyes in defiance. "Of course not," he said, though in truth, she had faded from his thoughts the night he met Kelsey. "She knew it was no use coming back here. Damn it, she knew the danger."

Meredith sighed. "A pity. I was certain she would be the one for you."

Cade made an impatient motion. "Shayla would have been the first of many."

His grandfather snorted. "As will the American, if you let yourself be seduced by that kind of magic."

"Kelsey is different." Shadows from the fire danced on the walls of the cottage, and Cade fell silent. In his mind, he saw Kelsey as he'd left her, dark hair fanned out across the white pillow, her lips curved in a contented smile as she slept. Was she awake now? Did she remember? Her thoughts tugged at him, and he tried to focus, but his grandfather's fury overrode the feeble connection.

"She is forbidden!"

Cade met his grandfather's anger with his own cool resolve. "If I made a mistake, then I ask your forgiveness. But I can't change what happened." He knew he wouldn't want to, even if it were possible. The image of Kelsey in the cave, her face glowing with passion, the way her body fit his, her taste, he knew these feelings would stay with him always, as well as the craving to experience them again. Even now, yearning coursed through him.

"You must undo what you have done. Before you cause

more harm. Before you completely lose sight of why you are here." Meredith sighed and sank into the wooden chair beside the bed. "Fortunately, I'm sure you were not her first any more than she was yours."

"Would that make a difference?" Cade's eyes fixed on a ray of moonlight peeking through the window, and he tried not to remember the little cry she'd uttered when he entered her. Tried not to think about her hot tightness, and the wonder of being enveloped in her body. He had no experience against which to judge, but Kelsey had been too passionate, too freely giving.

No, he couldn't have been her first. The thought gave him no relief but a twinge of jealousy for whomever she had loved before him. He wondered if she was promised to someone, as he had been.

But in another life, and she had died. Grandfather had made a lot of assumptions about him and Shayla. Luckily he didn't know she had never interested him in that way, although in time he was certain he would have done his duty by her.

Meredith appeared not to notice his attempt at diversion. "Can't you alter her thoughts?"

Cade shook his head. "I tried. But her will is strong."

Meredith pondered this for several moments. "Very unusual. Did you bring the sweater?"

Cade fingered the garment before handing it over. He should tell him, but the words stuck in his throat. "Grandfather—"

Meredith snatched the sweater and held it against his cheek, closing his eyes. The room grew deathly still, making the pop of the fire sound like the gunshot of an executioner. The bones in Meredith's hands stood out as his grip tightened on the ivory wool and his face furrowed in concentration. When he opened his eyes, his fury rendered Cade immobile.

"Did you know? Did you know before you took her?" His

voice began as a growl and ended as a bellow. "Did you know she was William Bouschour's daughter? The child of my greatest enemy?" The thatched roof shivered from his roar, and Cade was certain even the fish in the deepest depths heard.

He wished desperately for a lie, but knew it was no use. "Yes."

"You young fool! Bad enough that we have to outwit Bracken at every turn, what are you going to do if her father comes here? Everything we have planned, everything we've worked for will be destroyed."

Cade stood, ignoring the waves of dizziness, and reached for his clothes. "I'll find a way to make her forget." He nearly toppled over putting on his trousers. Only his grandfather's furious stare kept him going. "Or I'll find a way to make her leave."

Meredith folded his arms and fixed a stern gaze on his beloved grandson. "See that you do. And for God's sake, stay out of the sea. You're no good to us if you're lying on your death bed."

Kelsey woke slowly, her head heavy with sleep. Sunshine flooded the room, sending a rainbow of color dancing across the ceiling. She stretched and breathed in the scent of the sea.

The seashell captured her attention the moment she turned her head. Suddenly wide-awake, she leaped from bed and took the shell down from the top of the bureau. She carefully turned it in her hands, admiring the iridescent pink bands of color. Where had it come from? She hadn't seen anything like this the day she and Cade had gone to the other island.

She'd never seen anything like it before. Anywhere. Who had put it in her room? She'd have to ask Mrs. Devon later, but first she intended to find out exactly what it was.

She planned to research several things today, especially if Cade didn't return. If her room had a phone jack, she could do the necessary research here, where she didn't run the risk of someone peering over her shoulder, but the only phone in the building was in a small alcove off the great room. Fortunately, Dr. Bracken had the lab outfitted to handle a modem.

After downing a cup of coffee and a couple of raisin-cinnamon scones, Kelsey made her way to the lab. She hadn't dreamt the trip to the island, at least. The snails and mollusks she'd harvested were stored in jars of brine, neatly labeled in Cade's distinctive handwriting.

The live specimens needed to be fed. She sprinkled special food on the water, then checked the temperature of the tank. Satisfied everything was in order, she got out her laptop computer. It wouldn't be a good idea to leave a trail on the lab computers, or on the Foundation's accounts. Using her own account number, she accessed a toll-free number and began the search.

Dr. Bracken had said Cade had been at Dalhousie University in Nova Scotia. Once she accessed their computer, she'd have a lot more information on his research, if not on him. Perhaps that would even things up a bit, since he seemed to know a great deal about her.

He'd apparently been one of their most published scientists. Kelsey scanned the articles, pausing to study one on seal whiskers and how they are used to navigate and locate prey. Fascinating theory. Dr. Douglas definitely didn't take a traditional approach to his subjects, but his style was typically boring. Why did most scholars think they had to take the life out of their writing?

Resting her chin on her hand, she scrolled through another article. Yawning, she scanned a few paragraphs on the nutritional value of krill. Too bad scientific journals rarely had photographs of their authors.

The next one did.

Kelsey leaned forward. The connection was slow, making the picture take a long time to build. She slapped her hands against her thighs, impatient to see Cade's image. Here, he was the very picture of rustic casual, in jeans and sweaters, silver hair a tad too long. Thoughts of his hands and mouth working magic on her invaded her thoughts. *Stop it.* To linger on the memories would drive her crazy with questions and despair.

She focused on her task and squinted at the screen. What was his scholarly image like? The foggy image grew more substantial, then coalesced into the face of a complete stranger.

A knot of anxiety formed in her stomach. She double-checked the name under the photograph of a middle-aged man. C.D. Douglas stared back at her. C.D. Douglas. The names were similar, but this was definitely a different man.

A mistake. She'd made a mistake somewhere and wasted an hour researching the wrong person. Retracing her path, she came to the same information.

She swallowed uneasily. There had to be another explanation, but apparently there was no other Dr. Douglas at Dalhousie University. She downloaded the information and waited for the printer to spit out the hard evidence.

Perhaps the wrong picture had been printed with the article. If she called the University press, they could verify that.

She glanced at her watch. Noon, which meant it was eight a.m. in Nova Scotia, too early to be certain of reaching anyone. She'd wait until after lunch, then call. She had one more bit of research before she disconnected the modem, anyway.

The research on the shell was as disconcerting. Although she accessed several oceanographic institutions, the only creature that came close to the description of her shell had been extinct for a thousand years.

As wary as if someone had told her that seals could talk, Kelsey shut the computer down. She gathered up the papers she'd printed and stuffed them in the pocket of her lab coat.

These she'd keep in her room, away from where one of the other scientists would be likely to see them.

She walked slowly across the well-manicured grounds separating the lab from the inn. After lunch she'd call the University, find out that the picture of Dr. Douglas was a mistake. Then she could simply worry about how he could transport her from an island without her knowing he'd done it, and disappear into the night.

She ate lunch in the kitchen with the Devons. Barley soup accompanied thick slices of buttered bread with elderberry jam.

Mrs. Devon ladled another generous helping of soup into Kelsey's bowl. "Your research is going well, then?"

Kelsey savored the broth and returned the housekeeper's smile. "Yes, although I'm hoping to have a little time to do some personal research as well."

Gordon set his spoon down. "And what might that be, miss?"

"My mother was born in Orkney. She and my father lived on this island for a time when I was a baby. I'd like to see where they lived. Maybe find someone who still remembers her." She sighed and rested her chin in her hand. "I've even been hoping I'd discover a cousin or two."

Gordon exchanged a long look with his wife and shook his head almost imperceptibly. Mrs. Devon's mouth went white around the edges, as if it took every bit of will she had to keep from speaking.

"Been twenty-five years, you say?"

Kelsey nodded.

Gordon picked up his spoon before continuing. "Don't think you'll find anyone. Me and the missus only been here twenty. Folks find it hard to stick around such a remote place."

Mrs. Devon spoke at last, her breath gusting from her. "The last ones left before the scientists got here. Except for Meredith Douglas, of course. Cade's grandfather."

Maybe Cade's grandfather had known her parents. That would explain why Cade knew so much about her. Fresh excitement bubbled up. "Maybe he was here when they were, then. He might know if I still have cousins in the area. Where can I find him?"

Mrs. Devon stood and made a show of clearing the dishes. "I expect he'll find you. If he's willing to talk, that is."

"Then he can tell me where she lived while she was here."

Mrs. Devon wiped her hands on her apron. "Most anyone can do that. Not that it will do you any good, you see."

Kelsey chewed on a crust of bread gone dry in her mouth. She took a sip of water and swallowed. Scots. Why was it so hard to pry information from them? "Can you tell me?"

"Certainly, miss." But she cast a quick glance at her husband and fell silent.

"So tell me."

Mrs. Devon's hand swept towards the hill rising behind the inn. "There. You can just see a bit of chimney."

Enthusiasm surged through her. The house where her mother and father had lived and loved was a stone's throw from the inn. She could walk to it, maybe ask the inhabitants if she could see the inside. "Does anyone live there? Do you think they'd let me look around?"

Gordon shook his head and pushed back from the table. Narrowing his gaze at his wife, he excused himself and left the room. Mrs. Devon chuckled. "Gordon doesn't like anyone wandering around there. Not safe, and since it's part of our property, he feels responsible."

The sense of dread she'd had all morning returned and grew, setting her stomach on edge. "What's wrong with it?"

"Why the chimney is all that's left. Burned to the ground, it did." Silence as thick as smoke grew. Mrs. Devon picked up the plates.

Kelsey rested her head on her hands. Gone. The one thing she most wanted to see while she was here, and it was too late.

The housekeeper hesitated on her way to the sink. "I don't like being the one to say this, since I wasn't here, you understand, but if you go into the village, you'll likely hear the same story. Once people find out who you are."

"Tell me." Kelsey looked up and carefully folded her napkin.

"Well, now. I'm sure it was just another accident, like your mother's death, but some say in his grief or rage, depending on who's doing the telling, he set the fire on purpose."

"Who?" She forced the words out.

"Your father, of course."

"My father." She repeated the words, wanting to be certain she had not misunderstood.

"Yes, miss." Mrs. Devon reached down and patted her hand. "But it was all so very long ago. No sense in fretting."

"No, of course not," Kelsey murmured. So that was why her father didn't have a single picture of her mother, nor anything else from their life on this island. Why hadn't he just told her? She would have understood. She shared his grief over the loss of everything he held dear. Why didn't he see that?

Realizing she'd gotten as much information from Mrs. Devon as possible, Kelsey went to the alcove to use the telephone. Might as well clear up this mystery, too. After she gave her calling card information to the operator, the rotary phone clicked through a seemingly endless string of numbers. Finally the phone began to ring.

"Dalhousie University, College of Marine Science," a woman's crisp voice answered.

"I'd like to speak to Dr. Cade Douglas. If he's there."

"We have a Dr. C.D. Douglas on staff, but he's unavailable." There was a moment's pause. "Can I help you?"

"When do you expect him back?" Kelsey waited for the secretary to tell her he was on a leave of absence, out of the country for an indefinite period of time.

"In about an hour. He has a class right now, but his calendar indicates he'll be in his office after that."

Unable to speak, Kelsey sank to the small padded seat in the alcove. If Dr. Douglas was in Nova Scotia, then what was the name of the man who had made love to her on the beach?

"Miss? Do you want to leave a message?"

"No. Thank you. No message." Kelsey slowly replaced the receiver. What was going on? Had Dr. Bracken made a mistake? Who was Cade?

Chapter Seven

Kelsey shielded her eyes against the window of her room and peered out. Rain poured down in heavy sheets. Waves slapped the coast, shooting spray high above the craggy rocks. Two more days had passed since she'd been with Cade and still he hadn't returned to the inn. She had spent the time in the lab, wondering what he would tell her when he returned. If he returned. Although she'd accomplished a lot in the lab with the samples she'd collected, she felt as bleak as the weather.

She'd hoped Dr. Bracken and Dr. Norlund would have come back from the mainland as well, but their delay was probably related to the unceasing storm.

"Will you be dining alone again tonight, Miss?" From the open doorway, Mrs. Devon's lilting accents pierced Kelsey's thoughts. She let the curtain drop and turned away, but forgot the housekeeper's question as the shell on top of the bureau again caught her attention. She picked it up and held the cool smoothness against her cheek. It had been there when she first awoke after her strange adventure on the island. The question was, had Cade left it? And if he did, why? Where could he have found an ancient shell?

"Miss?" Mrs. Devon's voice turned anxious.

"I don't think this was in my room when I got here last week. Do you know where it came from?" Kelsey gestured with the shell.

"Can't say I do. Would you like me to ask Gwendolyn? She's the one responsible for the guest rooms."

"Yes, please." Kelsey continued to study the shell, sighed and placed it carefully on the small desk. If Cade had found it, why hadn't he left it with the other carefully prepared samples in the lab?

Mrs. Devon bustled around the room, straightening a picture frame that was the tiniest bit uneven, fluffing the feather pillows on the bed. "Now about dinner. Dr. Douglas didn't say he'd be needing supper this evening?"

"No," Kelsey murmured, turning back to the window. "He didn't say."

"Well, then. Why don't you come down at half past? Gordon's built a fine fire in the great room and you can have a little nip before dining. Poached salmon tonight. I think you'll like it."

"I'm sure I will. Thank you, Mrs. Devon." The housekeeper left. Kelsey sat at the desk and pulled out the sheaf of papers she'd printed from Dalhousie University. She studied the computer image. What was going on?

She buried her face in her hands as the throbbing pain at the base of her skull that had plagued her the past few days returned. It was as if her brain were trying to short circuit: she couldn't think, couldn't focus on the papers spread out in front of her. The smallest thought slipped away from her.

A strange skittering crept along her spine. The prickle of awareness on her skin made her jump up and run to the window. Cade was back. His presence surrounded her as strongly as if he were in the room.

The gray shape of a man made his way slowly towards the inn from the point of land jutting into the sea. Rain spilled off his head, but instead of being covered with a hooded slicker, like Mr. Devon always wore in the rain, Cade wore jeans and a sweater. Even his head was bare. He stopped, turning his face towards the sky, like an exuberant child, or....

An odd image tried to take shape in her mind, but was crowded out by a stronger picture. For a wild moment, Kelsey imagined herself standing with him, skin slippery with rain, Cade touching her, tasting a trail of raindrops.

Desire burst through her like sunshine after a storm.

Kelsey clenched her hand around her pearl necklace. She had to get out of this room. She couldn't stand here, letting her imagination create what was impossible. How she could still want him after he abandoned her and disappeared for days made her face burn. She didn't even know who he really was! The clasp on her necklace jerked free under her fingers, and she caught it just as it began a descent to the hardwood floor.

Her pearls, a precious gift from her father, one she wore daily, even when dressed in an oxford shirt or sweater and jeans. She carefully laid the necklace on the dresser. She'd inspect the clasp after dinner, but now she had to get out of this room, in case Cade was headed this way.

She took the back stairs to the kitchen, pretended an interest in dinner preparations, and after she was satisfied that Cade would have made his way to his own room, she ventured to the great hall.

Cade couldn't stop himself. Clothes dripping water on Mrs. Devon's immaculate floors, he made his way to Kelsey's room, although he sensed she had already fled. A folded sheaf of papers stuck out from a book on Kelsey's desk, as if she had been in a hurry to put them out of sight. Idly he picked them up, hoping for clues on what she had spent her time on while he was gone.

Dr. C.D. Douglas' picture stared up at him. His blood turned icy.

Damn it. How had she gotten this information? Why had she felt it necessary to research him? Even more important, what was she going to do about it?

How am I supposed to make her forget all of this, Grandfather?

Crumpling the papers in his hand, he touched her necklace, pearls still warm from her skin, still holding the essence of her, and closed his eyes.

Kelsey. But instead of being able to focus on blocking her memories, he found his mind transported to somewhere he'd never been, confronting a woman he'd never seen, except for the resemblance she bore to Kelsey. What memories besides Kelsey's had he tapped into?

Just as quickly the images shifted to the sea cave. Kelsey's thoughts swirled around his forcing him to remember her little gasps of pleasure, his sense of desperate triumph as he experienced his own release, then recalled the sensation of exhausted satiation until desire blazed once more. Swearing softly, he opened his eyes. Why couldn't he control this?

In the great room, the fire snapped. Kelsey took a sip of whiskey and staggered backwards as mind pictures flared to life as brilliant and heated as the fire raging in the grate. She sank into one of the overstuffed chairs and pressed a hand to the side of her head. Where did these overpowering images come from? Moments before she'd been engrossed in Mrs. Devon's island history when the sensation of Cade's hands on her was as vivid as if she were with him.

"There, now, have a seat." Mrs. Devon's voice soothed. "Just a wee bit strong for you, is it?"

The whiskey scalded her throat, but Kelsey took another bracing sip and nodded at the housekeeper. "It's very smooth actually. I'm just not used to drinking anything straight up."

"An American weakness, watering down good spirits."

Kelsey jerked her head towards Cade, standing in the doorway, accepting a glass of whiskey from Gordon Devon.

"Dr. Douglas." Mrs. Devon beamed at him. "So you made it through the storm, and just in time for dinner. We're having your favorite. Are Dr. Bracken and Dr. Norlund back as well?"

"No, but I expect they'll be here in the morning when the rain stops."

He spoke as if he had the weather report from the highest authority.

"What makes you think it will?" Kelsey couldn't help but ask.

"Here, I'll show you."

She joined him at the huge windows facing west and the restless expanse of sea.

"See that smudge of color on the horizon?"

Kelsey peered out the window. A tiny line of red streaked the edge of sea and sky. "Hmmm. Red sky at night. Very scientific, Dr. Douglas."

He smiled, and Kelsey realized it was the first time she'd seen his expression lighten since meeting him. Warmth curled through her, but she fought to keep her feelings from showing.

"Never underestimate the value of legends, Miss MacKenzie. Isn't that right, Mrs. Devon?"

The housekeeper nodded knowingly. "I was just telling her," she paused and sniffed dramatically. "Merciful heavens, Gordon's burning the sauce again. Excuse us." She and her husband hurried from the room.

Kelsey wrinkled her nose, but only the tang of peat stung her nostrils. "I don't smell anything unusual." She turned to Cade in time to see his furtively self-satisfied expression. "You wanted her to leave, didn't you?"

He shrugged. "Why would I?"

She allowed herself to hope that he wanted to touch her as much as she wanted him to despite the bewilderment and lingering feelings of anger that plagued her. "You tell me. Then tell me where you've been for the past two days when we were supposed to be working together. And finally, tell me who you really are."

He took a step back. "What are you talking about?"

"While you've been wherever it was, I decided I wanted to read your research on seals." Panic briefly flared in his eyes, then was gone.

"And what did you find?"

"A picture of someone who isn't you. A Dr. Douglas at Dalhousie University who isn't in Orkney, but is still in Nova Scotia teaching classes!"

Cade laughed out loud. "You're mistaken."

"I don't think so. In fact, I believe you're here on the basis of someone else's credentials."

His face darkened. "That's the kind of reasoning I'd expect from a novice. Jumping to conclusions on the basis of flimsy research. Which proves my point. We can't work together, Kelsey." His voice was so quiet she had to edge closer to hear and though he spoke her name like a caress, his words gave her a flurry of dismay.

"Why? Because you're not who you say you are, and you're afraid of what Dr. Bracken will do when I tell him?"

"Dr. Bracken is well aware of exactly where I come from."

"Then what are you so hung up about?" She studied his face, and although he was silent, he raised an eyebrow as if to suggest significant possibilities. Heat crawled up her neck. Defiance rushed in to counter her embarrassment. So he was sorry about what happened on the island. Well, she wasn't. She lifted a shoulder and took a bracing sip of the strong liquor.

"Look, we can't change what happened. Why are you trying to? Who are you? Why do strange things happen around you and you try to make me think I've been dreaming?"

"And what have you been dreaming, little one?" Ignoring her questions, he caressed her face in a mood shift that left her breathless. His gaze held hers, and he slowly lowered his mouth to hers.

His lips were like velvet. Kelsey's eyes fluttered shut and she gave in to bliss as her body awakened in slow degrees. This was what she remembered, the feel of his mouth, the taste of his kiss, the wind tossed scent of him. Her ears buzzed and for a moment, her mind blanked, sucking her towards a black abyss. Her eyes flew open in panicked awareness, and she jerked away from him, her will colliding with his like tidal currents. Memories coursed through her, bringing fresh heat to her face. Her glass crashed to the floor.

"What are you trying to do?"

Cade ran a hand through his hair and uttered a frustrated word she didn't understand.

"Call you to dinner, Miss. Is everything all right?" Mrs. Devon's concerned tones made Kelsey whirl toward the door.

"Yes, of course. I'm sorry about the mess." She knelt and picked up bits of glass, pricking her finger.

"Never mind that. I'll have Gwendolyn fetch the broom. You and Dr. Douglas go on to dinner."

Kelsey reluctantly placed the shards into the housekeeper's outstretched hand. Her finger stung, and she automatically raised it to her lips, then sucked gently. Cade stared, his eyes molten, before he abruptly led the way to the dining room. She had asked him a question. The answer was terribly important, she knew it was, but now she couldn't remember what she'd asked.

"Dr. Douglas," she broke off when he paused. What had she asked him? The edges of her thoughts were fuzzy, like a slightly frayed blanket. She'd just have to ask him again later.

Dinner was served family style by the Devon's and although they liked to share cocktails and coffee with their guests, they took their evening meal long after the last guest had consumed their fill. Sometimes people from the village came to dine, but tonight she and Cade would have the room to themselves.

Cade held her chair while she took a place at the oak table and laid her cloth napkin in her lap. He sat opposite. Mrs. Devon ladled bowls of cream of mushroom soup, then departed for the kitchen. Kelsey spooned a mouthful, but the taste barely registered. Cade kept his eyes averted and silence stretched awkwardly, the closeness and quiet giving the scene an odd sense of intimacy.

He looked tired and pale, as if he wasn't feeling well, and she became worried. Perhaps that explained his two day absence and like most men, he didn't want to admit he'd been ill. She remembered all too well her father's stubborn refusal to acknowledge that sniffles could be a cold, not a reaction to dust. Clearing her throat, she started to speak, but the swinging doors from the kitchen opened and Mrs. Devon returned with large bowls of salad, vegetables and fish.

Kelsey took small portions and picked at the food. The salmon had a sweet glaze on it, and she busied herself trying to guess the ingredients in Gordon Devon's secret sauce. At least she had a chance at that whereas trying to guess Cade's thoughts was like trying to break through currents at spring tide.

"Kelsey," Cade placed his hand over hers, startling her from her speculation. "I think it would be best if you went back to Baltimore."

The gruff tenderness in his voice brought tears to her eyes while the words pushed her further back into her chair. "What did you say?"

He moved his hand away and regarded her while he sipped water. "We've established that we're incompatible. On a professional level. Since we can only have four scientists on this project, I think it would be best if the slot was filled by someone more experienced. I know you have your heart set on working with Dr. Bracken, but perhaps back in the States you'll have an opportunity later. Something for which you're better suited. Or maybe your father has a place for you."

He had a place for her all right, miles behind, not beside him. Kelsey's mouth dropped open for a moment. How dare Cade suggest she wasn't qualified. And he couldn't know how much this position meant to her or he wouldn't even propose such a thing. "Just a minute, Dr. Douglas—"

He continued as if she hadn't spoken. "Tomorrow Dr. Bracken will be back. You and I both know we made a disastrous error in judgment the other day."

Kelsey glanced towards the kitchen, but the Devon's were safely out of earshot. So he regarded their afternoon of bliss as an error in judgment? How dare he.

She couldn't feel more wrenched if she were caught in an eddy. But at least he admitted it had happened, and she wasn't dream crazed. She took a deep breath and composed herself. "Please, don't try to break it to me gently."

She glanced up in time to see his anguished expression before he hid it behind a scowl. "It's stupid to keep playing with temptation, Kelsey. But as much as I want you, I won't let you risk yourself. And I won't jeopardize this project, either."

Oh, so he was going to be noble. She narrowed her eyes. A familiar sickening feeling bloomed in the pit of her stomach. Her father's voice echoed in her ears. *For your own good, Kelsey. When you're older, more experienced.* Always, always something standing in the way. Someone always thinking they knew what was best for her, without regard to what she wanted.

His tone softened, but she sensed the underlying steely resolve. "You can tell Bracken in the morning. It's better this way. Really. You can't afford to jeopardize your professional reputation."

She knew he was right, but oh the endless unfairness of it. Men could play around, "experience" life, but women had to carefully calculate each and every move unless they wanted to stay at the bottom of the career ladder. Cade had his nerve, taking what she offered so that she could never give it to anyone else, then making decisions for her.

When Kelsey remained silent, he pushed the knife deeper. "I know you're lonely, but I'm not what you need."

Kelsey tossed her napkin onto the table. "You want to

pretend it never happened, then by all means, let's just forget about it. If I can handle it, after—" her voice trailed off before she continued, not wanting to admit to him what he should already know. "Then you should be man enough to overcome your personal feelings. Or you leave. But I'm not going until the project is successfully completed." She pushed her chair back and left the room by way of the kitchen, passing the Devon's holding trays of tea and dessert, on her way out. The housekeeper's murmured words to her husband drifted up to Kelsey as she bounded up the stairs.

"He'll not be pleased. And she'll be another just like that first woman. Mark my words."

Chapter Eight

Kelsey dismissed Mrs. Devon's words and returned to her room, but the cozy space pressed in on her. The white painted brass bed looked lumpy and worn, the papers on her desk an uninviting mess.

As Cade had predicted, the rain had stopped. Against the still dark sky, a partial rainbow promised a better tomorrow. She'd go for a walk along the beach, clear her head and try to shake off the anguish Cade's words had given her.

Trying to decide on a sweater, she rummaged through the wardrobe, wishing she had been able to find her fisherman knit when her fingers closed around the soft, familiar wool. No, it couldn't be, the sweater had been missing ever since she had arrived, and she had finally convinced herself that she had forgotten to pack it before she left Baltimore.

She tugged, toppling a bright stack of folded sweaters and shirts to the floor. Scrambling to her feet, Kelsey clutched the ivory sweater in disbelief. Hers, yet somehow different. The damp wool didn't smell like her favorite perfume, but held a different scent, like… Cade. Her heart constricted.

Thinking she could have left the sweater in the lab or the great hall, she had even asked him if he had seen it.

He'd scowled and said no.

Why would he have taken something of hers? She wondered when he would have returned it, but the answer was obvious. While she was hiding out in the kitchen before dinner. That's why the sweater was slightly wet. He'd had it with him in the rain.

She buried her face in the damp wool and inhaled. Cade's unique scent of sea air and spicy musk wrapped around her and she was back in the cave, his strong arms around her, the beat of his heart steady beneath her ear. Her throat clenched as she fought back sudden tears, but the sobs welled up and were wrenched out as if driven by some force deep inside.

She didn't know what she had expected, had hoped for. Why should things have turned out any differently? She and Cade barely knew each other, yet the connection they shared was undeniable, and she'd given herself freely. He had taken, but left her with an awareness that even now cried out for fulfillment. She sank to the floor, powerless to hold back the torrent, the futile yearning and the utter despair.

In the lab, Cade hunched over the microscope, carefully reviewing Kelsey's work of the past two days. She'd worked hard and recorded her efforts meticulously while he was gone. She didn't deserve to be sabotaged, but it might be the only way to drive her away.

Something sharp twisted in his chest. He doubled over, mentally casting aspersions on Mrs. Devon's culinary skills when he heard Kelsey's tears. Soft, at the edges of his mind, but even from this distance, he tasted her pain.

He had hurt her, and she wept. Not tears of injured pride but a lost soulfulness that twisted his heart.

Grandfather was wrong. Modern women were not as free spirited as he insisted. Or maybe Kelsey was different, more caring, not one to give herself carelessly for simple pleasure. Or maybe....

He didn't dare contemplate the way in which Kelsey didn't match Meredith Douglas' suppositions about American women. Surely she had given up her innocence long ago.

He could go to her and simply offer comfort, then gently work on a solution to getting her away from the island. Away from his ugly truths, away from the project and, most importantly, away from Bracken's private agenda.

He turned the options over in his mind, worrying each one until an hour had passed, and he was still no closer to finding a solution.

He shut off the lights and walked the hundred yards to the inn. No lights shone from Kelsey's room, but he made his way there first anyway.

She had fallen asleep on the braided rug in front of the fireplace, and he started to turn away. Embers smoldered in the grate, but the room held a chill.

He couldn't just let her lie there, cold and alone. Searching out her dreams, he spun her a fantasy and watched a faint smile tug the corner of her enticing mouth as he carefully picked her up and placed her on the bed. She murmured but didn't waken so he removed her shoes and let his hands linger. She had lovely ankles, delicious legs. His fingers lightly traced the contours through her tapered jeans. If only….

If only what? He shook his head, angry with frustration. There could be no way to be together and not tell her the truth about what he was. She'd be repulsed. And even if she wasn't, sooner or later, she'd tell either Bracken or her father and the fate of Cade's family would be in worse jeopardy than they'd faced on the islands with the perils of nature that had taken the lives of his cousins. And Shayla.

No, there was no way, and his heart ached with misery.

Quietly, he drew the quilted comforter up to Kelsey's shoulders. Dark lashes cast shadows on her face. He wiped away traces of tears with his thumb, then touched his tongue to the saltiness on his own skin. Her pearl necklace circled her throat, their luster no more radiant than her creamy skin.

He couldn't stop himself from touching the cool luminescence, then let his fingers linger on her warmth. The heat of her struck him anew, and a vision formed in his mind, Kelsey wearing only the pearls and a smile, love shining in her eyes. He stifled a groan of hopeless longing.

Kelsey's eyes drifted open, her blue gaze sleepy, then

searching. With a jolt he realized her dream had woven itself into his thoughts, and now she lay watching him through wary eyes. He shivered from the recognition of desire.

She still wanted him. Even after the harsh words they'd hurled at each other, her need for him was as great as his was for her. He should go. He turned to leave but her fingers laced with his, and he found himself unable to move away.

And this was his chance. Her will blurred by sleep, he could make her forget what had happened at the cave. If he could make her forget, she could stay. Could he live with that?

He leaned over her, prepared to use every trick Grandfather had taught him. Kelsey simply returned his intense look, then her arms came up to circle his neck.

"Why do you really want me to leave the island?"

He groaned and sank onto the bed, forgetting any other purpose for being there the moment his lips brushed hers. "Kelsey, Kelsey," he whispered, her name a fire raging through his blood. "I don't want you to go. I only know that what I want from you isn't right."

She stroked his hair, let her fingers trail over his smooth jaw. "Tell me what you want."

"You." He buried his face against the warmth of her throat. The loneliness he'd felt for the past few years melted away when she was near. He didn't understand how. Or why. He knew her feelings paralleled his. Yet how could he tell her he wanted to feel her wrapped around him, needed her soft sighs filling his mind, longed for her heart to beat in rhythm with his?

She seemed to know as surely as if he'd spoken. Kelsey's fingers danced down the buttons of his oxford shirt, then she drew the sleeves down his arms, letting her hands rub against the fine hair before tugging the garment completely away. Her hands skimmed over his chest, then locked behind his neck. He lowered his mouth to hers, captivated by the soft, sweet feel of her.

"Do you realize what you're doing?" His words emerged as a gruff whisper.

"No." Honesty shone in her eyes, causing him physical pain. Her heart was so pure, so true. "I thought I was dreaming."

Grandfather was wrong about Kelsey. He ignored the blinding flash of realization and closed his eyes, not wanting her to see his doubts and confusion. His yearning. Again the image formed in his mind, Kelsey bare except for the pearls. His mouth melded with hers while she plucked at buttons and snaps until the image became reality.

Her dark hair fanned out against the white pillow. Cade wound a strand around his finger, then trailed a caress down her cheek to her neck. He rubbed a pearl between his fingers, astonished with the overpowering surge of need washing through him. He shed his clothes and took her in his arms, desperate to be inside her before the voices of reason returned to torment him. *This woman, this moment.* That was all that mattered.

She kissed him until he trembled, until he was unaware of anything but the feel of her flesh beneath his hands and her lips on his. He opened his eyes, astonished to realize she had shifted positions. Naked, she straddled his hips, her skin glowing like moonlight on a still cove.

"Is this what you wanted?"

Cade's heart hammered. "How did you know?"

She shook her head and her glorious sable hair brushed her shoulders. "I have these thoughts. Images really. Overpowering. I don't know where they come from."

"When did it start?"

She shrugged, a hesitant little gesture. "Soon after I arrived."

Cade's heart soared. Grandfather was wrong, he was meant to have Kelsey, if only for a time. There had to be a reason they were so strongly attuned to one another. He just didn't know if he could afford to risk his family to find out.

But they could have tonight. Let them have this one night together. If he could keep his wits and not run to Meredith like a wounded pup, no one would ever know he and Kelsey had one last night of passion. Tomorrow Bracken would return, and Kelsey would be forced to leave.

He raised his head and took the tip of her breast in his mouth. She shivered and closed her eyes, splaying her hands against his chest.

"Take me inside," he whispered, unable to bear the agony of being separate, yet so close.

She smiled shyly, hesitated for a heartbeat, then slid down his body and took him in her mouth. Cade tensed and cried out, then his limbs seemed to melt, and he couldn't have moved if he'd wanted to. He dug his fingers into the mattress.

A low moan ripped from his throat as she continued her gentle nipping and licking until he was sure he'd dissipate like mist in sunshine. Grasping her arms, he brought her up, settled her astride him and plunged inside. Velvety heat surrounded him, gripped him tightly. A deep shudder ran through him.

"Ah, Kelsey," he murmured her name like a caress, sure there was no sweeter sound. A soft, rain washed breeze wafted in the window carrying the aroma of the sea. Clean scents of starched sheets and wool blankets mingled with her delicate fragrance.

This was how it should be, a bed of linen instead of damp sand. The antique bed creaked with their sweet rhythm. He touched the pearls glowing at her throat, then ran his finger down the cleft of her breasts. His fingers dipped lower, stroking and encouraging her. Kelsey gasped and closed her eyes. Her hair spilled down her back. She clenched around him, and he joined her in tumultuous release.

Kelsey woke the next morning from the pale sunshine

peeking in her window. An odd sense of disappointment settled around her, overshadowing the night's pleasure when she realized she was alone. Cade certainly wasn't much for staying around for the after play. She'd believe she'd dreamed the interlude except she was unashamedly naked in her bed when she knew she'd fallen asleep fully clothed in front of the fireplace. She closed her eyes and stretched languidly.

"Good morning, sleepy head." Cade's voice startled her from pleasant remembrances.

She pulled the covers tight and glanced at the clock. "It's every bit of six a.m. What a slug I am."

Jeans unbuttoned, silver hair tousled, Cade stood before her, a steaming mug in his hand. He handed it to her. "For you."

"Coffee?" She made a futile attempt to keep the hopeful note from her voice.

He shook his head, but it was with affection instead of the exasperation he used to show her. "The finest English tea. And a bit of Gordon's whiskey."

When he remained standing, she patted the bed beside her, hoping he'd at least sit down and share a casual morning conversation while she drank the liberally sweetened tea. Instead, he shed the jeans, lifted the covers and slid in beside her. Kelsey blew on the tea. He wasn't wearing underwear, she noted, nearly burning her tongue on the hot liquid. He hadn't been last night either, or the afternoon at the sea cave.

He disappeared beneath the covers. "Cade!" Her voice squeaked. He emerged, gently took the mug from her trembling fingers and resumed lavishing kisses against her bare skin.

"What about breakfast? Mrs. Devon. Dr. Bracken. The others? Oh, sweet heaven." She dug her fingers into his shoulders as he playfully nipped her inner thigh.

He wrapped his arms around her waist and pressed his face against her abdomen. "Everyone's gone. We'll have to make our own breakfast."

Kelsey tensed. "Gone? Everyone?"

Cade pulled her down against him and massaged the tension from her neck. "Mrs. Devon left a note. She and Gordon have gone to Mainland Island. Some sort of family emergency. And apparently Dr. Bracken telephoned late last night to say he and Norlund hadn't concluded their business, so the Devons decided it was a good time to restock while they were in Kirkwall. Everyone will be back in a couple of days."

Kelsey let his supple fingers work her anxiety away. "What are we going to do in the meantime?"

"I just want to hold you." He cuddled her against his side, his hands gentle and caressing. "Later I want to show you some things about the island."

"We have work to do in the lab," she murmured, already relaxed and drowsy from the tea and his ministrations.

He hesitated, but his hands never stopped their hypnotic stroking. "I took care of it last night. Don't worry. Everything will be fine."

She awoke later to the aroma of frying bacon. Her stomach growled. Small wonder. This time the bedside clock read ten o'clock. That couldn't be right. Kelsey threw back the covers and slid out of bed. She never slept that late. She picked up the mug of tea on the nightstand and inhaled. A bit of whiskey, indeed. Now that it was cold, the smell of alcohol assaulted her senses. There was enough in there to scramble her mind even if she hadn't already been lightheaded from Cade's lovemaking.

What was he up to?

She shrugged into an oxford shirt and pulled on her jeans. Barefoot she made her way down the back stairs to the kitchen.

Cade stood at the stove, turning the thick slices of ham

Mrs. Devon referred to as bacon. "I knew you were up," he said, although Kelsey knew it was impossible for him to have heard her on the carpeted steps. He gestured with the tongs. "There's scones and fruit preserves. The bacon will be done shortly. Would you like eggs?"

"Fine." Kelsey rinsed out her mug, then sat at the table and refilled it with hot tea. She squeezed in lemon and added two spoonfuls of sugar.

Cade set a plate of bacon on the table. "I see you discovered the secret of making tea drinkable."

She took a sip and stifled a grimace. "Barely. What do the Scots have against coffee, anyway?"

Cade shrugged and returned to the stove. "I don't drink either one, so I couldn't give you an answer to that."

She considered him. His blue oxford shirt was only half buttoned. His silver hair still looked sleep tangled. "Really. What do you like for an eye opener, then?"

The quick look he turned on her stole her breath. Passion smoldered in his pewter eyes, making her pulse drum a frantic rhythm. Shared memories poured through her veins until her hand trembled, and she was forced to set the mug on the table.

Kelsey dropped her gaze. "Besides that." She dabbed at the spattering of tea on the polished oak and decided to change the subject before she found herself making love to him on the kitchen table. She could tell by the look on his face the thought had occurred to him as well, flustering her even more. "Where is Gwendolyn?"

"Enjoying a few days holiday, according to Mrs. Devon's note." He knelt before her and took her hands in his. "Why are you so troubled about being alone here with me?"

What a question. Despite the passion they'd shared, last night's conversation still played in the corners of her mind. Then there was something else. Some other question she'd had, but for the life of her, she couldn't remember what it had been. "Last night you said...."

He bought her hand to his face, rubbed her fingers over the smoothness of his cheek. Odd, how despite his otherwise rather disheveled appearance, he didn't have a trace of beard on his skin. He kissed her fingers, sucked gently on the tips. Heat pooled in her belly, poured through her until she felt deliciously languid.

"We were meant to have this time together, Kelsey. Whatever else happens later, these next two days belong to us. If you want it."

She did, more than she'd ever wanted anything. Even the determination and desire she felt about her work became a pallid imitation of emotion next to her jumbled feelings for this man. "The lab. There's so much to be done."

"It will still be there in three days time." He didn't quite meet her gaze, but instead cradled her face in his hands and kissed her. Kelsey closed her eyes and let the sensation of his mouth on hers overload her senses. His lips caressed hers, lazy and unhurried, igniting a response from her. Her arms went around his shoulders, her fingers slid into his hair. Thoughts coalesced into a kaleidoscope of sensations, the silkiness of his hair, the hardness of his chest against her breasts, the scents of warm bread and tea. At last when she couldn't think of anything except the feeling of his gentle caressing kiss, he pulled back and seated himself next to her. Still holding her hand in his, he fed her a tidbit of ham, the gesture so purely sensual she felt like snow dissolving on a warm pane.

"You must eat if you're going to keep up with me."

Warmth flooded her face before she realized he was, for the first time, teasing her. "Excuse me?"

A smile played at the corners of his mouth. He released her hand and rose, then moved to the stove. "I want to show you the island, particularly some rather remote places. We'll have to backpack." He turned, an anxious expression lurking beneath his nonchalant words. "That is, if you'd like to."

"Very much." She went to him then and wrapped her arms

around him. At last she'd have a chance to get to know the real Cade Douglas. "I want to see everything." She drew back and studied his face. "What about your family? I thought Mrs. Devon said your grandfather lived near here."

His relaxed mood changed like a storm-driven wind. A muscle tensed in his jaw. "Mrs. Devon is mistaken." He eased away from her and picked up the skillet, dropping it back on the stove and stifling an oath in a language she'd never heard before.

"Cade," she reached for his hand, trying to examine the palm and smooth fingertips before he snatched it away from her careful perusal. "Let me get some ice."

"I'm fine. Go sit down, Kelsey."

Stung by his harsh attitude, she picked up a potholder and removed the offending skillet from the stove. "I'll dish this up. Go put something on that. Mrs. Devon must have some aloe vera or burn ointment."

He nodded and hurried from the room. Deciding not to let her food get cold, Kelsey started eating when several minutes passed and he didn't return. She slathered preserves on a warm scone. Filled with seasonings she'd never heard of, food here had an unusual tang to it. The jam almost tasted as if the slightly bitter fruit had been sweetened with some type of flowers.

"Elderflowers." Cade took a seat beside her and began to eat.

Dumbfounded, Kelsey dropped her scone to her plate. "What are you talking about?"

"You asked what the jam was made with. Gooseberries flavored with sugar and elderflowers. The white flowers you've seen covering the hills. Mrs. Devon makes good use of the wild foods available on the island."

She was certain she hadn't spoken the question aloud. As certain as she was that he was intentionally distracting her from taking another close look at his hand. "How do you do that?"

"Do what?"

Kelsey gestured impatiently at him. "Know what I'm thinking before I can say it."

"I'm quite sure I don't know what you mean." He scowled, and the return of the Cade she'd first met filled her with a profound sense of regret for asking the question.

"Did you burn your hand very badly?"

"It's fine. A little of Mrs. Devon's homemade remedy and by the time we're ready to leave, it will be as if nothing happened."

She wanted to pursue it, but the look on his face clearly said no trespassing. She had so many questions. So many things didn't quite add up. Maybe if she was patient, by the time Dr. Bracken and Dr. Norlund returned she'd have the answers she needed.

Chapter Nine

After eating, Kelsey showered and dressed. By the time she finished, Cade had changed clothes, packed a picnic lunch and stood waiting somewhat impatiently in the great room.

"Half the day is already gone," he grumbled as she followed her out the front door.

"Well, why did you let me sleep so long?"

He stopped so suddenly, she collided with him. He turned, studied her upturned face for several moments before he tucked a damp strand of her hair behind her ear. "You look like Amphitrite—Neptune's wife—when you sleep. I couldn't bear to disturb you." He brushed a soft kiss to her lips, then took her hand and laced his fingers with hers.

She had to admit he was very good at keeping her exactly where he wanted, but how long could she be angry with a man who thought she looked like a sea goddess?

Instead of heading to the shore, where she had expected to spend the day beach combing, Cade led her through the verdant green of the fields towards the gray-green hills.

Overhead puffins wheeled and cried, spinning like pinwheels before heading out to sea.

"There must be hundreds of them." Kelsey shielded her eyes, mesmerized by the black and white birds, their tangerine feet and beaks brilliant against a cloudless sky.

"Wait till sunset. There will be thousands." Cade continued walking, carefully following a barely visible trail on the uneven green slope. "We're very near their nesting sites."

"How has the problem with the fish population affected

them?" She hurried to catch up. "Do they seem to suffer the same ailments as the seals?"

He stopped and gently placed his finger against her lips. "No more talk of work. I said I wanted to show you the island, not carry on a biology lesson."

"Cade, we can't forget why we're here."

"Later, Kelsey. Remember, the next two days may be our only chance."

Chance at what, she wanted to ask, but was certain he wouldn't know the answer any better than she did. She gazed into his gray eyes, as mysterious as a stormy sky, but now infinitely more peaceful.

"I have a place to show you very few people have ever seen. Come along now." He took her hand again and helped her over the boulders, although she didn't need it. Kelsey allowed his solicitude. The bandage on his hand rubbed against her palm and she wanted to ask him about the burn, but decided it wasn't important. Like most men, he probably resented being fussed over for having a slight accident. Her father certainly became impatient whenever she tried to.

"Tell me about him."

Kelsey stumbled. "Who?"

Cade tightened his grip on her hand. "Your father. You were going to tell me about his latest project. Something you might participate in, perhaps?"

He was sneaky, she had to give him that. For the past few hours, she'd begun to hope he'd abandoned the idea that she should leave. She could confront him again, rehash last night's arguments, but found she had no interest in it.

A soft wind teased her hair, the sun shone warm on her face, and Cade's firm grasp on her hand made her glad she was at this moment in time, this place. She took his question at face value.

"He's in the Mediterranean, filming a special on Monk seals for public television. He's made it very clear that he has no use for me." The thought stung, although why it should still bother her after all these years, she didn't understand.

Cade squeezed her hand. "Then he's as bullheaded and foolish as my grandfather remembered." He seemed to regret the words the moment he spoke them. Using their joined hands, he gestured towards the puffin burrows. "You asked about the puffins. Each pair has only one chick and each one is in a separate nest."

"I thought you said you didn't want to conduct a biology lesson." She studied his profile, wishing he'd look directly at her so it would be easier to gauge the truth in his eyes. "Your grandfather knows my father?"

"Who doesn't know of William Bouschour? He's made quite a reputation for himself over the years."

An answer, yet not quite complete. How could she get him to be open with her? "Does your grandfather know Dr. Bracken, too?"

"Yes, although his impression of your former professor is less flattering."

Again, not a very informative answer. Although it made sense, she supposed. Dr. Bracken had said Cade's grandfather made his fortune in shipping. It would be only natural for a businessman to find himself at odds with environmentalists. And Cade's family could know a lot about her father and Bracken without ever having actually met either one. "How does he feel about your career?"

Cade paused as her question puzzled him. "He's very pleased, of course, and why not?"

Kelsey shrugged. "It seems like you might be at cross purposes at times."

"We both want what is best for our family."

Dozens of questions sprang to her lips, but before she could speak, Cade broke into a jog, dragging her with him.

"We're almost there. See that slight break in the elder bushes? That's our path."

Path to what, she wondered as branches caught at her hair,

scraped against her jeans. What Cade called a break in the dense vegetation was barely big enough to squeeze through without risking looking as if they'd tangled with a coral reef. Cade moved through the undergrowth with the practiced ease of a forest creature. Finally, he stopped, blocking her view of whatever lay ahead.

"Close your eyes."

Kelsey tried to peer around him. "Why?"

He turned and gave her a tentative smile that melted her questions. "Please?"

When she nodded, he placed one hand over her eyes and wrapped his arm around her shoulders, guiding her forward. "No fair peeking."

"As long as you don't let me fall."

"Trust me," he whispered against her ear, transporting Kelsey back several days to when he'd emerged from the sea and saved her from the tide. Or at least when she thought he'd rescued her.

"Cade." She wanted to ask him about that day. About the day at the sea cave. How could he take her places and she not remember the trip? But this was real, this was now. She felt the warmth of his body next to hers, smelled his distinctive scent of sea and fresh air. His hand was smooth and cool against her face. "Cade," she said again.

"Now you can look." He took his hand away but didn't move.

For a moment, Kelsey felt dizzy and disoriented, as if he had transported her to some mystical place. She blinked and the world slowly swung into focus. Sunlight danced across a pool of clear water surrounded by huge standing stones covered with moss and lichen. A small waterfall cascaded from the gray-green hill into the pool. Shimmers of light dazzled her eyes. She took a tentative step forward.

"Oh, Cade. It's beautiful." The words seemed so inadequate for such a magnificent setting.

He seemed as pleased as a child sharing a secret hiding

place. "We can have lunch here, if you'd like."

Kelsey squeezed his hand. "Very much. I'd like to do a little exploring, first, though." She peeled off her backpack and set it on the flat rocks near the water's edge. "It's so clear, I feel like I can see forever." She knelt and scooped up a handful of cool water, then splashed it on her warm face. "Aren't you hot?"

Cade dropped his sweater and backpack beside hers and stretched out, leaning against one of the standing stones. "Not really. Take your shoes off and go wading. I seem to remember you like cold water on your bare feet."

It was the first reference he'd made to the day they'd spent at the sea cave. Kelsey let the water trickle through her fingers. It was cold, but not icy. She had a sudden wild impulse to shed her clothes and feel the cool water envelop her.

His gaze burned into hers while a pulse thrummed in his throat. "Do it, Kelsey."

"I'm not that crazy." She sat back on her heels and studied him, wondering how she could have answered him when she had no way of knowing for sure what he was referring to.

Cade opened a flagon, took a sip and handed it to her. Kelsey held the flask and drank, feeling the imprint of his mouth more than the bottle against her lips. Wine, warm, fruity and musky, trickled down her throat.

"Mrs. Devon's homemade wine?"

"Elderberry." Cade leaned on an elbow and considered her. The wine made her lips even more crimson, more enticing than they already were. He watched her take another slow draught and resisted the urge to kiss her.

Kelsey trailed her fingers in the water, longing evident on her face, and handed the flask back to him.

"Do it, Kelsey," he whispered again.

"It's not safe to swim alone." She unlaced her sneakers, pulled off thick socks and rolled up the legs of her jeans. She dangled her legs in the water, a momentary shiver passing through her.

He knew she was thinking of Lana and wondering: was this what had happened to her? Was this how an innocent outing had turned to tragedy? "I wouldn't let you be hurt." He hoped she believed him. Her pensive expression told him she wanted to.

This time he didn't even try to fight the overwhelming desire. Cupping the back of her head, he pulled her close and kissed her, slowly and deeply, letting his tongue taste the intoxicating blend of her and wine.

Reluctantly, she broke away from him. "Swim with me." Her words were a gentle plea.

He brushed his thumb across her lower lip and felt her tremble. "I can't. But I'll watch you."

Dark with desire, her eyes looked like the midnight sky. Her fingers worked the buttons of her shirt, then the snaps of her jeans. She stepped out of her clothes and stood naked before him. Goose bumps dotted her delicate skin.

"How do you make me do such crazy things?" Her voice was as soft as the breeze that floated around them.

He took her hand, kissed the fingertips. "You do what you wish, of your own free will." He released her hand. "Show me what you do in Baltimore."

"In Baltimore, I wear a wet suit." She dipped her toes into the water. "Cade, this is insane. I'm going to freeze."

He was silent, letting her find her own way. She crept from the rock into waist deep water and rubbed her arms. Her nipples tightened, red nubs against white skin. Cade gripped the flagon of wine and tamped down the lust that made him want to dive in after her. Foolish, foolish thoughts. If he got into the pond, the game would be over for sure.

Kelsey took a step backward and disappeared beneath the surface. Cade rose, panic forcing him towards the water's edge when she emerged sputtering and laughing. Her dark hair plastered her head like a sleek cap.

"You could have told me there might be a drop-off."

Turning her back on him, she swam towards the waterfall, slicing through the water without a splash. She disappeared from sight around a large outcropping of rocks.

Clenching his hands, he watched where she had gone and waited for her to reappear, impatience growing stronger with every passing second. It was wrong. It was stupid and risky, but the urge to join her was overwhelming. He shed his clothes and carefully placed them out of sight, then dove into the cool, fresh water.

Kelsey stood under the waterfall, letting the water pound on her back. She shivered. She was freezing and no doubt certifiably crazy. She edged back around the rocks. "Cade?"

No answer.

Her clothes remained piled near the water's edge, but the blanket Cade had stretched out on was empty. Where had he gone? He'd promised to watch out for her, but what good was that if he couldn't even swim? Again she thought of Lana and wondered if this was the kind of foolishness that had cost her life.

Something shimmered beneath the surface, a flash of silver in the dappled sunlight. Something slippery brushed against her thigh. Kelsey choked back a scream. Images of the Loch Ness monster and creatures of the deep bubbled into her mind. Then she realized how ludicrous the idea was and burst out laughing. Years of scientific training down the drain simply because a fish had rubbed against her leg. The pond wasn't deep enough to host anything except small vertebrates, and she knew the lochs in Scotland, particularly one so remote, teemed with trout.

Still, her unease spoiled the pleasure of a moment before. She swam back towards where she'd entered the water. The creature emerged several feet in front of her. Kelsey shrieked, then relaxed when she recognized a seal.

Not just any seal. One unlike any she'd ever seen. *Bracken's legendary silver seal.* Cold chills raced through her. So her professor wasn't just chasing a flight of fancy.

But what was such a creature doing here, in a fresh water pond a mile from the sea?

Slowly she extended her hand. He rubbed a cold nose against her palm, then dove beneath the surface. Kelsey took a breath and followed. Sunlight filtered through the water, casting the rocks into strange shapes. She followed the turning, twisting sleek body, resurfaced for a breath, then let him follow her across the pond.

Kelsey floated on her back, the seal a few feet from her. "Whatever you're doing here, you certainly are a friendly fellow." He gave her a wide grin and swam beneath her, brushing his slippery body against her rump.

This wasn't possible, she must be dreaming, but the bright sky and bracing water told her it was real. He played like the dolphins did back at the aquarium in Baltimore and although she'd worked with seals as well, she'd never encountered a wild one so friendly, so human.

"Cade!" She shielded her eyes and searched for him in the thicket surrounding the pool. "You've got to see this." No response. An uneasy feeling surged through her. What if he'd left her here? How would she find her way back?

The seal nudged her, plainly wanting to continue their game of tag. He dove again, and Kelsey followed. The water was deeper here, but light played on the bottom, making shadows of her and the seal. Shadows merged, her distinctly woman outline blurring into an imitation of the seal.

Selkies. The idea rose unbidden and wouldn't subside. What if….

She swam quickly to escape her thoughts, but the seal was faster. One minute he was in front of her, the next gone. Her lungs burned with a need for air. She pushed upward towards the surface, too late seeing the outcropping of rock. A breathless feeling burst in her chest, then the world turned black.

Chapter Ten

Kelsey moaned and put her hand over her eyes. Cade hovered over her, pressing a cold cloth against her forehead. "Kelsey. Wake up. It's soon time to start back."

She levered herself to a sitting position, startled to find herself fully dressed. The world swayed around her. She pressed her hands to the side of her head. "What happened?"

Cade's eyes twinkled with a mixture of sympathy and mischief. "Too much of Mrs. Devon's elderberry wine, I'm afraid."

She ran her hands down her sides, clutched the oxford shirt then smoothed over her jeans. "I went swimming. I hit my head on a rock."

Cade laughed out loud. "Did you now? Swimming, in this cold water? And it's hardly the weather for it in any case."

Anger poured through her, and she jerked away from his gentle hands. "Yes. And you disappeared. There was a silver seal."

Cade's brow furrowed. "A seal. Silver, you say. Kelsey, my love, you've been listening too closely to Bracken's fantasies."

"My hair is wet." She reached up and touched her hair. Dry hair. She ran a hand through shoulder length strands, searching for a trace of dampness. A knot formed in her stomach. How could this be happening to her again? "I didn't imagine it."

He took her chin in his hands. "No, but it sounds like a fine dream."

She searched his eyes, a dark silver like pewter. Like the seal. Involuntarily, she shrank from his touch.

Disappointment flickered in his eyes, then he released her and turned away.

Feeling cold, alone and incredibly frightened, Kelsey threw her arms around him. "Just hold me, please, Cade."

Sighing, he wrapped his arms around her and rested his cheek against her hair. "What troubles you, little one?"

Kelsey choked on a sob. "How can this keep happening to me? How can something be so vivid, so real, yet you tell me it's just a dream? I feel like my mind is slipping away."

He stroked her back, tenderness and concern in his voice. "Sometimes dreams are all we have."

Kelsey closed her eyes and tried to find the meaning hidden behind his words. When he released her again, she let him go.

He handed her a roast lamb sandwich made with thick slices of homemade bread. "Eat now and you'll feel better. Then we should head for the inn."

Kelsey sat back and bit into the bread, although she had no appetite. The meat had a strong flavor to it, unlike what she was accustomed to.

Cade reached into the pond and withdrew a string of trout. He held it up triumphantly. "Supper. While you were sleeping I caught our dinner."

She couldn't help but wonder how he had accomplished this when she'd seen no evidence of fishing gear. "Very resourceful. Who's going to do the cooking?"

Cade looked surprised. "I am. I don't expect you to wait on me, Kelsey, just because we've become lovers. In my family, responsibility for meals is shared."

She nodded, wishing she could find a way to draw him out more. Maybe if she told him about her own family, such as it was, he'd share stories about his. "Sounds like a good plan. In my family, meal responsibility was shared with whatever fast food restaurant was convenient."

He raised an eyebrow, compelling her to explain.

"My mother died when I was very young. I barely

remember her. And of course, my father was always more married to his work, anyway."

"He's made quite a name for himself." He tucked a strand of hair behind her ear and let his hand linger. Kelsey leaned into his palm. Strange, how she found his touch alternately comforting and unnerving.

"He matters very much to you, doesn't he?" His voice was soft, his eyes full of sympathy. "Don't fret about it, Kelsey. You're just on the threshold of your career and you've accomplished a great deal. One day, he'll admit to you how proud he is of you."

She skipped a flat stone across the pond and watched it turn and arc before hitting the water with a small splash. "I hope you're right, but there's not much chance of that happening if I can't work with Bracken."

"What difference does it make who you work with? Or where?" Cade brushed crumbs from his pants legs, then took a sip from the flask and handed it to Kelsey.

She shook her head. "I think I've had enough wine for one day. Besides the fact that Dr. Bracken is one of the most respected scientists in his field, my father and he go way back. They were on a research project in Australia when I was a baby."

"There are other scientists. Other, better projects." He stood and extended his hand to help her up. Rising, she linked her hands behind his neck and gazed into his eyes.

"You still want me to leave this island, don't you?" Despite the pleasure they found together, despite the pleasant day they'd shared, she knew he still wanted her to leave as certainly as she knew the glade would soon be plunged into a dusky twilight.

His eyes held a hint of misery. "I just don't see how I can ultimately give you anything but heartache. Don't ask too much of me. I'm afraid you'll be very disappointed."

"But we can work together. Dr. Bracken doesn't need to know what's happened between us."

"And how would we hide it? When I'm near you, every cell in my being cries out in recognition." He gently disentangled her hands from his neck and moved away. After settling her backpack over her shoulders, he picked up his own. "Hell, woman, I don't even need to be near you. Your scent reaches out to me when we're at opposite ends of the island until I can't think of anything else."

If he needed her that much, she didn't understand how he could want her to leave his life forever. He answered as if he'd read her mind.

He brushed past her, his shoulders slumped as if he carried a great weight. "It wouldn't last, Kelsey. And if it did, it would destroy us both."

She followed him silently down the trail, ducking below the branches, her tortured thoughts miserable company. What happened in Cade's life to make him so certain a committed relationship would be his ruin? She certainly had no reason to think it was the answer to her loneliness, either, but the difference lay in that she was willing to give it a try.

Despite the unhappy marriage that she had long suspected was the reason for her mother's death, Kelsey had seen other couples who were able to go the distance. The Devons were the most recent example. Mrs. Devon had confided that she and Gordon had been married for thirty-five years. They seemed quite content with each other.

Several paces behind him, she emerged from the thicket onto the sloping hillside. Below, the inn looked like a mound of gray rocks silhouetted against an iridescent sea. Overhead, countless puffins wheeled like jets stacked in a holding pattern over Heathrow. White plumage reflected the fading afterglow of a brilliant sunset of reds, purples and oranges. Reaching for Cade's hand, Kelsey stopped, unable to take her eyes off the spectacle. "Where are they going?"

"Some roost at sea. Others along the cliffs below us."

They stood together, watching until the last bird circled and disappeared. From far away, a seal barked. Cade tensed, his grip on her hand becoming painful.

"What's wrong?" She couldn't quite make out his expression in the unearthly half-light.

"Nothing." He didn't release her hand and practically dragged her down the trail.

She wriggled her hand away and stood, resting her hands on her knees, trying to catch her breath. "I'm sorry. If you've got a reason to be in such a damned hurry, go on ahead. Personally I can't think of a single reason to be in such a rush to get back to a cold, dark, house."

"No? Then maybe I should remind you." Crushing her to him, he kissed her thoroughly, punishingly, as if trying to exorcise a demon from his soul. The seal's cry became louder and more plaintive, then abruptly ceased.

She pushed at his shoulders and turned her head, trying to catch her breath. "What is the matter with you?" Cade's breathing rasped against her ear.

He buried his face against her neck. For an uncertain moment, she thought she felt tears. "Are you all right?" She strained to hear his answer.

His lips moved against her skin, muffling his voice. "I do want you, Kelsey. More than just physically. But being with you requires a great price. I don't know what I'll do when the time comes to pay it."

What on earth was he talking about? Did he mean his career in general or working with Bracken? Maybe he was afraid of what her father would do if he found out Cade had been taking his daughter lightly. She almost laughed at the thought. Her father wouldn't even notice what she did unless she developed the ability to live underwater. She stroked the back of his head.

"If you're worried about my father—"

Releasing her, he scrubbed at his eyes and continued his descent down the hill. "It's not your family that concerns me."

She hurried to catch up. "Yours, then?"

"I'm afraid I'm a great disappointment to mine."

She took his hand, anxious to reassure him. "I can't believe that. You're one of the most respected biologists in Scotland. I've read some of your papers and your work is unequaled." The odd thought buzzed through her mind that she'd wanted to discuss his other work, at length, with him. Now she couldn't remember why.

"My family does not measure success the way you do."

She felt like she'd been doused with ice water, uncertain of how he meant the last remark, certain it was meant to be unflattering to her or her father. Probably both. "Look, whatever your grandfather has told you about my father has nothing to do with me."

He gave her a sad look and again she was struck with an image of the seal at the pond. Her dream, she corrected herself. No matter how real it seemed, she had no proof it had really happened. All she had was his word. She looked out towards the sea, unable to meet his gaze.

He let her fingers slip from his. "We are part of what they are, no matter how hard we try to deny it."

She supposed he was right. If she really wanted to live a different life than her father, she would have chosen some other career. Instead, she seemed doomed to work in his shadow, even when they were at opposite ends of the world.

The sky hung over them like a smoky gray bowl. The star of Venus winked faintly, barely visible above the last rosy streaks of sunset. Clasping her hands and closing her eyes, she made a crazy, impossible wish. She shouldn't hope for something to last that wasn't meant to be but couldn't stop the yearning. All her life she'd longed to be part of a family and have a real home. Since her father couldn't give that to her, why couldn't she have one of her own?

Cade continued on, apparently unaware she no longer followed. "Kelsey?" His voice drifted over the heather. "Come along, love."

Love. That's what she really wanted, but she knew Cade

wasn't willing to put a name to their feelings for each other any more than she was. Still, the rightness of being his refused to leave her.

Back at the lodge, Cade insisted on preparing dinner himself. Kelsey used the time to take a long bath, soaking away the aches and strained muscles the day's activities had left her with. He was a confusing man, tender and loving one minute, the next a chilly remote stranger she didn't know at all. When he said he was wrong for her, she should take him seriously. He was certainly in a better position to know.

Kelsey squeezed out the washrag and dragged it over her skin. But she cared about him and his gentle concern for her said he cared for her as well. If the next two days weren't enough to change his mind, maybe once the project was completed, they'd be able to get to really know one another.

Kelsey sighed. No telling where she'd be once the project was over. The aquarium director in Baltimore had assured her she'd be welcomed back, but things changed. Funding could be cut. A new project could be started. Hers could be restaffed.

No, she and Cade would be smart just to cherish whatever time they had together now. Whatever happened later, at least they had these few days.

That night she dreamed of a silver seal with dark, pewter colored eyes. Lured by the promises in his eyes, Kelsey dove into the pool and followed him down, down, into a shimmery world of shadow and light. Marveling at her ability to swim so long underwater, she turned her head. Instead of her legs and arms, she saw a long cylindrical body. With flippers instead of hands and feet. Her father and Dr. Bracken swam alongside her, approval evident in their expressions.

No! She bolted upright, a scream frozen in her throat.

Cade gently shook her shoulder. "Kelsey. Wake up. You've been dreaming again."

She smoothed her hair back with trembling fingers. Another dream so vivid it seemed real. She'd become very adept at that the past few days. "What time is it?"

He moved to the window and spread the curtains. A pale glow illuminated the room. "Dawn. We must hurry if we want to miss the tide."

She dragged in a shaky breath. Just a dream. Best to put it from her mind. She climbed from the bed and pulled on a shirt and jeans. Her fingers fumbled with the buttons while she slid her feet in her tennis shoes.

Cade knelt and tied the laces. "You said you wanted to try winkling."

No doubt a result of too much of Gordon Devon's fine whiskey. "Yes, well. That was last night."

He stood and chucked her chin, then pressed a light kiss to her lips. "Nevertheless, I'm a man of my word. Come along now. I fixed a thermos of tea for you."

"I can hardly wait." She fumbled for a sweater and came upon the fisherman knit. Cade watched her, his expression unfathomable. Now was the time to ask him, even if her mind was still sleep-clogged. "Why did you take my sweater?"

"Why would I?"

She clutched the sweater in one hand and scrutinized him. "You tell me. It was here the first day, then gone. It reappeared when you did, smelling like you do."

Cade laughed out loud. "I'm not sure whether to be insulted or amused. Kelsey, love, why didn't you just ask me? I have a sweater exactly the same. I found it on the beach and picked it up by mistake. Imagine my dismay when I tried to wear it!"

"Why didn't you just tell me?"

A dull flush rose from his neck, whether from embarrassment or from the weight of a lie, she wasn't sure. "I see now that I should have. I'm sorry. Can we go now?"

"I suppose so." She could think about his explanation later and decide if it was one more story she should buy into. Leaving the sweater and grabbing a sweatshirt instead, she followed him from the room.

They trudged along the shore in silence, the crunch of rocks, and the lap of the waves the only sound in the still morning. Kelsey's pulse hammered when she recognized the path as the one she'd trailed him on the morning she'd been stranded by the tide. Several types of seaweed draped the rocks, making them treacherously slippery but Cade didn't seem to be bothered by it. He picked his way across the crevices, looking for periwinkles, a small shellfish, growing among the fronds.

He scooped up a handful of shells and shook his head. "Too tiny. We'd need a hundred to make a meal. Winkling is much better in the winter, although you have to fight the rain."

"Is this what you were doing that morning?"

He turned his full attention on her. "When?"

"Shortly after I first arrived. I tried to follow you and got stranded by the tide. You appeared out of the water and rescued me."

Cade dumped the shells into the bucket she carried and rubbed his hands on his jeans. A grin spread across his face. "What a fine imagination you have, little one. Was I carrying Neptune's triad?"

She clenched her hands, suddenly determined to know the truth, even if it meant he was right and she'd dreamed all these strange events. "Cade, I know the difference between reality and a dream. Or maybe I've been dreaming since I got here. Please tell me the truth. I need a logical explanation. It's insane to even consider buying into tales of magic."

"So you don't believe in magic." He shook his head as if saddened, then took her face between his palms. His mouth brushed hers, and she held her breath. Longing stabbed deep into her, making her knees wobbly. "What about the magic between us? Do you believe in that, or have the past two days been an ordinary occurrence for you?"

She dropped the pail and gripped his wrists. "I have never felt this way before."

"Never?" His gaze chided her. "You're a beautiful woman, Kelsey. You've been on your own for many years. Would you tell me you've never been with a man before?"

She shouldn't have to tell him. He should know. Astonished more than affronted, she placed her hand over his heart. "There's your answer, Cade. I don't need to tell you." She slid her arms around him and waited for his response.

Watching her face, seeing her eyes darken to velvet in anticipation of his kiss, he knew that was the best answer he could expect for such a rudely intimate question. Still, he didn't want to accept what he'd suspected. For if Kelsey had been a virgin, he was doomed as certainly as the sun would make its slow and deliberate ascent across the sky.

Chapter Eleven

After supper, they sat on the lawn watching the sun drop into the sea. Cade stretched out on the blanket and watched Kelsey, her head tipped back, following the sea birds dip and swoop down to the ocean, then dart up. A few puffins floated in the water, bobbing on the gentle waves.

"I wish it was always like this." She closed her eyes and inhaled. The light breeze tossed her sable hair around her shoulders.

"Ah, but that's the way of magic. Now you see it—" He tickled her nose with a piece of sea grass.

She glanced at him, then hugged her knees to her chest and rocked. "Is that your way of saying that what we've found will disappear in the morning when the ferry arrives with Dr. Bracken and Dr. Norlund?"

He raised himself on one elbow and studied her. "As you know it must."

"Do you think Dr. Bracken would care that we've developed a close friendship?"

The problem, as he saw it, was that was precisely what Bracken was hoping for. Cade just didn't want Kelsey to know that, certain she'd find the knowledge as disturbing as he did. "I think it would be a mistake, for both of us."

"As you've said, several times." She seemed to be weighing something in her mind and come to a conclusion. "I know this is after the fact for this discussion, but," she hesitated and her face became pink. "What if I were pregnant?"

"You're not."

"How can you be so sure?"

He gestured impatiently, as flustered by the conversation as she appeared to be. "I can't give you a child, Kelsey. It's not possible."

She let out a pent-up breath and for an instant he thought he saw a flash of disappointment. "Can you tell me why?"

"Let's just say there are medical reasons and leave it at that."

"Fine." Kelsey stood and dusted off her jeans. "I'm going to my room. There's some material I need to review before the morning, and I'm tired."

So she was going to walk away from him in as cool a manner as the evening breeze that lifted her hair and swirled it around her face. "Do you want me to join you?"

Already several feet away, she hesitated. "Do you really think that's a good idea? I mean," she looked away from him, towards the sea, "we don't know when they will return."

He wadded the sea grass into a ball and tossed it away. "Yes, of course. Goodnight, Kelsey."

"Goodnight, Cade."

Her footsteps on the grass barely made a sound, yet the finality of her leaving made his heart clench. But he let her go just the same.

Hours later, Kelsey turned restlessly onto her side. She thought of what he'd said about not being able to get her pregnant. Naturally, a pregnancy now would be an absolute disaster, and she scolded herself for being so careless in the first place. Thank goodness she didn't have to be worrying and counting the days, but her relief was tinged with regret, a sure sign she was in deeper than she liked to admit.

Ridiculous thoughts, foolish dreams. She and Cade didn't have a future together. He'd made that plain from the first.

But she wanted him, the feel of his strong arms around her, the beat of his heart beneath her ear.

He hadn't protested much when she'd gone to bed alone. She wondered if he was having as much difficulty sleeping as she was. Every creak of the old inn made her start up in bed, hoping to see Cade silhouetted in her doorway. She punched her pillow and turned towards the wall. She had to stop being so spineless where he was concerned. She'd taken her stand, and by God, she was going to stick with it. Cade could toss and turn all night, she was going to get a peaceful night's sleep. Her mind made up, she drifted into an uneasy slumber tormented by dreams of a silver seal.

Cade lay on his back staring at the ceiling. The unearthly gray light of never ending twilight cast strange shadows in his room. He hadn't heard the seal tonight. Maybe he was finally going to get a respite.

His thoughts stubbornly returned to Kelsey. She'd looked so fragile, yet so determined when she'd walked away from him. He wondered how much it bothered her that he couldn't give her children. Better for her to know that than to know the rest of the truth about him. Maybe it would be enough to keep her from dreaming the sweet imaginings he knew flitted through her mind.

The same exquisite longings coiled in his belly, made him hard with desire. The suppressed hunger burned at him. One more night. What difference could it make?

She was right. With Bracken due to return in the morning it was too risky to spend the night together.

But the need to be enveloped in her warm softness fevered his mind. Her troubled dreams permeated his thoughts. Seeing the seal at the pond disturbed her a great deal. He should have known better than to do something so crazy. As grandfather always said, yield to the impulse of the moment, spent a lifetime in regrets.

Maybe he should have used the opportunity to tell her the truth about himself.

No, her scientific training would be overwhelmed by the knowledge. She'd tell her father. Or worse, Bracken. He couldn't let that happen.

The image of Kelsey swimming resurfaced. Again and again he saw her white skin, pebbled from the cold, her smooth round breasts rosy, her eyes wide with curiosity and trepidation. He imagined taking her on the bed of leaves and grass near the water's edge until he could feel her beneath him.

Stifling an oath, he threw the covers back and crept from his room. She'd left her door unlocked and hope surged through him. With the curtains drawn tight, Kelsey's room was in even deeper shadow, but he made out her still form on the bed, heard her soft, even breathing.

He said her name without speaking, and she stirred, rising partway.

"Cade?" Her voice trembled, whether from anxiety or desire he wasn't sure.

"Yes."

"I thought we were in agreement."

He moved to the side of the bed, drawn by forces stronger than his conscious will. "Are you asking me to leave?"

She hesitated and all his hopes and fears narrowed into one endless moment while he hovered on a precipice.

Then she reached out her hand and laced her fingers with his. "I can't."

With a groan of relief, he sank to the bed and gathered her in his arms. Pressing kisses to her throat, he murmured her name. Kelsey trailed her fingers down his back and laughed shakily. "We're both going to hang for this, I know. But I can't bear the thought of not being with you our last night alone."

He rolled onto the bed with her, stroking his hands over her soft curves and plucked at the oversized T-shirt she wore. "Get this thing off. I have to see all of you."

"All in good time. Do you always run the halls naked? She ran her hand down over the flat plain of his belly into the thatch of hair and teased him with her fingers.

He throbbed in response and closed his eyes. "You torment me, woman. I think you delight in it."

She traced the contour of his ear with her tongue, and he sucked in a breath. "I do."

His hands swept up her sides, taking the shirt and pulling it off over her head. "Then be prepared to pay the price."

Hovering over her, his fingers slid inside and found her wet with readiness. She touched him, guiding him, and he eased inside her. "Ah, Kelsey, but you do feel like heaven."

She smiled up at him. Her hair spread over the pillow like a dark halo, and her eyes were dark with promises. Her hands skimmed up his smooth chest and locked behind his neck. He bent his head and kissed her, plundering her mouth with the same deliberate strokes with which he took her body, coaxing a response from her.

The brass bed creaked and groaned in syncopated rhythm to their intimate movements until the sound and her soft sighs were all that filled his mind, the only things that mattered. He felt her climax build, and his chased after until they tumbled together in blissful completion.

Well past midnight, Dr. Bracken trudged up the darkened stairway to his room, Dr. Norlund two steps below him.

"We're days behind schedule, Dennis. What could we have possibly accomplished by being away? And how will we be sure it was long enough?"

"Listen." Bracken laid a hand on Norlund's arm. A faint creaking echoed in the corridor. He loved old houses and the old furniture that usually went with them. The shadowy and otherwise quiet inn swelled with an erotic, intimate rhythm. Kelsey's antique brass bed. Now there was no doubt she was with Cade. The thought filled him with a rush of accomplishment.

He almost rubbed his hands together in glee. There'd be no turning back now, for either one of them. And with a little help from Mother Nature he'd see evidence of results by the end of the summer. "We were exactly where we needed to be for our experiment to succeed."

"But, Dennis," Norlund persisted, apparently oblivious to the passion permeating the air.

A woman's muffled moans escaped the closed door. The creaking increased in intensity. Even in the dim glow of Mrs. Devon's flickering night-lights Norlund's embarrassed flush was highly visible. What a prude the Swede was. Bracken allowed himself a satisfied chuckle. If he was right about the attraction between Kelsey and Cade, the two of them would be at it all night. "Put your ear plugs in and go to bed, Erik. Everything is proceeding just as I'd hoped it would."

Erik Norlund stood inside his darkened room and waited for the sound of Bracken's door closing. From next door, voices murmured softly, words inaudible over the incessant squeaking of bedsprings.

How disgusting.

He wondered if Cade and Kelsey had accomplished anything of merit during the week he and Bracken had been gone. And what did he and Bracken have to show for it? A meeting with the Foundation revealed their patrons were getting restless for results, as he was. Bracken, meanwhile, seemed intent on chasing after some fantasy, probably borne of one too many "wee drams."

He strained to hear something other than the noises of lovemaking emanating from next door, but heard nothing else. Bracken, the voyeur, was probably still standing in the hallway, picking out names for Cade and Kelsey's mythical children.

How disappointed he'd be when they turned out to be as ordinary and uninspired as Kelsey MacKenzie. He had a difficult time seeing her as the daughter of the eminent William Bouschour. He did, however, have a great deal of respect for the oceanographer despite his reservations about Kelsey. Perhaps everyone was entitled to one mistake, and he knew too well where his own weaknesses lay. An idea took seed in his mind. If Bracken were to see what a miserable failure the girl was as a scientist, he'd have to get rid of her, obsession or not, or The Foundation might decide to cancel the whole project.

Anxious to get to the lab, he cracked open his door. Bracken was nowhere in sight. Perhaps he'd made an extra effort to be quiet, not wanting to squelch the passion they couldn't help but be privy to.

Despite his intentions to be indifferent, the soft sounds of Kelsey's muffled moans reminded him all too clearly of his own recent romantic adventure. His blood stirred in spite of himself. Now there had been an interesting, enthusiastic woman. Too bad she'd insisted on having her own way.

Norlund pushed the thoughts aside. What was done was done. He had to get away to a quiet place where he could make plans, perhaps do something that would force Bracken back to the reason they were all here in this godforsaken place.

Chapter Twelve

Kelsey awoke early, alone, as she had known she would. Deep contentment from a night of being well-loved overshadowed disappointment at facing the day by herself. The musky scent of lovemaking hung in the air, clung to the rumpled linens. If she was planning to maintain even a tiny degree of discretion, that would never do. She rose, stretched and opened the window wide. Mackerel clouds presided over a leaden sea. Apparently another storm was brewing. She wondered if Dr. Bracken would make it back after all and found herself hoping he wouldn't.

She stripped the bed and wadded the sheets up. After a shower, she raided the linen cabinet and remade the bed herself. The thought of Mrs. Devon or the demure Gwendolyn doing it sent a surge of embarrassment through her.

Chores taken care of, perhaps she and Cade could at least have breakfast together before Dr. Bracken and Norlund arrived.

Spurred by anticipation, Kelsey dressed and practically skipped down the stairs. She burst into the kitchen, a bright smile on her face, and skidded to a halt.

Dr. Bracken sat at the oak table, sipping tea and perusing *The Scientific Journal*. He glanced up and gave her a kindly smile. "Well, well. Good morning, Kelsey. You look as if you had a good night."

A rush of heat spread up her neck. Kelsey quickly turned her back and rummaged through the cupboard, although she couldn't have said what she was looking for. "Good morning, Dr. Bracken. Do you know if Mrs. Devon—"

"Everything's on the table. Sit down and tell me what you and Cade have been up to the past few days." Unbidden, an image of Cade's hands stroking her thighs, his mouth devouring her, unfolded. She sank into a chair and poured a cup of tea. "We went over to one of the other islands. I brought back samples and prepared tests. Perhaps after breakfast you can go over the results with me."

Bracken peered over his bifocals at her. "Ah, yes. I am most certainly interested in results."

Again, a rush of warmth suffused her face, and she sought to hide it by raising her teacup and lowering her eyes from his curious, penetrating gaze. The kitchen door slammed and she looked up to see Erik Norlund, face as forbidding as a bull walrus.

"I warned you, Dennis. Turn important research over to a novice and disaster would strike. Months of work down the drain because of you!" He hurled an accusatory stare at Kelsey.

She straightened in her chair. "Good morning to you, too, Dr. Norlund. What's the problem?"

"I'll tell you what's wrong. You. You shouldn't be here. You don't have the experience, the training. All you have to offer is—"

Bracken waved a dismissive hand. "That's quite enough, Erik. I can see that you're upset, and I'm sure you have good reason. But we function as a team here, not as competitors, not as judge and jury." He patted Kelsey's hand. "Finish your breakfast, then we'll all go to the lab and discuss what needs to be done. Where is Douglas?"

Norlund planted himself in the chair opposite Kelsey's. "In the lab, trying to assess the damage."

She forced herself to look him in the eye. She'd done nothing wrong, so why did she feel like a flock of sea birds had been turned loose in her stomach? Forcing herself to eat, she spooned up a mouthful of mueslix. The cereal made her want to gag, but she chewed slowly and washed it down with

the strong tea. Norlund glared at her, but Bracken calmly
continued reading the Journal and munching on toast and
marmalade.

She wished Cade had come back with Norlund. Surely,
he'd vouch for her work. Sometimes, despite the most
careful preparations, samples spoiled, test results were
skewed. There must be a perfectly logical explanation.
Besides, she wasn't the last one to work in the lab.

Cade was.

A chill crept up her spine as his words returned. "Don't
worry. I took care of everything." He wouldn't, couldn't
destroy valuable research just to be rid of her. Not after what
they'd shared.

Would he?

Suddenly nauseous, she pushed her bowl away and looked
up to find both Dr. Bracken and Norlund intently eyeing her.

"What's the matter, Kelsey?" Norlund's voice held a
slight taunt. "A bit queasy this morning?"

He knew. Obviously, they had returned last night, not this
morning, and because his room was next to hers, Norlund
had heard her and Cade. Frantic, her mind raced, trying to
remember every sound, every nuance he might have
overhead. Oh, why hadn't she and Cade used common sense
and stayed away from each other?

Because they couldn't.

Cade had tried to warn her, but she was stubborn and
foolish to think strength of purpose would be enough.
Bracken would dismiss her once Norlund had a chance to tell
him. Mortified, she held her head high and returned his stare.
"No, I just don't seem to be very hungry this morning. And
the food here takes a bit of getting used to."

Bracken chuckled. "There's an understatement. You
probably haven't been getting enough sleep, either."

Norlund snorted and poured himself a cup of tea. Kelsey's
face burned, and she wished herself to the other side of the
island.

Bracken turned a page of the journal and glanced up at her. "Is Cade proving to be a good teacher?"

Again, images of him at the sea cave poured through her mind. Cade, skin slick, looming over her, thrusting inside her, over and over, until she had cried from the sweet pleasure. She crossed her legs and folded her hands in her lap. "Yes, sir."

"Good. Good." Bracken nodded approvingly and closed his magazine. He glanced at Norlund. "Well, then. If you're ready, let's all go to the lab and see what needs to be done."

Cade ran a hand through his hair and peered into the microscope for what seemed like the hundredth time. It couldn't be. It just couldn't. But the results were unmistakable. All Kelsey's careful preparations for nothing.

The inner door rattled on a draft, then opened. Kelsey stood before him, her eyes imploring, hands tightly clasped in front of her. Bracken and Norlund followed close behind.

"Good morning, Dr. Douglas." Her words were even, calm, but he sensed her inner turmoil.

"Good morning, Miss Mackenzie. I take it Dr. Norlund alerted you to the problem here?"

She pulled up a chair beside him. "Not specifically. I'd like to take a look, please."

He swept a hand towards the microscope and studied her profile as she bent her head. "Obviously the samples have become contaminated. I'm sorry."

"Are you?" She raised her head. Blue eyes glittered, then she blinked, and he was certain he had imagined her tears.

Why was she so upset? Certainly, she didn't suspect him of ruining her work? "I know how hard you worked on this."

"Will you vouch for my work?"

Sensing the Swedish biologist studying them, Cade chose his words carefully. "I wasn't here when you prepared the samples."

"But you reviewed—"

Norlund shouldered himself between them and squinted through the microscope. "A disaster," he muttered as he picked up another slide and studied it. "Not only have you ruined the samples you collected last week, but by not following basic laboratory procedures, you've jeopardized the ones we've been studying for months."

Kelsey's mouth opened, then she hastily closed it. Cade could almost see her mentally counting to ten. "Dr. Norlund, I assure you, I was extremely careful—"

He silenced her with a scathing look, but before he could say anything, Dr. Bracken interrupted, taking his arm and steering him to the jars of saline, shellfish and small sea creatures lining several shelves. "Now, now, Erik. You know as well as I do that slides can carry bits of contaminants and can even be subject to changes in the weather, as well as the specimens carrying unseen bits of residue that will skew the test results. We still have samples of everything we collected."

He stopped in front of the tank of live specimens. "Good heavens. They're all dead."

All three scientists stared at Kelsey. Denial sprang to her lips, but she knew it wouldn't do any good to protest. The tank had been her responsibility. She rose and went to look. A foul scum floated on the surface. "Dr. Bracken. I don't know what to say."

His cheeks puffed out with a deep breath. "Well, it needs to be cleaned up. Disinfect it thoroughly. Tomorrow we can take the boat out and retrace your footsteps from last week."

Cade shot a quick glance at Kelsey. He hoped not. Pink stained her cheekbones, but she refused to meet his eyes. Just as well. He knew her thoughts paralleled his. He saw her in the cave, lying beneath him, opening to him like a sweet flower, taking him in. His nostrils flared with the fragrance of her, the tang of sea air and the memory of the hot, tight feel of her.

"Isn't that right, Douglas?" Bracken's hand rested heavily on Cade's shoulder, and he started. "We'll go out in the morning, make a day of it."

"As you wish." But what he wished for was what he knew he couldn't have and to let Bracken see him staring at Kelsey like a besotted teenager would never do. "If you'll excuse me, I think I'll go have breakfast."

Sick at heart, Kelsey barely heard him leave. Slipping on a lab coat, she thought about the unusable samples she'd collected. What had happened? But the answer was painfully obvious.

Cade. How could he have done such a thing?

Surely he wouldn't have tampered with everything in the lab, but there was only one way to be certain. Kelsey took a fresh box of slides from her work station. She'd start with the first jar and examine every shell, every fish, every piece of seaweed until she had satisfied herself that what had gone wrong wasn't just a mistake.

"Obviously, the slides were improperly prepared. And the tank was allowed to stagnate." Norlund's voice was haughty.

Kelsey bowed her head, refusing to argue with him and make a bad situation worse. "I'm sorry, Dr. Bracken. I don't understand what happened, but I won't leave this room until I know. I'll do some new slides, then clean the tank."

Dr. Bracken patted her shoulder. "Don't fret about it, Kelsey. These things happen. I have the utmost confidence in you. I'm going for my morning stroll, then I'll join you." With that he nodded a farewell and headed out the door.

Dr. Norlund lingered a moment longer, his expression grim and penetrating. "I know what's going on here, MacKenzie. Don't think you're fooling me. I don't know what your father holds over Bracken's head, to force him into taking you on for this project, but I'll see to it the Foundation hears of this latest setback. Then let's see you find a position in the field of marine biology. Other than on your back, of course." He slammed out of the room.

Outrage and humiliation washed over her. How could she have been so stupid? Oh, Cade had warned her of the dangers of being involved with him. And for a few all too brief moments, she'd thought she'd found heaven in his arms.

What a fool she was. With sterilized tongs, she extracted a mussel from a jar of brine, carefully laid it on a clean cutting board and neatly sliced off a minuscule piece of tissue. She'd work till she dropped, if that's what it took and she wouldn't let Cade Douglas distract her.

Despite her indignation, the realization of never being with him again filled her with melancholy until the impact of what he'd done slammed into her.

He'd betrayed her, in the most basic of ways. She would show him she wasn't to be taken lightly. Anger fueled her resolve and filled her with determination. It might not stem the longing, but anger would sustain her and maybe that would be enough.

As she slid the specimen under the microscope another thought nagged at her.

Why hadn't Dr. Bracken been more upset?

Kelsey spent the rest of the day in the lab, not even taking a break at noon when the others left for the inn. Long after suppertime, she stood, stretched and rubbed the back of her neck.

Dr. Bracken appeared in the doorway. "Ah, Kelsey. Taking a break finally. Why don't you call it a night? You missed a tasty dinner, but I'm sure Mrs. Devon wouldn't mind heating some up for you."

Her stomach growled, reminding her she hadn't eaten anything since the few bites of mueslix she'd had at breakfast. "That sounds great, but if you don't mind, I think I'll come back after dinner. There's still so much to be done. Would you mind taking a few minutes to go over what I spent the day on?"

"Certainly, certainly." Dr. Bracken looked over the new slides, held the bottles of saline packed samples and glanced at her meticulously detailed notes, but his review held the hurriedness of a cursory examination. Had he been out of the research field too long, spending his time instead on funding and recruiting so that the rudimentary aspects no longer appealed to him? Nevertheless, if he could tell the others that he'd gone over her work, she would be protected from another "accident."

He beamed at her. "Exceptional, as always. I expect we'll have some interesting review work in a few days, perhaps next week. Run along now and have a bite, maybe go for a walk and clear the cobwebs. I believe I saw Cade heading for the shore."

The sound of his name rippled along her nerve endings. Cade. They hadn't spoken a dozen words to each other all day and she missed the musical sound of his voice, the soft burr of his accent. Why was Dr. Bracken so anxious for them to get along? "I'll just come back to the lab. Leave the lights on for me, please."

"As you wish, Kelsey, but the work will still be here in the morning, and as Mrs. Devon would say, it's a pet of an evening."

Feeling more and more awkward from his unsubtle hints, she excused herself and hurried across the lawn to the inn. She found Mrs. Devon in the kitchen. The housekeeper bustled around the room, muttering under her breath.

"Losing two days work, laundry and dishes piled to the ceiling and for what?"

"Good evening, Mrs. Devon." Kelsey hovered in the doorway. "I thought I might fix myself something to eat. That is, if you don't mind."

Mrs. Devon straightened from placing tea towels in a drawer. "Mind? Of course not, dear. But you just go sit down in the dining room. I'll fetch it to you straightaway."

"But I can see you're busy and it is past the usual dinner time—"

Mrs. Devon laid a hand on Kelsey's arm and steered her into the dining room. "Don't have a care about it. I'll be glad to serve you. Poor wee thing, working till dusk while those men take it easy."

Kelsey stifled a smile. No one had "taken it easy" all day. But the others had left for meals while she, burning to recapture the lost work, had been too involved to leave. "Is everything all right with your family?"

Mrs. Devon sniffed. "Right as rain. Family emergency, indeed. Leave a full inn and rush off to Kirkwall to see my dear sister, only to discover she was as surprised to see me as I was distressed to think she was lying ill and needing my help with her little ones."

An ominous feeling settled in Kelsey's stomach, stealing her appetite. It was odd that the Devons were called away at exactly the same time Dr. Bracken was left, but was it more than a coincidence? "What made you think something was wrong?"

"A telegram." Mrs. Devon planted her hands on her hips and shook her head. "Delivered by the ferry captain himself. Had me so rattled, if Gordon hadn't been watching out for me, I would have forgotten to pack so much as a toothbrush."

Kelsey folded her arms across her stomach, trying to stifle the noisy rumblings. Mrs. Devon chuckled.

"There, now, you poor thing. Here I am rattling off while you're about to faint from hunger. I'll bring you some bread and some of my homemade elderberry preserves." She bustled from the room.

Odd things were going on here. Who would have wanted the Devons away from the inn? Kelsey stared out the window at the white capped sea a hundred yards away. A man's silhouette emerged from the shadows. Her heart raced in recognition. Cade.

Maybe he'd engineered the Devons' impromptu trip. But what could he have accomplished with them gone that he hadn't already done?

As if she'd spoken his name, he looked up, his gaze piercing despite the distance. She remembered the heat in his eyes, felt the caress of his glance and gripped the arms of the chair to hold back the overwhelming longing. Little flames of desire licked at her resolve to maintain her composure.

If she went to him now, what would he do? What would he say? Would he deny he'd been the one to sabotage her work? Or would he say he was only doing what he thought was best for her, by ensuring that she'd have to leave?

It hadn't worked, at least not in the way he'd planned. Bracken was totally understanding. As far as Dr. Norlund was concerned, she'd have to work to regain the initial acceptance he'd given her, and that would take time, but she was certain she could do it.

The weight of awareness pressed on her, and her breath lodged in her throat. Kelsey pushed back her chair, narrowly missing Mrs. Devon. She tore her gaze away from the window and Cade.

"Goodness, I nearly spilt the tea on you. I've got some warm bread here. You just sit back and enjoy. I'll have the soup out quick as I can get to the kitchen and back." She poured tea, then left.

Sighing, Kelsey arranged her napkin in her lap and glanced up. Cade was gone. The beach stretched out, empty and chilly looking, but not nearly as cold and barren as she felt.

Chapter Thirteen

Cade kicked at a clump of seaweed and tried to push thoughts of Kelsey from his mind. He needed to focus on this latest setback. What was going on? Why had Erik Norlund seemed to have developed a sudden dislike to Kelsey? Bracken, enmeshed in his own schemes, seemed oblivious to the tension reverberating in the lab all afternoon. Thankfully, Norlund wasn't much for working late at night. Usually. Cade couldn't help but wonder if the scientist had worked last night after he and Bracken returned from the mainland. Or was the mishap with the slides and the tank simply an accident?

He knew Kelsey suspected him. The thought pained him and did nothing to ease his guilty conscience. He'd even deluded himself that he and Kelsey could find a way to be together in the quiet darkness of night. Now there was no way she would welcome him into her bed.

Just as well. The more he needed her, the more difficult it would be to do what must be done and for his family's sake, he couldn't forget what his purpose for being here was.

Mrs. Devon returned with a steaming tureen of soup. Kelsey's appetite perked at the tantalizing aroma of broth, onions and pepper. The soup tingled in her mouth while the housekeeper hovered anxiously. "It's delicious, Mrs. Devon."

She beamed. "Nettle soup. My own recipe. You enjoy and I'll be out straight away with the roast and potatoes."

Kelsey spooned up another mouthful. Food here often

used strange ingredients, from stinging nettles to flowers to—

Periwinkles.

The bucket of small shellfish she and Cade had collected yesterday. What had happened to it?

Mrs. Devon brought a platter of roasted lamb, potatoes and turnips. She dished a generous portion onto Kelsey's plate.

"There you go, dear. And if you be needing anything else, I'll be in the kitchen."

"I looked for periwinkles yesterday. How are they used?"

Mrs. Devon halted at the swinging doors. "Oh, winkles make a lovely supper. I usually boil them in bouillon with a touch of garlic. Then you scoop the meat out and sprinkle with a bit of salt and vinegar. But it's not the season. Any you'd find now, even if you could, are much too small. You need to be here in the winter, then I could show you."

"Thank you, Mrs. Devon." The housekeeper nodded and left the room.

Most likely, Cade had simply dumped the bucket out. But if he hadn't, maybe there was something she could use in her experiments. Anxious to look, she hurriedly finished her dinner and brought her dishes to the kitchen.

She found the bucket near the back door, so close to the steps she was surprised she hadn't tripped over it on her way to the kitchen.

Except it hadn't been there.

The thought became a certainty. Seaweed covered the meager collection of shellfish clustered in the bottom. Kelsey shifted the handle and tried to decide where to take it. The lab was the most logical place, but it obviously wasn't the most secure. She'd have to chance it. There was no where else she could test the winkles without risking contamination to the samples or herself. Still, she could conduct a few experiments privately. Away from prying eyes. Safe from sabotaging fingers.

As promised, Dr. Bracken had left a light on, but the lab was deserted. She prepared the samples in specimen dishes and locked them in her desk to keep them from prying eyes.

Deciding to take advantage of the quiet, she spent an hour pouring over reference books and preparing notes and lists of work to be accomplished the next morning. An hour melted into two. Kelsey blinked at her watch, astonished at the passage of time. By now, the others would be in their rooms and she wouldn't have any problem returning without being noticed. After placing her equipment into the sterilizer, she shut off the lights and locked the door.

A three quarter moon hung over the sea, bathing the hills with a dappled light. Shadows swayed in the wind. Hugging herself, she hurried the short distance to the inn, stealthily crept through the kitchen and up the back stairs.

Opening the door to her room, she stopped short. Although she'd been absent all day, a light glowed from the desk lamp. Odd, she wouldn't have left a light burning in the morning and that was the last time she'd set foot inside the room. Gwendolyn must have left it on when she cleaned.

Wind burst through the window, rifling the pages of a book sitting open on the desk. Kelsey slowly made her way across the room. Someone wanted her to look at the book. The uncanny feeling grew. She shrugged the sensation away.

She was being fanciful again. Something about this island, made her think things, made her want things, she knew to be impossible. The book was probably another treatise on the malaise afflicting the seals, and Dr. Bracken thought she needed the information.

She picked up the well-worn book and turned it over in her hands. *Scottish Folk-tales and Legends.* A knot formed in her stomach. Her mother had shared many of these stories with her. As young as she'd been when she lost her mother, Kelsey still recalled her voice, as warm and welcoming as hot chocolate on a winter night lulling her to sleep with tales of her home. Wispy memories floated at the edges of her mind, teasing her to remember.

She thumbed to a dog-eared page and settled into the wicker chair near the window. "MacCodrum of the Seals." She skimmed through the story. The fairy tale gave her an odd, unsettled feeling in the pit of her stomach, although why it should have she couldn't imagine. She moved on to the next marked page, "The Wounded Seal," then to the "The Seal's Skin." Shape shifter stories. Men or women who donned their seal skins and became seals in the water. She remembered hearing about the seal legend from her mother's dreamy voice. The hair prickled at the back of her neck, as if someone watched over her shoulder, nodding encouragement at her unscientific thoughts.

A picture of the silver seal at the pond surfaced. One minute Cade had been with her, the next gone. The seal had been the same color as the dead seal she'd discovered her first night here. Where had he come from?

Cade insisted he hadn't seen him. That was an understatement. He said she'd been dreaming.

It couldn't have been a dream.

The sensation of cool water on her bare skin was too strong, too real. The seal had nuzzled her hand with a velvety nose, rubbed his smooth coat against her. She remembered.

She remembered!

The urge to retrace their path to the pond nearly overpowered her caution and good judgment. Kelsey stood at the window, looking out over the sea. The midnight light, shadowy and eerie on the beach, would be even more ghostly away from the water. And the moon wouldn't be bright enough to guide her through the hills. She'd have to wait for daylight.

Turning away, she concentrated on other tasks, re-reading her lab notes, studying a text she'd brought from the States. Her eyelids drooped. It was nearly midnight and she was so tired. If she didn't get some sleep, she wouldn't be able to focus on the tedious details of test after test in the lab.

She pulled back the quilted coverlet on the white antique bed, trying not to see the images of herself and Cade, bodies entwined, skin glistening in the afterglow of their lovemaking.

It wasn't just the physical aspects she craved, although God knew, that was a major part of it. She longed for his whispered voice, words spoken in a language she didn't need to know to understand the most tender of endearments. She could almost feel his gentle stroking on her skin, the brush of his fingers through her dark hair.

Stop it.

He'd used her, then betrayed her. That was what she needed to focus on, not the fantasy of a love that had never happened and was never meant to be.

Kelsey awoke before dawn. She ached all over and although she would have given anything for a few more hours of rest, work concerns pressed in on her and made it impossible to go back to sleep. She found hot tea and warm scones on the sideboard in the dining room. No one else seemed to be stirring. Just as well. If she could get a couple of hours of work done before she had to face Dr. Norlund, she'd breathe easier. As for Cade… If she didn't have to see him again, ever, that would suit her just fine.

She pulled her hair back and deftly braided it as she walked the short distance to the lab. Her hopes of working alone were dashed as soon as she opened the door.

Cade stood in the lab, monitoring a tank of live specimens. Kelsey moved forward, careful to keep her distance from him.

"Where did those come from?"

He jotted something on his clipboard and didn't look up. "Does it matter?"

"Considering we lost everything yesterday, I'd say it matters." She studied him, hoping to find a trace of guilt or denial in his expression but found neither.

He glanced up, but the spontaneous glimpse of tenderness in his eyes was quickly hidden behind his too familiar scowl. "I was out earlier this morning."

"And you just happened to collect all this?" Her hand swept towards the tank. "Looks like most of what we lost."

"Some. Not all." He turned a piercing frown on her. "Bracken expects us to take the boat out today."

"Can we retrace our path to that island?"

"No!" The word exploded from him. His fingers bit into her upper arm. "I never should have taken you there."

Kelsey jerked away from his painful grip and the layers of meaning in his words. "What is the matter with you? What was so special about that damn island?" Besides everything, the loss of her innocence, the awakening of her soul.

"You don't understand," he muttered, turning away, not meeting her eyes.

"At least we agree on one thing. I don't understand." She bent to examine the tank and check the temperature of the water.

Weariness etched fine lines around his eyes. "Your father is coming. Just like you wanted."

His words shredded the small measure of composure she'd managed to draw around herself. "What?"

The door to the lab flew open. Dr. Bracken burst into the room, excitedly waving a sheet of paper. "He's on his way, Kelsey. Here. Before the week's out, I'd wager."

"Who?" She responded automatically, reaching for the telegram Dr. Bracken thrust towards her.

"Your father, of course." Bracken rubbed his palms together. "Ah, yes. Everything's coming together nicely." He clapped Cade on the shoulder. "Wait till you meet him, Douglas. We'll get the notice we need for this project to succeed. I must tell Dr. Norlund." He hurried from the room.

Cade's eyes had darkened like thunderclouds. "Why did you send for him?"

Kelsey's mouth dropped open. "Send for him? Why would I do that?" She read the telegram. *Got your message. Exercise caution. Will leave here ASAP. Bouschour.* No tender sentiments here. Not even a love, dad. "I don't know what he's talking about. I certainly didn't ask him to come here." She had however, written to tell him she was returning to the islands she hadn't seen since her mother died.

Was that the message he referred to?

"We don't need him here."

That was an understatement, but she resented his attitude. "Afraid of facing my father, Cade?"

He shook his head. "You still don't understand what they are trying to do to us, do you?"

She rested her hands on her hips and faced him, eyes blazing. "No, I don't. And who are 'they,' Cade? Dr. Bracken? Dr. Norlund? My father? The Devons perhaps? Whoever left the book in my room last night?"

"What book?" He turned towards her, his eyes as guileless as silvery pools, but even more mysterious. "What book are you talking about?"

If Cade had been the one to leave the book, he was doing a terrific job of playing ignorant about it. Kelsey pushed by him, intent on returning to the inn and having some breakfast to replace the two lumps of rock the scones had turned into. "I should have known it wasn't you who left it. You don't have any interest in happy endings."

His fingers wrapped around her wrist, holding her in place next to him. "You can't expect a happy ending for something that was doomed from the beginning."

She forced herself to relax although her pulse drummed beneath his fingertips. His grip eased, but the pain shadowing his expression hurt worse then the pressure of his hand. "And why exactly is that? We're both adults. Other people enjoy each other without it being the end of the world. Other men seem comfortable enough with the arrangement."

"We're not other people. I'm not like other men."

Although his voice was quiet, his words thundered through her. She agreed, whole heartedly, but the anguish in his eyes made her realize there was a depth of meaning she couldn't begin to comprehend. She eased away from him and walked to the door. "Well, for the record, I never asked you for more."

His sigh held unfathomable weariness. "Perhaps you should have, Kelsey. From all of us."

Instead of returning to the inn, she found herself following a trail opposite to the path she and Cade had taken two days before. Needing time to think, she returned to the hill overlooking the sea where she had stood her first night in Orkney. The inn looked ancient, peaceful, able to withstand centuries of turmoil. It would still be there long after she had returned to the States.

Where would Cade be? Would he continue his association with Dr. Bracken, or would he go to Glasgow?

Heather purpled the hill and sent a sweet fragrance swirling around her. Overhead a lone puffin battered the air with its wings, then dive bombed into the cliff below.

She should return to the inn, have some of Mrs. Devon's oat bread, then get back to work, but the need to find a small piece of her past proved overwhelming. Kelsey followed a faint trail, encouraged by the bent branches of the elder bushes that marked a path in the direction of the chimney Mrs. Devon had said belonged to the house Kelsey's mother and father had shared.

The sun shimmered from behind gray clouds like a sterling silver platter. Kelsey shed her sweater and tied it about her waist. If she could find the ruin, maybe she could rid herself of the idea she'd get answers for anything other than the research project.

Maybe by coming to terms with the past, she could forget

what she'd seen at the pond or what she'd dreamed every night since. Perhaps she'd understand what she was searching for.

The trail ended in a small clearing. A crumbling chimney rose above her. Spreading plants of ground elder and flowering weeds choked through a decaying foundation.

A sense of loss pervaded her, filled her with regret for the loss of the family she couldn't remember. She picked her way through the ruins and sank to a half-wall covered with moss. Closing her eyes, she focused on hazy memories. Her mother's soft voice, the gentle touch of her hand. A lullaby of a faraway island where seals shed their coats to become men and women. Her eyes flew open.

Why did she keep coming back to that? Selkies were no more real than stories of Hansel and Gretal. Why was the folk tale the only thing she remembered about her own mother?

Faint memories tugged at her, Mother taking her by the hand, promising her a picnic lunch if she played quietly. The tang of gooseberry tarts flavored with elderflowers and sugar, cool water tickling her toes as she dangled her feet in a pond. Her mother disappearing into the thicket.

Someone else had been there, too. Kelsey tensed, then blew out a breath. Of course, her father had been with them. But why couldn't she picture his face in the tranquil scene?

The pond Cade had taken her to was the same one she'd played at as a child. Why hadn't she remembered that a few days ago? If she went back now, maybe she'd find the rest of the memories.

Behind the ruined cottage a small stream glimmered like a bright ribbon. The stream probably led to the pond. Kelsey pushed through the bushes. She had to find that loch again.

Time dragged until she lost all sense of how long she'd struggled against the wilderness, how much further she had to go. Thistles clutched like tiny hands at her clothes. Twigs slapped her arms, but she refused to give up. The crunch of rocks beneath her feet echoed like thunder.

Perspiration misted her face, hair straggled from her braid, but she pushed forward through the dense growth. Just when she'd begun to suspect she'd lost her way completely, the bushes thinned, and she found herself in a clearing. Cade's pond glinted like a jewel.

Kelsey pulled her sweater off and crouched by the edge of the water. The pond looked placid and peaceful, yet the shadowy depths hinted at great secrets. She trailed her fingers in the coolness and scooped up a handful to splash her face.

"You look warm."

The man's voice startled her and drew her attention to the opposite side of the pond. He looked familiar. Almost like an older version of…. One instant he was across the water from her, the next he materialized beside her.

Or so it seemed.

"You're some distance from the inn. How did you find your way?"

For some reason, his friendly attitude warmed her like the sun on her face and made her relax despite the peculiarities of the situation and the man himself. "I was here the other day. With a friend."

"Your friend wouldn't happen to be Cade Douglas, would he?"

"Yes." Kelsey rose and found herself at eye level with the man. "Do you know him?"

The man chuckled and chewed at the edge of a very impressive gray moustache that completely covered his upper lip. "Sometimes not at all. He's my grandson."

No wonder the man had looked familiar. Recognizing his resemblance to Cade, she held her hand out. "I'm Kelsey MacKenzie, Mr. Douglas. It's nice to meet you."

"Ah, yes. Kelsey." He spoke her name as if he were closely acquainted with her, took her hand and held it for a moment. Kelsey's ears began to buzz. Black flecks floated in front of her eyes. She jerked her hand away and closed her eyes until the dizzying sensation passed. She sank down to a large boulder.

"You can call me Meredith." Seemingly unperturbed, he settled himself on the rock beside her. "So like your mother," he murmured, half to himself.

Kelsey's languor vanished. "You knew my mother?"

"The most beautiful of the MacKenzies." Meredith's gaze became distant. "Eyes the blue of a Scottish sea." He returned his attention to her. "Like yours. Do you remember her?"

"Only a little, I'm afraid." For some reason, the memories of her mother were stronger in this place. The wind rustling through the bushes might have been the swish of her mother's polished cotton skirt, the sigh of branches her mother's voice.

There were other sounds, the spill of water over rocks, the cry of birds. She might have noticed that the other day if she hadn't been so focused on Cade and a silver seal. She trailed her fingers in the water. "This is a magical place, isn't it?"

His gaze bore into her. "Some think so."

His words held meanings she could only guess at. If there was a seal here, would Meredith know? Would he give her a truthful answer if she asked?

"You want to know about your mother."

She nodded, her other questions fading into insignificance. Kelsey leaned forward, suppressing a shiver of apprehension about him, Cade and this place. Perhaps Meredith could give her all the answers she needed.

Meredith considered her. "I hope you'll forgive an old man, but I find it difficult to reminisce on an empty stomach. I've a pot of soup waiting on the stove. Why don't you join me? My cottage is just a stone's throw."

She should return to the inn, but Meredith's offer proved too tempting. With her father due to arrive, this might be her best chance to learn something about her mother. Besides, with his warm, friendly manner, it was difficult to think of Meredith Douglas as a stranger, although she was certain he wouldn't approve of her close "acquaintance" with his grandson.

Maybe he knew.

The thought made Kelsey's face heat up. Cade had been gone for several days after their interlude at the sea cave. If he'd been with his grandfather, perhaps he'd confided in him.

Meredith's expression was kindly as he waited for her answer. No, he couldn't know what had happened.

Wary of his touch, she ignored his outstretched hand and got to her feet. "Soup sounds wonderful, although I can't stay long." At his inquiring look, she continued. "I need to get back to work. The project."

"Ah, yes. The project. Still, you must eat lunch." Meredith led her to a trail that went the opposite direction of the one she'd taken from the inn. Skirting the pond, the path led downhill through a thick growth of tall grass, scrubby trees and elderbushes. They walked a long time in silence.

Kelsey began to question the wisdom of following this strange old man on such a long hike when a break in the undergrowth revealed a glimpse of sparkling sea. A crofter's cottage clung to the hill at the edge of the shore.

Kelsey's footsteps slowed. Dr. Bracken had said Cade's grandfather had made a fortune with his fishing fleet, but his modest dwelling belied this.

As if sensing her hesitation, Meredith Douglas put a hand on her elbow and guided her towards his humble home. Still finding his touch disquieting, she eased away from him.

"It's not the Gleneagles, or even Murdoch Castle Inn, but I find it easier to live simply at my age, especially with all of my family gone."

He ushered her through the door, and Kelsey stepped inside the dwelling. This must be what her parents' cottage had been like. Narrow wooden windows provided a minimum of illumination, while the thatched roof gave the cottage a distinctly musty odor. The scent of simmering spices threaded through the air. "Where is your family?"

"Moved on to other islands, for the most part. As your mother's family did many years ago." His gaze pierced through her. "I'd join them, if I were able."

For an instant, she felt a stab of guilt, as if she were somehow responsible, but since Meredith Douglas seemed to be particularly fit for a man his age, Kelsey could only guess at why he'd decided to remain here.

He insisted she be seated while he ladled soup into two ironstone bowls. At his direction, Kelsey topped hers with chopped parsley and something that smelled like basil. He seated himself across from her and she picked up a pewter spoon. Tingling spiciness assaulted her tongue. Stinging nettle soup, but unlike Mrs. Devon's, the highly seasoned broth made her mouth feel slightly numb.

"I hope you like it." Meredith waited, gauging her response.

She didn't really, but something in his eyes made her certain her rejection would hurt his feelings. She smiled and swallowed another mouthful. "Very tasty."

Seemingly satisfied, he began to eat.

Kelsey longed for a tall glass of iced tea, but had already discovered that people here were surprised at the idea of icing down their strong tea. She was certain Meredith wouldn't have enough ice cubes, providing he even had refrigeration in the rustic cottage, but she'd settle for a glass of water. Her mouth burned as if it had been attacked by jellyfish. "This is very good."

Meredith looked pleased. "My own special blend. I gather the ingredients from the sea."

How odd. Mrs. Devon had told her that stinging nettle soup was made from the weeds that choked most of the hillside. Kelsey ate another mouthful, her eyes watering. With his obvious penchant for seasoning, Meredith Douglas could be the chef at any Mexican restaurant in her home state of Texas. She wondered if his recipe for nettle soup included a case of Tabasco sauce. "Could I trouble you for a glass of water?"

"Certainly, child, certainly." Meredith rose from the table and went to the sink in the far corner of the room. He primed a pump and filled a tall glass with water.

Watching him, Kelsey had a difficult time reconciling her impression of Cade as a brilliant, successful scientist with the humble lifestyle of his grandfather. She wondered why anyone would chose to live as if on a permanent camp out, but maybe at his age, Meredith Douglas craved the simplicity of a life uncomplicated by modern conveniences.

Kelsey gulped down half of the glass, savoring the coolness of the water against her tongue. She shot a quick glance at Meredith. Instead of looking concerned over her reception of his cooking, he looked amused, almost... calculating. She dismissed the thought and forced herself to finish the soup. She set her spoon down and blinked. The room shifted in and out of focus.

"You said you knew my mother. What about her family? Do you know if they live near here? I must have... cousins, or something. I had wanted to—" Her mind blanked. What had she wanted?

Meredith brought a plate of butter and homemade bread to the table. "There have been no MacKenzies on Orkney for thirty years."

Thirty years. She frowned, trying to collect her thoughts. Her parents had married thirty years ago. Or was it longer? She tried to reason through it. She was—How old?

Kelsey tried to butter a slice of the thick bread. The knife slipped in her hand, and she buttered as much of her fingers as she did of the bread, but Meredith acted as if he didn't notice. She surreptitiously wiped her fingers on the napkin in her lap but most of the butter went on her jeans.

Lethargy stole through her until she longed to lay her head

on the table and sleep.

"Miss MacKenzie." Meredith's voice seemed to come from the end of a very long tunnel. "Have you had enough?"

She'd had enough, all right. Enough of pretending polite interest in conversation that made no sense when what she really needed was a nap. Enough of his soup that could probably clean the barnacles off a boat.

She tried to thank him, but the words didn't want to emerge past her swollen tongue. She stood, wanting to smile and communicate her need to leave, but her knees buckled, and the packed dirt floor rose up as conscious thought slipped away.

Chapter Fourteen

For the rest of the morning, Cade concentrated on his work and tried to ignore his growing uneasiness about Kelsey's absence. Where could she have gone? Disappearing without telling anyone wasn't like her, and the last time... His uneasiness increased as he recalled how she had become stranded by the tide. What if....

From his work station, Norlund muttered several disparaging remarks about the morals of American women in general and Kelsey's in particular.

Finally goaded beyond endurance, Cade threw down his pencil and strode over to Norlund's desk. Brimming with the need to wipe the smirk from the Swedish scientist's face, Cade grabbed him by the lapels of his lab coat, lifting the big man off his chair. Norlund towered over him by half a foot, but despite his height advantage looked startled and fearful.

Bracken caught at Cade's arm. "Now, Cade. I'm certain Erik didn't mean what he said. We're all just touchy about losing so much of what we'd done. Take a little break. Get some fresh air. We'll meet you for lunch in half an hour."

Cade shook his head and maintained his grip on Norlund. "He needs to apologize and keep his blasted comments to himself."

"Erik? Tell him you meant no harm." Bracken's voice was gently persuasive.

Norlund hesitated, swallowed and nodded. "My apologies, Douglas. I had no idea you were taking your little dalliance so seriously."

Stifling the urge to flatten the big man's nose, Cade lowered him to the floor and released him. He dusted off his hands as if the gesture were enough to rid himself of the ill feeling touching Norlund had given him. Norlund harbored dark secrets, Cade had no doubts about that, but the problem lay in proving what he sensed to be true. "Perhaps my soul isn't as black as yours, Doctor."

Turning on his heel, he strode from the room. Norlund's comment drifted to him as the door swung shut.

"You really ought to put a leash on him, Bracken, or we'll end up with another incident like Lana Reynolds."

Lana. Norlund couldn't blame Cade for that. Putting the man's viciousness from his mind, Cade turned to the sea for solace, hoping to find some sign of Kelsey on the rocky shore. Nothing. Not a sign that she had been there at all, no trace of her footsteps having disturbed the rocks, nor a scent of her. The wind carried only the tang of salt and the taste of sea life.

A burning sensation radiated upward from his stomach while a sour sensation filled his mouth. He rubbed the center of his chest. Apparently, Mrs. Devon's golden flapjacks were making a reappearance, but he wasn't usually troubled by what he ate.

He walked further along the shore, searching for Kelsey's small footprints. Water foamed around his shoes. The tide was coming in. If she had come this way, the sea could have already obliterated signs of her passage.

The heartburn that had plagued him since mid-morning increased in intensity. Perhaps if he had lunch, the discomfort would ease, but he couldn't make himself return to the inn. He had to find Kelsey. Somehow he knew she wasn't in her room or the dining hall. Despite the fact Norlund had been in the lab all morning, Cade didn't trust the Swedish scientist any further than he could throw a walrus. What if he had tried to harm her? Could his jealousy and anger be out of control?

If only he knew where she had gone, it would be a simpler matter to focus his attention and reassure himself that she was safe. Again he remembered her mishap with the tide shortly after she had arrived. Rescuing her had cost him a great deal physically and earned him grandfather's displeasure as well. He didn't want to go through that again.

He considered calling out to her, but didn't want to draw the attention of Bracken and Norlund in case they had decided to walk to the shore, or were strolling about the lawn. He stopped and pressed his fingers to his temples, concentrating in the way grandfather had taught him.

Burning pain slammed into his chest, spread up to his throat, sizzling his tongue. He staggered, falling to his knees in the sand. The sea eddied around him and tugged at his pants legs. His mind cried out to her, but he felt no response.

Grandfather, what have you done?

Breaking free of the fragile connection, he lurched to his feet. He had to get to her before Meredith did something Cade was sure to regret. If anything bad happened to Kelsey, he wouldn't be able to bear it.

Heedless of the rising tide, he struggled over the boulders, making his way along the shore to the small cottage where Meredith Douglas had lived since the day the rest of the family had found it necessary to leave the islands.

His lungs burned, and he wasn't certain if it was from his closeness to the sea or if it was Kelsey's pain he felt. The waves licked like fire at his legs, but he pushed on, knowing it would take twice as long to reach her by going over land. He didn't dare try another way, knowing he wouldn't be able to help her if he became ill himself. At last the thatched roof of Meredith's cottage came into sight.

Grandfather sat on the porch as he always did, rocking slightly in his wooden chair and contemplating the sea. He frowned at Cade struggling up from the beach.

"It was understood you would stay out of the sea." Meredith's voice sounded as forbidding as his scowling face looked. Disapproval radiated from his tense posture.

"It was understood you would let me handle Miss

MacKenzie. I've kept my word." His tone made the accusation respect for his grandfather wouldn't let him put into words.

Meredith's frown deepened, and he looked away. "I've not harmed the lass. She's inside. Resting."

Cade trudged up the steps, and waited until he'd caught his breath before he spoke again. "What have you done to her?"

Meredith rose, drawing himself up to his grandson's height. "Only what you refused to do."

The argument sprang out before he could stop it. "Her will is too strong."

"Strong, yes. Too strong, Cade?" Grandfather's voice gentled, and he laid a hand on Cade's arm. "Or is it that you don't want her to forget?"

Cade swallowed a denial and looked away. How could he explain to his grandfather that making Kelsey forget what they had shared would be like tearing his own heart out? How could he ever hope to make her forget when in his soul he wanted her to remember their time together forever?

Meredith patted his arm. "You know it's best. Time for you to start thinking with your mind again, instead of letting nature and instinct rule you."

"I never—" The words ripped harshly from his throat, before he acknowledged the truth of what grandfather said. It was true and useless to deny to his elder. Lately, he'd thought of nothing except being with Kelsey. He bowed his head. "Forgive me, grandfather. I know you only want what is best for the family. As I do. But I won't see her hurt."

Meredith guided him inside. "You don't want her hurt? All the more reason to put it behind you. Without the memories to drag her down, she can see that Bracken stays on his task here. You can accomplish great things, both of you, now that this incident has been purged from her mind. Perhaps it will even be possible to persuade her to leave the island. That would be best and in your heart you know it."

Cade looked down at Kelsey, asleep on the pallet his grandfather used as a bed. Dark shadows circled her eyes and her face looked unnaturally pale. "You're certain she's not ill?"

Meredith shrugged. "A good night's rest certainly won't hurt. Either one of you."

Heat flooded his face, and he refused to meet his grandfather's eyes. How could grandfather possibly know how he and Kelsey had been spending their nights? Was he as transparent as a school boy? But perhaps Grandfather was right. Despite the ecstasy he shared with Kelsey, being together wasn't worth the pain it caused both of them.

The pain which could only get worse until it destroyed them.

"You'll see," Meredith continued. "There will be another for you. One much better suited to what you are, what you must be. You'll see."

Watching Kelsey sleep, her dark lashes setting off the paleness of her complexion, he longed to feel her soft skin beneath his hands. No, he couldn't accept Meredith's convictions, even though he wanted to believe his grandfather was right. For the thought of ever being with another female instead of Kelsey was as unappealing as the idea of never being able to return to the sea.

Kelsey kept her eyes closed and tried to concentrate. Men's voices seemed to come from a great distance, but the words drifted out of reach of conscious thought. Gradually, she realized they spoke in a language she had never heard before.

Or had she?

They argued about her. She understood that even though she didn't know why. One voice was younger, insistent and pleasantly familiar. The older was more measured, calmer. Hypnotic, but not as compelling as the younger man. Unable to resist the pull of the younger voice, she followed it into deeper slumber and a dream from which she didn't want to awaken.

Kelsey blinked and sat straighter in the unyielding wooden chair, wondering why she felt as groggy as if she'd been sleeping when she'd merely let her attention wander from Meredith's discussion of the merits of using local ingredients gathered on the hillside for blanc mange.

"I'm sure you're right," she murmured, compelled to make some sort of response. How on earth had she ended up here? Discussing recipes when she couldn't even make toast without burning it? She looked up to see Cade Douglas enter the cottage.

His smile was remote, measuring. How odd. "I'll walk you back to the inn, if you're ready."

She wondered why he would think she wasn't ready to leave. There was just so much culinary information a person who specialized in microwave dinners could absorb in one sitting. She pushed her chair back, and Dr. Douglas was immediately there to assist her, his grip almost—intimate on her shoulder. Despite the warmth of the cottage, she shivered but put the strange sensation from her mind. It was almost as if her body recognized his touch, but that was impossible.

"Thank you for lunch, Meredith. I enjoyed meeting you."

Meredith's expression was friendly, his smile warm. "Come see me again, Kelsey. Perhaps next time you'll tell me about where your mother's family lived."

She'd tell him, that didn't seem right. The idea that he already knew much more than she did teased the edges of her mind where a slight headache was blooming. There must be something in the air here she was allergic to. She couldn't remember having as many headaches in her life as she'd had since she arrived in the islands. She rubbed her forehead.

Again Dr. Douglas was at her elbow, his tone solicitous. "Are you quite all right, Kelsey?"

She wobbled with her first step, but his concern irritated

her. "I'm fine, thank you, Dr. Douglas. If you want to walk with me, then let's get going. I know we left a great deal of work in the lab and most of the afternoon is already gone."

She thanked Meredith again and left the cottage. She didn't look to see if Dr. Douglas was behind her, she sensed him. His presence followed her like a shadow, although he made no effort at conversation.

She skirted the pond. Something about the shimmery depths flirted with her memory, then drifted away. The headache became aggressive, making her struggle to focus. Kelsey stopped and squeezed her eyes shut.

"What is it, Kelsey?" Dr. Douglas' hand on the back of her neck felt familiar and improper all at the same time.

Unnerved by the sensation, Kelsey shrugged away from him. Why was he touching her? He was a colleague. Having his hands on her was totally inappropriate.

"Nothing. I have a headache, that's all." Why was he so concerned? Especially since he was the one who took such pains to avoid even the appearance of being within touching range of her. Usually, he had the uncanny ability to make her feel as if she carried some contagious illness, or something.

"Look," she turned to face him. "I know you don't like my being here, but you're going to have to live with it. And I think it would help if you kept your hands off me. We don't need to give Dr. Bracken any reason to think we've engaged in anything improper. Especially when we haven't," she added for emphasis.

Cade couldn't believe what he was hearing. Dazed, he searched her face and felt as if she'd hit him between the eyes with a two-by-four. She didn't remember. She actually had forgotten everything except the animosity they had towards one another. He stared at her for several long moments, resisting the urge to gather her in his arms and give her something to remember. Angry regret overpowered his astonishment, his building need. So he'd been wrong and grandfather right. She could be made to forget. The knowledge made him feel as if his heart had been ripped out.

But if this was what was meant to be, so be it. He pushed past her, leading the way along the narrow trail. "As you wish, Miss MacKenzie. As you wish."

To Kelsey's surprise, Dr. Bracken made no complaint about her being gone most of the afternoon. She checked the cultures she was growing, fed the live specimens in the tank and adjusted the temperature. Everything looked in good order, which was just as well. The way she was feeling, there was no way she could work late into the evening as she'd been doing for most of the past week since Dr. Bracken and Dr. Norlund had returned.

Dr. Bracken stopped by her desk on his way out. A look of concern furrowed his brow. "Are you feeling ill, Kelsey? You've looked rather pale the past few days."

She smiled up at him, grateful for the consideration he'd always shown her. "Just a little tired, is all. I'll be glad when we've caught up to where we were before everything was lost."

Dr. Bracken shook his head. "Well, don't overdo it. Good research takes time. Rushing it is of no use. Besides, I don't want your father to think I'm working you too hard."

Her father. As if he'd even notice. He lived and breathed for his work and expected his crew to work the same long, hard hours he did. Kelsey wouldn't want either her father or Dr. Bracken to think she couldn't hold up to the same rigorous standards. "I'd like to have some definitive results to show my father when he arrives."

"Ah, yes. Results." He peered more closely at her. "Make sure you get plenty of rest. It's amazing how much more difficult a problem can appear if one is too tired. Why don't you run along to the inn for tea? Mrs. Devon is serving her wonderful shortbread."

To her surprise, Kelsey realized she was hungry.

Apparently Meredith's nettle soup wasn't much on staying power. "I think I will. I'll come back before supper and finish up here."

"No need for that." Dr. Bracken practically shooed her from the lab. "We're going to put in a full day tomorrow. I've arranged for a captain and a larger boat to take us to those islands you and Cade visited. If we knew when your father was arriving, perhaps we could press his crew into service, but I'm anxious to replace those specimens we lost."

Kelsey looked up from her research notes to find Dr. Douglas' gaze fixed intently on her. A lock of silver hair tumbled across his forehead and for a moment, she had an inexplicable urge to smooth it back, the gesture seeming almost like something she had actually done.

He frowned. For some reason, he seemed annoyed by Dr. Bracken's plans. "The wind is from the west."

Kelsey looked out where the bright red and green flags carrying the Murdoch crest flapped in a stiff breeze. "And your point is...."

"By morning, the sea will be too rough to set out. We might just as well not make any plans until the moon passes into the next phase."

Kelsey looked at Dr. Bracken to see his reaction to Dr. Douglas' pronouncement.

Dr. Bracken simply smiled genially. "Well, you're our local expert, Douglas. I'll alert the captain we may not be requiring his services for a few days. Why don't you go on to tea with Kelsey? I'll shut down here and join you in a few minutes."

Cade looked as if he would protest, then shut his notebook and took off his lab coat, carefully hanging it up near the door.

Kelsey waited until they were outside before she spoke. "He doesn't have a clue, does he?"

Dr. Douglas walked beside her, an arm's length away, keeping a safe distance between them. "What do you mean?"

Kelsey gestured back to the lab. "Dr. Bracken. He has no idea how much you'd like me to leave, does he?"

Cade stopped, moved closer as if to touch her, and her heart flipped into double time. How could he make her feel as if the universe centered in his molten pewter gaze? She involuntarily held her breath and waited—for what she wasn't sure. Abruptly, he dropped his hands away from her and stepped back, leaving her with a deep sense of disappointment and dismay at her reaction to the brief closeness.

"He has plans of his own, Miss MacKenzie. You'd do well not to forget that for a moment."

Two weeks passed with no further word from her father. Kelsey immersed herself in work and tried to ignore the hurt his delayed arrival caused, but couldn't quite push the disappointment and feeling of rejection away any more than she could ignore the way her heart hammered whenever Cade Douglas was within reaching distance. He went out of his way not to touch her or even brush against her, but that didn't stop her breath from catching, or a shiver of anticipation from sliding across her skin when he was near. It was as if her body knew something her mind refused to recognize, but when she tried too hard to analyze the feelings, the headaches she had come to expect began to bloom and soon pushed out all thoughts except for her lab work.

But at night she tossed and turned, caught up in dreams she wanted to forget as much as she wanted the reality.

One night, she stood at her bedroom window, letting the breeze cool her sweat-drenched skin. The perpetual twilight dappled the ripples on the sea and cast the shore in a frosted silence. A ghost of a moon, barely discernible in the odd light, hung low in the sky. For the past two weeks, she and Dr. Douglas had barely exchanged a dozen words.

Why then had her erotic dreams of him increased in intensity? How could she imagine making love so vividly when she had never been with him? Or any other man?

She rubbed her hand along her arm, but it was his hands she felt on her body, his sweat that cooled her skin. She took a ragged breath and let the dream images wash over her again, felt the climax she knew she'd never experienced build to a level of tantalizing frustration. What was happening to her? Cade must be aware of it and that was why he went out of his way to avoid contact with her. How humiliating.

During the day it was much easier to ignore the chemistry between them. Much easier under the watchful glare of Dr. Norlund, the bemused observance of Dr. Bracken to pretend she didn't have deep desires for Cade.

Alone, nights were unbearable. Sometimes the dreams were so intense, she swore she could taste the salt of his skin, hear his voice softly encouraging her, his breath on her face, feel him hard and demanding inside her.

Clenching her hands, she took a deep breath. She needed something else to think about, something besides work to be concerned about. If only her father would hurry up and get here. Although his telegram had promised an imminent arrival, a week had passed, then another, with no further word. She wished he would show up and get the fireworks over with. But as had happened many times, something more pressing than his only child had probably come up.

Sighing, she turned from the window and switched on the desk lamp. Settling into the chair, she opened the textbook on North Sea seals Dr. Bracken had asked her to study. If she couldn't sleep, she might as well work. According to the text and her own research before she'd arrived, several species of seals inhabited the various islands. Why then, hadn't she seen even one since she'd arrived?

Her thoughts drifted. Dr. Douglas had taken her to one of the outer islands several weeks ago. She pictured it clearly. The cool breeze on her face, the dark shadows on the beach she had thought were seals. Getting caught on the sand bar when the steering cable broke. Closing her eyes, she leaned her head back. Warm sun bathed her face, icy water stung her bare feet when she'd jumped from the boat to look for samples. They'd had some mechanical trouble with the boat.

Cade had stayed with the boat while she explored the island, then…. Her head began to pound.

Why was the rest of the afternoon an indistinct blur?

Chapter Fifteen

Cade threw back the covers and climbed off the too soft mattress. Naked, he strode to the window and pulled the curtain aside. From a great distance, a seal cried, its plaintive voice cutting through the dusky light. Summer was already half over, and they were no closer to a solution to save the seals than when the project had started. Dr. Bracken's promises of two more scientists had been nothing more than vague talk about securing the necessary personnel. So far nothing had been said about anyone else joining the team.

He wondered if Bracken had even done any recruiting in the time he and Norlund had been gone or if the whole trip had merely been a ruse to push him and Kelsey together. It had worked, but now, thanks to Meredith, the time he'd shared with her he could treasure only in the darkest depths of night. Grandfather expected him to forget what had happened as easily as Kelsey had.

As if he could.

Kelsey had the benefit of Meredith's strange blend of magic. She also had a new found reserve Cade couldn't seem to bridge. Not that he made much of an effort.

No, it was better this way. Better she not remember, even though he went crazy with wanting if she got even three feet from him, and he caught her scent.

Just the slightest whisper of her and he could taste her on his tongue, feel her hair tease his bare skin, feel her wet, tightness envelop him.

His body tensed into painful readiness, and he again felt betrayed. By himself, by his grandfather. But mostly by the woman he wanted more than anything. The woman who gave herself so casually that Meredith's simple spell could erase from her mind the moments Cade knew he'd treasure forever.

Dawn streaked the sky with pink and orange when Kelsey woke from where she'd fallen asleep over Dr. Bracken's dry textbook. She yawned and stretched, trying to ease the kink in the middle of her back. Dumb to have fallen asleep in the chair, but at least she felt a little more rested than she had for several days. She took a quick shower, fighting the erratic plumbing to keep from alternately freezing and scalding herself, then dressed in a sweater and jeans.

Dr. Douglas was seated at the table closet to the window when she entered the dining room. Kelsey helped herself to fruit and porridge from the sideboard and wondered what she should do. Except for Dr. Douglas the dining room was empty. She could have her choice of tables, except she preferred to sit by the window. Besides, going too far to avoid Cade Douglas was certain to appear rude. She pulled a chair out to sit with him.

He wiped his mouth on a linen napkin. "Good morning, Miss MacKenzie. I hope you won't think it ill mannered of me, but I was just about to leave."

"Don't go on my account." She emptied a packet of coarse dark sugar on her porridge and hunted for the cream pitcher. He placed it near her, exaggerating his movements to avoid brushing her fingers.

He looked faintly annoyed. "I wasn't. Dr. Bracken asked me to draw some blood samples from the live specimens this morning. He'll be wanting you to run a series of tests this afternoon."

She took a mouthful of cereal and rolled the gritty texture on her tongue. Noticing his gaze fixed on her, she paused before swallowing, then bit into a muffin. He followed every movement, seemingly obsessed with watching her in the ordinary task of eating. "He hadn't mentioned it. Do you have a few minutes to stick around and tell me about it?"

She regretted asking the minute the words emerged. If he didn't stop scrutinizing her, she was going to end up with her bowl of hot cereal in her lap. For an instant, an image of Cade's mouth on her, coaxing her to ecstasy made a rush of heat flood her body. She trembled. Jerking her gaze from his, she set the spoon down and reached for her tea cup, rattling it against the saucer before she got the cup to her lips. Hot tea burned her tongue.

"Whatever are you thinking about, Miss MacKenzie?" His voice was little more than a whisper. "You look as if you'd spent too much time in the sun. Which certainly isn't possible here." His hand swept towards the sky, where another bank of thunderclouds formed on the horizon.

What was there about him that made her blood sing, that hummed along her nerve endings, as if every cell could imagine his flesh rubbing against hers, as if she could feel his hard thrusts inside her? All the dreams she'd had in the past two weeks poured through her mind.

She took a deep breath. "The day after Dr. Bracken and Dr. Norlund went to the mainland, you took me to one of the outer islands." She glanced towards the door to the kitchen to make sure they were still alone. "What happened there?"

He sat back in his chair. "Why do you ask?"

Kelsey twisted her fingers together in her lap. "I know this is going to sound odd, but the last thing I remember is some kind of trouble with the boat. I don't remember what type of specimens I collected, or how long it took to get back here. Part of the afternoon is just a blank."

He seemed to choose his words carefully. "Nothing special."

For a fleeting instant, Kelsey saw him looming over her, his eyes squeezed shut, the muscles taut in his throat and chest, heard his hoarse shout as he poured himself into her. She brushed her napkin to the floor so that she'd have the pretext of retrieving it in order to hide the scarlet heat staining her face. How could she look at him and risk him seeing what she couldn't seem to purge from her mind?

She straightened and took a sip of water. "Why can't I recall what we did?"

His expression a study in nonchalance, he shrugged. "You dozed off on the way back. What is it you think you should be remembering?"

She tried to meet his gaze, but the fear he'd read the longing in her eyes made her quickly look away. Ever since she'd had soup with Meredith Douglas, the persistent sense of some kind of memory lapse plagued her.

Still, with Dr. Douglas being as distant as he'd been, she could hardly ask him if she'd simply forgotten that they'd made love. She'd be mortified if he knew what she'd been dreaming about. And lately, the dreams seemed to follow her more and more into wakefulness.

"Nothing." She looked up in time to see a fierce pride light his eyes before he scowled and rose.

"Then I wouldn't waste any energy worrying about it. If something significant had happened, you'd certainly remember, wouldn't you? Now if you'll excuse me, I'm going to the lab."

He felt her gaze on his back long after he knew she could no longer see him. Instead of going immediately to the lab, he skirted the far side of the inn and headed for the shore. Tipping his head back he inhaled the myriad smells of the sea and let the freshness wash through him. Flinging his arms wide, he longed to roar in triumph.

She remembered.

Oh, not everything, yet. And she still thought she'd been dreaming about what had happened. Night after night he'd shared in those dreams, waking up hard and sweating, aching for the taste and feel of her.

She remembered, on some level, what they had shared. In time, she would recall everything. He was as certain of that as he was that each night the moon continued its course across the dusky sky.

Gradually his elation seeped away, swept out on the tide receding from around his feet.

She remembered.

They were doomed.

Kelsey pressed her cold hands against her hot face. Judging by the look on Dr. Douglas' face, he'd guessed, at least in part, the scandalous turn her thoughts had taken lately where he was concerned. And he was amused by it.

How humiliating.

The only consolation was that, with typical male arrogance, he was flattered. Well, all she could do was to make sure she maintained the distance she'd cultivated so carefully over the past weeks. Her stomach clenched, unexpectedly threatening to dislodge her breakfast.

Kelsey squeezed her eyes shut and rested her head in her hand until the sensation receded. She'd felt this way yesterday, too. After several weeks here, she really should know better than to drink Mrs. Devon's horrendously strong tea on an empty stomach. And of course, talking with Dr. Douglas had a way of making her insides feel like the center of a storm cloud.

A door opened and closed behind her, and she looked up, hoping to see Dr. Douglas, although why she was anxious to have him return, she didn't want to think about. When Dr. Bracken greeted her instead, she sank back into her chair and forced a smile.

"Good morning." He pulled out the chair Cade had vacated, pushed the used dishes aside, then eyed her as if she were a hot house flower. "Sleep well?" When she nodded, he smiled and continued. "Any more news of your father?"

Kelsey took a cautious sip of water and willed her queasiness away. "No, but that's nothing unusual."

Dr. Bracken's eyes were full of sympathy. He patted her hand. "I expect he'll be along as soon as he's able. He's made quite a name for himself since the days when we were both here as fledging biologists, determined to make a tidal wave." He chuckled at his own joke. "Don't fret, Kelsey. I'm certain he always tried to do his best by you, but it hasn't been easy on him, losing your mother the way he did."

The familiar sense of desperation filled her. Somewhere there had to be someone who had the answers she sought about her mother. "You weren't here when she died, were you?" She asked the question, even though she already knew the answer.

Dr. Bracken fiddled with the flatware, rolling the handle of a table knife over and over between his fingers. He shook his head. "You really ought to take the time to visit with Meredith Douglas. I believe he could tell you a great deal about your mother. He lives in a crofter's cottage on the east side of the island. Not far from here."

"I know." At his questioning look, she explained. "We met one day when I was out walking. He invited me to lunch and we chatted." Kelsey laughed ruefully. "He certainly makes a wicked nettle soup."

"Is that right?" Dr. Bracken sat back in his chair, but his posture remained rigid. "When was this?"

Kelsey considered how much time had passed. She had been working such long hours in the lab her visit with Meredith seemed as if it must have been in another life. "About two weeks ago. I think it was the day I received the telegram from my father."

"Interesting," he murmured, then sat forward, resting his arms on the table. "How have you been feeling?"

She found his inordinate interest in her health lately very perplexing. But she dismissed the oddity of it when she thought about the extreme consideration he'd always shown her. A kindly man and a long-term colleague of her father's, Dr. Bracken had been concerned with her welfare since she had first come to know him on a personal basis as a student at Texas A&M University.

"I'm fine," she assured him, knowing it would be a mistake to worry him with details of the bouts of headaches and queasiness she'd been experiencing lately. She couldn't very well tell him about the dreams which had been keeping her awake, either.

Mrs. Devon entered the dining room and set a plate of coddled eggs on the table in front of Dr. Bracken. "Just the way you like them, Doctor." She turned to Kelsey. "Is there anything else you'd like this morning? Some eggs, perhaps?"

Kelsey watched Dr. Bracken attack the runny eggs. Yolk the color of marigolds flowed over the plate. He forked up a dripping mouthful with obvious enjoyment. Her breakfast curdled in her stomach.

"No, thank you, Mrs. Devon." She pushed her chair back, anxious to leave before she embarrassed herself. "I'm going to get some fresh air before I get started on those specimens." She left the room.

She forced herself to stroll until she was out of sight of the dining room, then ran to the shore. Cool sea air stroked her face, and she gulped in a steadying breath, but it was no use. Tears stung her eyes. Unable to fight the bile rising in her throat, she vomited. Waves curled around her toes, carrying away the evidence.

Kelsey wiped her mouth on the back of her hand and breathed slowly and deeply. As soon as the queasiness passed, she stumbled from the water's edge, sank down onto a large boulder, tucked her legs up and rested her forehead on her knees.

No doubt about it, she was going to have to quit drinking the witch's brew Mrs. Devon called tea.

From the point of land west of the inn, Cade stood on an outcropping of rocks. She was ill and the urge to rush and offer comfort warred with his promise to his grandfather. He relaxed when she turned from the sea and sat. In her hurry to find a comfortable place, Kelsey hadn't noticed him, and he used the opportunity to study her. She looked pale, her creamy skin contrasting starkly with her dark hair.

Not too surprising, considering the frequent sleepless nights she'd had. He hoped she wasn't suffering any lingering effects from grandfather's soup. Meredith had assured him he had not harmed her, merely wiped out the memories of their time together. "Like removing a few pages from a book. Certain events may be lost, but the context of the story stays the same."

He supposed that meant Kelsey hadn't forgotten her chief purpose in being on the island. As he watched, she untied her shoes, pulled off her socks and scrunched the legs of her jeans up to her knees. She rose, walked to the sea and let the water flow around her ankles. Longing stabbed through him. She had such beautiful legs, such exquisite feet. Recalling the smooth, delicate skin covering the graceful curve of her limbs, his lips tingled, remembering the warm, soft feel of her flesh.

She reveled in the water, like a sea nymph. It was one of the things he found the most irresistible about her. An image of her bounding from the skiff into the cold water on the isolated island came to mind, followed by memories of her provocative swim at the inland pond. In the water, she was incomparable grace, as if she belonged there. He gave his imagination free rein and pictured the two of them slicing through the ocean, side by side. How he longed to share the secrets of the sea with her. Would she let him, if she knew?

Just as the thought brought a flicker of hope to him, the realization of what he was asking crashed over him like a North Sea wave in winter. Others had tried, with disastrous results. Stories passed from father and son, each a warning to those who would defy nature.

No, he couldn't tell her. He couldn't bear seeing the look on her face. Still, he longed to go to her and tell her his story, even if there was only the tiniest fragment of hope that she wouldn't reject him.

He felt the presence of his grandfather before he turned and saw him approaching from the beach opposite the one where Kelsey waded in the surf. His attention immediately strayed back to Kelsey.

"You must stop pining after the girl." Meredith's strong voice rang with authority, making the words a command, instead of a suggestion. "Put her and the incident from your mind."

Cade tore his gaze from Kelsey and faced his grandfather. "It isn't that simple."

Meredith snorted, his expression skeptical and long-suffering. He rested a hand on Cade's shoulder. "You're not the first to believe that, but the fact remains, she's beyond your reach. Come, walk with me and I'll tell you the story of another young pup who sought to defy the laws of our kind."

Cade sighed, certain Meredith would launch into another dire story he'd heard a hundred times. "You've told me. Many times."

Meredith raised a shaggy brow. "Ah, but I'm certain you'll find this story particularly interesting. It's about your father. And a beautiful woman named Annabelle MacKenzie.

Chapter Sixteen

"Miss MacKenzie!"

Kelsey turned at the eager sound of Mrs. Devon's voice and watched the housekeeper speed across the grass as quickly as her stout legs would allow. In her hand she held an envelope, which she clutched to her bosom while she tried to catch her breath.

"The post just arrived."

Kelsey regarded her curiously. What could be so urgent it couldn't wait till she returned to the inn? "Thank you, Mrs. Devon, but you didn't need to go to such trouble. I was just about to return."

Mrs. Devon handed the letter to Kelsey. "Priority mail. Didn't make sense to have him go to all that trouble to get it here in a hurry if I couldn't stir myself to walk across the lawn and give it to you."

Kelsey murmured another thank you and glanced at the return address. Her father.

"We watch all his specials on public television." Mrs. Devon's enthusiasm was palpable. "Look, the postmark is from Barcelona. Maybe he's heard what a fine scientist you are and wants you to work for him. Wouldn't that be a coup?"

It would be a miracle. Kelsey ripped the envelope open, wishing the housekeeper would take her kindly presence elsewhere, surprised Mrs. Devon didn't know William Bouschour was her father. Cade had known. Why would he if it weren't common knowledge here? She hesitated before drawing the folded letter out. "Was there anything else, Mrs. Devon?"

She finally seemed to remember herself and drew back. "Oh, no, dear, except that if you wish to respond to your letter, you'd best do it while the captain lunches at the inn. Once he's gone, it may be several days before you'll be able to post a letter. Do let us know what your good news might be, though. And you be sure to tell him if he wants a first rate place to stay, we've got the finest lodging in all of the British Isles right here."

"I'll do that."

The housekeeper turned and headed back to the inn, humming, no doubt imagining the humble Murdoch Castle the background for a television special.

Kelsey smiled and shook her head, then unfolded the paper. *Daughter, Regrettably I won't be able to join you as quickly as I had wanted. I wish you had consulted me before taking on this assignment. Of course, Dr. Bracken's given you excellent guidance over the years, but choosing you for his current project shows a grievous lack of judgment. I'll be in port here for a week and will be expecting you on the next flight out. Orkney is not the place for you. We'll discuss more suitable options after you arrive. There are many good reasons why we left there twenty-five years ago, and I would caution you against interacting with the islanders. Bouschour.*

Her hands trembling, Kelsey stuffed the letter back into the envelope. He still thought of her as a child, incapable of choosing her work, her companions. *I would caution you against interacting—* What in the world was that supposed to mean? Avoid eye contact with any Orcadian? Don't have an affair with a crofter's son? Grabbing up her shoes and socks, Kelsey stalked back to the inn to draft a reply.

For years, her father had taken little interest in her life. Why the sudden need to issue edicts?

Well, she wasn't leaving. It was bad enough that Cade Douglas thought she was ill equipped for this project and that Dr. Norlund regarded her work skeptically. Dr. Bracken, at least, had complete faith in her abilities. She intended to do nothing to shake his confidence.

After procuring paper and pen from Mrs. Devon, she headed to the dining room, hoping to ask the ferry captain to delay his departure just long enough for her to answer her father's summons and tell him she had no intention of leaving Orkney. She paused at the door to redistribute the items she carried in order to have a free hand, when she heard Dr. Norlund's voice drift down from the staircase.

"The inn's been peculiarly quiet at night, Dennis. Is it possible your well-laid plans are foundering?"

Dr. Bracken's chuckle echoed off the tall ceiling. "On the contrary, I expect to learn any day that the experiment 'took'." She could almost see him shrug. "And if not, there are ways of helping things along. We still have the rest of the summer." The front door creaked shut and the voices faded. Kelsey stood in the hallway, trying to make sense of what she had just heard.

What kind of experiment had Dr. Bracken been conducting? And what was he expecting to learn?

Could it possibly have something to do with her?

For the next several days, Kelsey immersed herself in work, applying herself diligently in the lab. At night, she read the books Dr. Bracken provided for her until weariness completely overtook her, and she collapsed into bed.

Some of the reading material had nothing to do with marine biology, but instead covered Scottish history, including another book on legends and myths. Reading another version of a selkie story, Kelsey paused and tried to figure out why Dr. Bracken would have her reading something so far afield from the project. Perhaps he wanted her to lighten up a bit and not spend all her time poring over dry textbooks and research articles.

"So ask him already," she muttered, slipping on a pair of

jeans and hunting for her shoes. She glanced at the bedside clock. Although it was nearly eleven p.m., she knew Dr. Bracken rarely turned off his lights before midnight. She tugged at the waistband of her Levi's, trying to fasten the brass button. Obviously she'd been indulging herself with too much of Mrs. Devon's wonderful cooking, particularly the shortbread. Although she hadn't yet worn this pair of jeans since she'd arrived, they had fit perfectly before she left the States. Kelsey shrugged away a twinge of guilt and pulled her sweater over the waistband.

She left her turret room and paused outside Cade's door. The temptation to see if he shared her insomnia nearly proved overwhelming, but no light shone from underneath his door.

She couldn't very well ask him to wake up and discuss ancient Scottish legends with her, especially when what she really wanted from him was... she didn't even want to admit it. Her erotic dreams about him were more and more consuming even though they hadn't shared two words since the day she'd sat with him at breakfast. He might not have much of a reason for keeping a distance, but obviously he intended to stay well away from her.

In fact, he scarcely glanced at her, but when he did, his eyes were haunted, as if by a great sorrow she didn't share and didn't understand, but somehow felt as if she should. Perhaps once the project was over, they could get to know each other without feeling like a conversation was a conflict of interest.

Kelsey shook her head at the far-fetched idea and continued down the hall. Cade Douglas had given her no reason to think he ever wanted to have a friendly relationship with her. Trying to convince herself that he did only proved she needed to work a little more at her personal life once she returned to the States.

Dr. Bracken answered on the second knock. Pipe in hand, his pullover shirt unbuttoned and leather slippers on his feet, he looked every bit the fatherly figure she'd learned to appreciate.

"Kelsey, what a pleasant surprise. Come in, come in." He ushered her into the cozy sitting room of his suite, and she took a seat on an antique sofa. "Can I offer you a cup of tea?" He gestured to the tea service on the cherry coffee table.

Kelsey suppressed a shudder. "No, thank you. I'm sorry to disturb you so late."

Dr. Bracken puffed on his pipe, obviously enjoying the sickeningly sweet tobacco. "Not at all. We haven't had much chance to chat the past few days, and I was just wondering if everything was well with you."

There he went again, inquiring after her health. "I'm fine," she assured him, then wondered if his curiosity came from the same concern her father had about her being in the islands. Instead of asking him about the books she'd come to discuss, she blurted what had been on her mind since she'd received her father's letter nearly a week ago.

"Dr. Bracken, do you know why my father is so opposed to my being in Orkney?"

He eyed her as if trying to decide what he should reveal against what she might already know. "You know your mother died here."

Kelsey nodded. "Yes, but I've never been told why. Was there something that made her ill, or did she misjudge the sea the way Lana did?"

Dr. Bracken scraped out his pipe, then refilled it. Kelsey watched him, finding comfort in the ritual she knew he only indulged in once a day.

"Perhaps you'd call it an error of judgment. I've always wondered if she might have been clinically depressed. I'm sorry I can't be more specific, but I feel these are questions you must address to your father."

"Perhaps, although I doubt I will get an answer there either." She rolled the hem of her sweater between her fingers. "Why isn't she buried here?"

"Kelsey." His tone was gentle. "Your mother is buried with her family. You know they didn't live on this island."

"But then where?"

He held up a hand as if to ward off further questions. "I really can't say any more." He leaned forward and changed the subject. "Tell me. How are you and Cade getting along?"

Kelsey shrugged. "Fine, although I suppose you've noticed we seem to have a bit of a personality conflict."

Dr. Bracken chuckled. "I don't think that's what I would call it." At her raised eyebrow, he continued. "Actually I believe he's quite taken with you."

Heat stole up her neck. "I'm sure you're mistaken."

"Oh, no. I don't think so. I thought perhaps at first you two would make magic, but it seems of late that I was mistaken. Was I?" His gaze searched her face.

Embarrassed, Kelsey plucked at the nubby texture on the arm of the wingback chair and decided to avoid a direct answer. "I can assure you, I won't let anything stand in the way of my work."

Dr. Bracken laughed. "Sometimes I think you're much too serious, child. It wouldn't bother me if you and Cade decided you wanted to 'explore' this attraction you have for one another. It certainly wouldn't be the first time colleagues have taken a fancy to each other, either. Nor is it likely to be the last. So go ahead. Indulge. Dr. Norlund might be a bit old-fashioned about such matters, but I like to think of myself as a progressive man. Whatever you and Cade have decided to do behind closed doors is your business."

"Thank you, Dr. Bracken," Kelsey murmured, too shocked to know what else to say. Silence permeated the room for several minutes while she pondered how best to communicate the purpose of her visit.

"The breakthrough we could make if only you were—" he muttered, half to himself. "It could be a miracle of genetics."

Abruptly, he focused on her. "One must always

remember, Kelsey, that the sea holds limitless possibilities. For all the scientific logic we possess, there are mysteries and wonders beyond our wildest imaginings." His eyes lit with a fanaticism she had never seen before.

She shifted uneasily in her chair and wondered what he was thinking or if he was still referring to Cade. "I suppose Dr. Douglas would know more about the sea here than just about anyone."

He nodded slowly and seemed to come to a decision. "I've something I really think you should see. Wait here." He rose and went into the bedroom while a half-dozen scenarios played out in her mind. For a moment, she considered if perhaps she should leave. But Dr. Bracken had never behaved inappropriately towards her, and her curiosity about what he wanted her to see was strong.

He emerged from the bedroom carrying a pelt over one arm. "I debated over sharing this with you for some time now, but worried it might still be too soon."

Too soon for what, she wondered as Dr. Bracken draped the pelt over her lap and took a seat opposite her. "Touch it, Kelsey. Have you ever felt anything so luxurious? Have you ever seen such a glorious color?"

She poked a tentative finger at a silver seal skin. Oh, she'd seen something this delicate shade before, the color of moonbeams on water, shimmering more brightly in Dr. Bracken's suite than it had on the beach her first night here many weeks ago. No wonder she hadn't been able to find the dead seal the next morning. Why would he have taken it and not turned it over to the team for examination?

"Where did you get this? How?"

He waved a hand as if her questions were irrelevant. "For twenty-five years, I've waited for my chance to prove there were more of these. That the creature inhabiting that skin wasn't merely a freak of nature."

What an odd choice of words. Kelsey wanted to shrink away from the hand that stroked the fur pelt over her knee, but Dr. Bracken was so deep into his thoughts it was as if she weren't in the room.

His attention jerked back to her. "Do you understand what this is about? Do you realize what an important discovery you and I are about to make?"

She shook her head vigorously, wondering just what Dr. Bracken was smoking in that pipe of his.

"The silver seals, Kelsey. They live somewhere in these islands. Your father has known it for years."

Impossible. For a moment, all she could do was gaze at Dr. Bracken. "He's never written about it. Never mentioned it." Besides, if she knew her father, he'd be the first to explore the waters with a full crew and complement of TV cameras if he had any notion he might discover a breed of sea animal others might think extinct. The protests rose desperately from a throat gone dry. "Wouldn't he have told someone?"

He shook his head and his eyes narrowed. "He's afraid, especially after what happened with your mother. But you and I aren't. We're not too timid to prove a legend."

"Legend?" She glanced down at the folk tale book she still carried in one hand.

"It's your destiny, Kelsey. The one your mother wasn't strong enough to face. But you are. Maybe I'll even win the Nobel Prize."

"I don't understand."

"You will." He gripped her arms so tightly, she winced. "We'll be famous, the most sought after marine biologists of all time. The selkies. They exist. All you have to do is help me find them."

Chapter Seventeen

He had to be joking. Her breathing suspended, Kelsey stared at Dr. Bracken and tried to form a response.

As if someone had thrown a switch, Dr. Bracken slapped his hands on his knees and gave her an engaging smile. He plucked the book from her limp fingers and thumbed to the well-worn page she'd studied night after night.

"An intriguing concept, isn't it? I would imagine the legend began from seeing a seal such as this one." He gestured to the pelt still half-covering her lap.

He'd been joking. She exhaled, took a deep breath and returned his smile. What a peculiar sense of humor the man had. "Then you don't believe in a creature who can metamorphose into a human?"

He shrugged. "As a scientist, of course not, but who can say? Shape shifters certainly have held a place in legends from all over the world. Werewolves, vampires. Swan princesses. Tell me: have you enjoyed the stories?"

She couldn't say she had. It was more like an unwilling fascination, somewhat like the feelings she had for Cade Douglas. "I found them quite intriguing, if a bit bizarre." Like the conversation she and Dr. Bracken had been having for the past thirty minutes. She handed the silver pelt to him and rose. "Well, I'd better get some sleep if I'm going to be at my best tomorrow."

"Absolutely." He stood and escorted her to the door. "In the morning, we're taking that trip to the other islands I've been promising you."

A deep feeling of unease gripped her stomach. "I'm looking forward to it. Will Dr. Douglas be joining us?"

"Most likely not. He's been called away for a few days. I'm hopeful he'll catch up to us, however." The unease increased. "To help us find the selkies?" Dr. Bracken laughed heartily. "Well, if anyone can—" He trailed off, his expression becoming serious again. "The silver seals, Kelsey. They're the key to what we're searching for."

The silver seals are the key. Kelsey pondered Dr. Bracken's words as she rolled onto her side and punched her pillow. Once again, sleep eluded her, but not because of Cade and his molten pewter gaze. Tonight, remembering the fanatical glow of her former professor made her too uneasy to even close her eyes.

He'd been kidding her, of course. Back at the University he'd been known for his strange sense of humor. Why did his behavior surprise her?

Rather, his excessive interest in her relationship with Cade Douglas disturbed her. Not because such interest seemed unseemly, not to mention just plain prurient. Something more....

Sighing, she rolled onto her back and stared at the ceiling. "Really, MacKenzie," she muttered. "The man's been like a father to you." More than a father, she corrected, thinking of her only parent. Dr. Bracken probably recognized her loneliness better than she did and merely wished for her to enjoy some companionship.

Fatigue weighted her limbs, and she forced herself to relax as once again her thoughts followed a well-worn fantasy about Cade Douglas. He had the most incredible hands. In her dream world only, of course. Smiling, she turned to her side and hugged the pillow, pretending she held his strong body next to hers and that his caresses soothed her into much needed sleep.

Cade stood at the window of Meredith's cottage and watched the eerie twilight play over the ripples of water in the bay. Again, Kelsey's dream reached out to him. Night after night, it was like this, her dreams firing his blood, the longing to possess her threatening his self control.

Clenching his hands, he took a deep breath and focused on the sea, but the soft, sweet feel of Kelsey continued to plague his thoughts. If only grandfather's nettle soup would bless him with forgetfulness, he'd drink a cauldron full.

How much longer could he stand the agony of having to be near her every day, remembering every tiny detail of her, but knowing she remembered only when she slept. With great effort, he pushed Kelsey's image from his mind. He could ill afford to let grandfather see the sorry state he was in. Behind him, Meredith moved about the dwelling, heating stew and grumbling.

"Did you understand a word I told you?"

Cade ignored the question and continued watching the sea. "Bracken is running out of patience. I believe he plans to take the crew out. If not tomorrow, then the next day."

Meredith snorted. "Good. Maybe this time you'll use the opportunity more wisely."

Cade scowled at the reminder of how he and Kelsey had spent the week Bracken and Norlund had been gone. Maybe that wasn't what they should have done, but he still couldn't find it in his heart to be sorry. "You don't even know he has what you seek."

Meredith shrugged. "Who else? Unless Bouschour torched it along with his cottage."

"You don't know that he did that."

Meredith raised a bushy brow. "I don't believe in coincidences. His wife dies a violent death and later their dwelling burns to the ground?"

"That doesn't mean he set the torch."

"Then who? Bracken?" Meredith chuckled. "He would have had no reason to. Then. Now? Who's to say? I only wish that damned Frenchman would show up. Then we could settle things once and for all. Sit down and eat."

"What is there to settle after all this time? Father has been dead for twenty-five years. Nothing can bring him back." Cade took a seat at the rough-hewn table, then dug into the fish stew. "It would be better for Kelsey if her father were here."

"And worse for you." Meredith brandished the serving spoon at him. "Mind what I told you and remember one thing: if he ever finds out about you and his daughter, it will be your hide he takes away as a trophy."

Cade's ears burned. "Well, there is no chance of that now, is there, since she can't remember." Breaking off a chunk of barley bread, he dipped it into the spicy concoction and nearly had it to his mouth when he looked up into Meredith's narrowed gaze.

"Then you had best stay well away from the lass, especially after Bouschour arrives. All he needs is one look at your face when she is near and it will be your undoing. Mind what I say and put her from your heart once and for all."

He wanted to. He truly believed that nothing would make him happier than to forget Kelsey MacKenzie ever existed. But later that night as he lay on his pallet in a corner of the cottage, when Meredith's breathing had fallen into the even pattern of slumber, Cade's body again caught fire until he was consumed with the memory of Kelsey beside him, beneath him, her body melding with his until nothing in the world mattered except the welcoming warmth of her.

The next morning dawned clear and bright with a gentle west wind that barely rippled the water. Perfect weather for an excursion. Any hopes Kelsey had of the expedition again being postponed vanished. She supposed it was just as well to get the trip over with before her father arrived and had a chance to interfere. He would be sure to try and run the show, as he always did. Dr. Bracken wouldn't take kindly to the interference. And as for Dr. Norlund—she suspected he wouldn't miss the opportunity to discredit her before her own father.

Despite the fact that Dr. Bracken had told her Cade was gone, Kelsey stopped by his room on her way to breakfast. She rapped lightly on the door and waited.

To her embarrassment, Dr. Norlund chose that particular moment to step from his room. "Forget your toothbrush, Miss MacKenzie?"

She frowned. For the past few weeks, Dr. Norlund seemed to delight in making innuendoes about her and Dr. Douglas. It was small comfort to know he was fishing in the wrong pond. Even though she knew she had done nothing to be ashamed of, Norlund's attitude irked her, and she knew it wouldn't further her cause any to argue with him.

She straightened her shoulders and faced the scientist. "Dr. Bracken told me we were going to explore the outer islands today. I was hoping Dr. Douglas would be able to join us."

"I'm sure you were." Norlund brushed past her on his way to the stairs.

Rather than hang around Cade's door like a love-sick puppy, Kelsey decided to accompany Norlund downstairs. "Do you believe we'll find a new breed of seals, like the silver ones Dr. Bracken thinks inhabit these islands?"

He stopped so abruptly, she nearly crashed into him and had to grab the railing to keep from losing her balance.

"What do you know of this?" He turned and glared up at her, his usually icy blue eyes even more reminiscent of a glacier.

She'd always thought Scandinavian people were noted for their cool tempers, but Dr. Norlund was as volatile as an angry squid. "Very little, actually. Dr. Bracken was merely explaining his theory to me last night, but I told him I'd never heard or read about silver seals."

He nodded stiffly. "It would be most unwise to encourage him in this endeavor, Miss MacKenzie. See that you don't." Without giving her an opportunity to respond, he proceeded down the stairs. What in the world was going on? Was Dr. Norlund turning against his other colleagues as well as her?

Dr. Bracken was already in the dining room, sipping a cup of tea and gazing out the window.

Kelsey saw no need not to continue the conversation. Let Dr. Norlund defend his position himself. If he wasn't supportive of their endeavors here, Dr. Bracken should be made aware of it. "Good morning, Dr. Bracken. I was just telling Dr. Norlund about our discussion last night."

Dr. Bracken's heavy brows shot up, giving him the look of a startled hare. "Oh? And what does Erik think about our hypothesis?"

"He hasn't had a chance yet to tell me if he shares your theory about there being an undiscovered species of seal here."

Bracken visibly relaxed, setting down his teacup and sitting back in his chair. Mrs. Devon came in from the kitchen, bearing coffee pots and plates of toast.

"I believe it to be highly unlikely." The Swedish scientist scowled, cast a superior look at Kelsey and poured from the silver urn on the table.

Kelsey avoided even looking at the tea and bit into a piece of dry toast.

"Marmalade?" Dr. Norlund pushed the jam pot towards her, a smile verging on a sneer visible below his pale moustache.

Kelsey's stomach gave an unaccustomed lurch. She liked jam, but after a month here, still hadn't gotten used to the tartness of Mrs. Devon's homemade marmalade. "No, thank you," she murmured, looking up from her plate in time to see Dr. Bracken and Dr. Norlund exchange a significant look.

She patted her abdomen. "Trying to watch the calories. I think I've put on a couple of pounds from Mrs. Devon's wonderful cooking."

The housekeeper paused as she set a plate of oat cakes in front of Dr. Bracken. She beamed at Kelsey. "Not that you couldn't stand to, child. Can't I tempt you with something else this morning? I've got some lovely stewed apples."

"Yes, thank you."

The housekeeper bustled off to the kitchen.

Kelsey studied her former professor and tried to think of the most tactful way to broach the question that had kept her awake. Like a high diver, she decided to plunge in. "Dr. Bracken, aren't you worried the foundation might become concerned you're spending more time on your silver seal search than on the cause of death of the other seals?"

He dug into the oat cakes and regarded her for several moments. "What about you, Kelsey? Do you think your search for answers about your mother's life has diminished your effectiveness on the team?" He turned towards her, the words hard, but the friendly, fatherly light never left his eyes.

Feeling chastised, she chose her next words carefully, but continued to meet his gaze. "I don't believe so, but I hope that my colleagues wouldn't hesitate to tell me if they thought I was misdirecting my energies."

Dr. Norlund snorted, but made no reply.

Dr. Bracken rested his elbows on the table and leaned towards her. "Well, I believe that if we can discover where the silver seals are, we will have all the answers we need. It may even be of help to you."

Mrs. Devon, laden with the apples for Kelsey and another plate of oat cakes for Dr. Norlund, entered the room in time to catch Dr. Bracken's words.

"If you can find the silver ones, then you'll have solved the riddle."   ·

"What riddle?" Kelsey took the bowl of stewed apples and looked expectantly at the housekeeper.

"Well," Mrs. Devon lowered her voice, although it was just the four of them in the dining room, "some say the silver ones are the selkies. That's why no man has ever seen them."

"You mean no one has ever seen a silver seal?" Kelsey thought about the pelt she'd seen in Dr. Bracken's room last night. Certainly, he couldn't be the only person to ever come across one. What about the dead one she'd found on the beach her first night here, or was it a result of the grimlins, the mysterious twilight, as Cade insisted?

Her voice just above a whisper, Mrs. Devon nodded. "That's right, Miss. No one has ever seen them. Oh, we know they are here. Some folks say they have even heard the sound of their laughter when the moon is full. But not a soul has ever laid eyes on one.

"And lived to tell about it, of course."

Chapter Eighteen

Without another word, the housekeeper turned away and disappeared into the kitchen.

Mrs. Devon's remarks raised chill bumps on Kelsey's arms, and suddenly the last thing she wanted to do was spend the day on the water with Dr. Norlund and Dr. Bracken, but she couldn't think of a single reason to convince Dr. Bracken they should postpone the expedition.

Superstitions and folk tales, that's all it was. Her scientific mind should automatically reject them. But her mind filled with all the strange things that had happened to her since arriving on the island and the persistent sense of blank areas in her memory continued to plague her while Dr. Norlund and Dr. Bracken finished breakfast and continued a genial discussion about other research they'd done in other places.

A short time later, standing on the jetty, she watched the boat Dr. Bracken had chartered dip and rise on the small waves. The craft looked sound, the captain and first mate experienced. Why did a knot of apprehension keep her standing on the dock when everyone else was already on board?

"Kelsey!" From the deck, Dr. Bracken waved and motioned to her. "Come along, now!"

Casting a longing look at Murdoch Castle, Kelsey started down the pier and boarded the boat.

"I already told you, he's not coming." Dr. Norlund's patronizing tone made heat rise in her face as he extended a hand and helped her on the boat.

"And I'm sure that's going to lessen the amusement value of this trip for you, Dr. Norlund. What a pity."

Apparently surprised at her retort, he refrained from making further comments and moved to the opposite side of the boat as the crew cast off, and the boat moved away from the jetty.

Kelsey stood on the port side with Dr. Bracken and watched Murdoch Castle grow smaller and smaller. Her apprehension increased with each bit of distance they put between land and the boat. Why was she so uneasy when the day was so perfect?

Out of the protected cove, the wind kicked up froth as the three foot waves of the harbor gave way to ten foot swells. The first mate hoisted the mainsail while the captain cut the engine. The boat plowed on.

Sunshine sparkled on the vast expanse of water. As far as Kelsey looked, she could see nothing but the sea. Usually she liked unlimited expanses of water and the accompanying sense of freedom and adventure. Today her feet longed for dry land as much as her insides wished for relief from the rolling, pitching motion of the boat.

"It's a little rough out here." Kelsey had to shout at Dr. Bracken to be heard over the snap of canvas, the rattle of the rigging, and the smack of the sea against the wooden hull.

He leaned against the rail, closed his eyes and smiled. "Ah, but feel that sun. A perfect day."

Right. A perfect day for being perfectly sea sick. "Where are we going?"

"Around the North Sound. Among other areas, I'd like to find the island you and Cade visited. You would recognize it if you saw it, wouldn't you?"

She nodded, although she wasn't sure she could and didn't think she even wanted to try. Concentrating on concrete details of what she could only remember as a pleasant afternoon made another headache threaten. "It was quite sandy and very low-lying, except for the rocks at the shore. You know, I almost thought I saw seals on the beach, but by the time I picked up the binoculars, they were gone.

Cade said I was mistaken."

Dr. Bracken laughed, but made no comment. Kelsey brushed a loose strand of hair away from her face and looked towards the bow. Rise, slap, rise, slap, the boat rode the waves like an awkward swimmer. Unlike the day she and Cade had gone out, the sea seemed to resent their presence, making the boat strain to make headway. Her stomach churned, like a cork caught on an eddy.

The captain shouted something in what sounded like Norwegian to the first mate, who nodded and hurried over to Kelsey.

Blond hair tied back in a stubby ponytail, he bobbed his head at her. "Beg pardon, miss. Captain thinks you're looking a bit green. You might want to watch the horizon instead of the bow. Find a point to fix on and don't pay no heed to the motion of the boat."

Kelsey murmured a thank you and turned away. How embarrassing. She was a good sailor, usually. As much time as she'd spent on boats when she was a child, she ought to be.

Dr. Bracken patted her hand. "The North Sound has some of the most treacherous waters in the Atlantic." He dug in his pocket and pulled out a packet of saltines. "Here. Try these. The way you've been picking at your breakfast lately, I thought it would be a good idea to bring some food along. Mrs. Devon packed box lunches for later."

The thought of food nearly made her gag, but Kelsey nibbled at a cracker and willed her insides to stop colliding. "Thank you, Dr. Bracken. This does seem to help."

"You know, Kelsey," Dr. Bracken braced his feet and looked out towards the horizon, "if you have some sort of problem, I hope you know you can count on me as your friend."

A piece of cracker stuck in her throat. She coughed and Dr. Bracken gently patted her back. What in the world was he talking about? What kind of problem did he think she could have?

Images of her dreams with Cade flared. For an instant, she was in his arms, feeling him touch the center of her. Cade, in her room at the inn, the antique brass bed singing with their movements. Cade, sitting beside her on the front lawn of the inn. *I can't give you a child, Kelsey. It's impossible.*

Of course it was impossible. You had to have sex to get pregnant. And why would he have said that to her? He couldn't have. It was just part of the dreams.

She gripped the rail and took a steadying breath. Why were the dreams as vivid as any reality she'd experienced here on these islands? What was wrong with her? Dr. Bracken laid his hand over hers. "Anything you want to tell me. I would understand and I would do everything I could to help you."

She thought about the queasiness she'd been having during breakfast the past few mornings. Obviously, Dr. Bracken had noticed as well. Then today, she'd mentioned she'd put on a few pounds.

He thought she was pregnant! No wonder he'd gone out of his way last night to tell her he understood about her feelings for Dr. Douglas. No wonder he acted sympathetic about the attraction he realized they shared and had wanted to reassure her. Oh, my God. What had she actually done to make him think something so completely unbelievable?

She fought down a feeling of outrage and searched for the right words that would convince him he was·jumping to erroneous conclusions. "I appreciate your concern, Dr. Bracken, but I want you to know, there's not a problem."

Dr. Norlund had moved from the opposite side of the boat and edged a little closer. If she was going to convince Dr. Bracken that she and Cade hadn't been misbehaving, now might be her best chance before Dr. Norlund had an opportunity to make any more disparaging remarks.

She lowered her voice. "Despite our conversation last

night, I want you to know that Dr. Douglas and I," she swallowed. "Well, there is no Dr. Douglas and I." At his puzzled expression, she rushed on. "What I'm trying to say is that we haven't been intimate."

From the corner of her eye, she saw Dr. Norlund raise a disbelieving brow. Damn the man, anyway. Why did he have to come over here now? What gave him the right to act so superior? "So if that's what you're anxious about, then you have no cause to worry. But I do appreciate your concern."

"Kelsey," Dr. Bracken's voice was gentle. "At the risk of embarrassing you, I must tell you: it's been quite, ah, obvious that you and Cade have been enjoying each other's company. At least you seemed to be the night Dr. Norlund and I returned from the mainland."

Kelsey fought the fog clouding her memory and tried to focus on what he meant. She remembered coming down to the kitchen and finding the other two scientists at breakfast. Dr. Bracken had been friendly, but distracted. Dr. Norlund had been surly and had remained so ever since.

Her face flamed. "You're mistaken." She concentrated harder but other images remained just out of reach. A sharp pain stabbed her head. Kelsey's eyes blurred with tears. She shrugged off Dr. Bracken's assistance and staggered away.

She needed to think. Away from Dr. Norlund and his insinuations. Away from Dr. Bracken and his misguided notions. The boat lurched and heeled sharply. Kelsey stumbled and lost her precarious balance.

Something struck her across the back, and her feet left the solidity of the deck. The first mate shouted, then she fell through the air towards the choppy sea.

Chapter Nineteen

On the beach where he relaxed with his cousins, Cade stretched, reveling in the feel of the sun on his strange skin. He twitched his whiskers and took in the scents of damp sand, mollusks and fish. How he had missed being with his family and being this other self.

Meredith sat on an outcropping of rocks, watching them alternately rest and frolic in the sand. Maybe grandfather was right. This was where he needed to be from time to time to help him keep his center and remind him of what was important.

A cloud passed over the sun, casting the shore in gloom for several minutes, but even after the sky cleared the sense of disaster found its way into his awareness.

Kelsey. Something had gone wrong.

All morning, he'd felt the faint tug of her anxiety, but not wanting to earn more of Grandfather's disapproval, he'd managed to push the sensation away and focus on his family and what he needed to be doing to help Meredith. A search of Bracken's room had not yielded what he sought, so at his grandfather's urging, they'd taken the small skiff and headed for the outer islands to spend the day with his cousins.

A sharp pain stabbed his chest, making it hard to take a breath. She was in trouble. And Bracken was expecting him to extricate her. Fury thundered through his veins. Had Bracken lost all perspective in his quest for the silver seals? How could the man be so cold-blooded that he'd risk sacrificing the girl he treated as a daughter?

Cade couldn't let it happen. No matter what it cost him, Kelsey's life was beyond measure.

He surged up and headed for the sea. Grandfather's voice rang harshly in his ears, his cousins voices rose in a babble of noise, but Cade continued to plow through the sand until he felt the first sting of salt on his nose, then he let the ocean swallow him and carry him to his fate.

Her lungs burned. Kelsey fought the weight of her water-logged sweater and struggled to the surface. The boat disappeared behind a swell of water that washed over her head. Coughing and sputtering, she battled to shed the sweater and wished she could as easily rid herself of the hiking boats she wore. Why hadn't they thrown her a life preserver?

Eyes stinging, she tread water, closed in by a gray-green canyon. She forced herself to relax enough to ride the next mountainous crest, instead of letting it crash over her head.

The water was so cold. The chill penetrated her jeans, made her teeth chatter. Soggy boots made it hard to keep her head above water and finally dragged her under. Emerging, she fumbled with the laces, gulped in a lung full of air and let herself dip below the surface while she yanked off one boot, then another. If only she had something to hang on to, she could make it until the boat could circle back and pick her up.

They knew she'd gone over. They had to come back for her. Pumping her legs, she worked on staying afloat. The sun was directly overhead, and she was lost in the trough, making it impossible to get her bearings. Waves scudded over the crest of each swell, making swimming out of the question. Besides, if she started to swim in the direction she guessed the boat had gone, it might make it even more difficult for them to find her.

She dog paddled, riding each new swell, trying to keep warm, but still the chill seized her. So cold. She didn't think she'd ever been so cold. Gradually, panic was edged out by a growing sense of euphoria accompanying the onset of hypothermia.

She wouldn't last much longer.

A sharp pain knifed into her side. She doubled over, clutching her middle. A wave rolled over her head, dunking her. She wasn't going to make it. If the waves didn't take her, then the hypothermia would. Or the excruciating cramp seizing her.

Something silver flashed in the water beside her. Startled, Kelsey cried out and gulped another mouthful of water. She was dreaming again. She could have sworn she saw a seal. Hysterical laughter bubbled up. Her life was slipping away, and she was dreaming of seals.

The creature bunted her, sliding under her and lifting her higher in the water. Kelsey coughed out a mouthful of water and took a shallow breath, then ran her hands down the sleek body and gazed into the whiskery face of a seal.

A silver seal.

Images of a picnic by an inland pond played through her mind. She'd shed her clothes, gone for a swim. A seal had joined in her water play.

A seal just like this one.

He seemed to grin at her and barked a greeting, then supported her while she struggled to find a handhold on his slippery skin. Exhausted with the effort, Kelsey rested her cheek on his back while he skimmed effortlessly through the water as if she weren't even there and kept her close enough to the surface to keep her head above the water.

The day at the pond, Cade had insisted there had been no seal, and had told her she'd had too much of Mrs. Devon's elderberry wine. Why would he lie to her?

Unless he'd heard Dr. Bracken's theory and thought she was trying to trick him into admitting he knew more about Bracken's strange ideas than he was willing to acknowledge. She pushed the thoughts away and concentrated on survival. She could deal with that later. Right now her fingers were stiff with cold, and survival was the only thing that mattered. She hoped she could continue to hold on.

She wondered where the seal was taking her, then wondered why she thought he was taking her anywhere, and not just offering her something to cling to. The sea rolled and pitched around them, but remembering the dolphins at the aquarium, she relaxed into his rhythm and let him take her.

Time became a meaningless measurement. How long had it been since she'd fallen overboard? Half an hour? An hour? A day? How much longer could she last?

Voices filtered into her awareness. Kelsey raised her head. Shouts resounded from the boat now coming into sight, its engine sending off a stream of black smoke as it battled the waves to pull alongside her.

Dr. Bracken leaned half over the side, his face gray with worry while the first mate threw a life preserver.

"Kelsey, thank God! Hold on, we'll get you back on board."

He peered more closely at her, but as Kelsey reached for the orange ring, the seal disappeared. She clutched the life ring, sliding it over her head and draping her arms over the sides. The first mate began to haul her up. The worry on Bracken's face instantly vanished, replaced with a look of wonder and excitement.

"Erik! The net! Pull it up!"

She hung on with a desperate grip. The captain assisted the first mate in fetching her from the sea, but Dr. Bracken and Dr. Norlund appeared to have forgotten she existed. Hoisted out of the water, Kelsey let the first mate pull her the rest of the way into the boat where she collapsed on the deck, shivering uncontrollably.

The captain bundled her into a blanket and hustled her to a sheltered area, all the while muttering in Norwegian. She couldn't understand a word of what he was saying, but from the dark looks he cast at Dr. Bracken and Dr. Norlund, she guessed he wasn't pleased with either one of them.

At Dr. Bracken's request, the captain brought the boat sharply about. Kelsey stumbled back out on deck, grabbed the lower beam of the rail and tried to steady herself as the vessel heeled, then righted itself.

The first mate pressed a mug of hot tea laced with whisky into her hand. "You need to drink this, Miss, to warm yourself."

She forced down a mouthful of scalding liquid. Fire seeped into her iced blood, spread through her.

"You there." Dr. Bracken gestured to the first mate. "Give us a hand with the net. We've got it trapped. We just need to bring it in."

Clutching the rail, Kelsey continued to stand. Huddled in her blanket, she looked down into the vast blue sea. Silver flashed through the water. Her seal. Dr. Bracken was trying to capture the seal that had saved her life.

No. This couldn't happen. He didn't deserve to be trapped, but they had caught him. And if they let him live, he'd be subjected to all kinds of tests and experiments. If they let him live.

The animal thrashed wildly, looking for a way out, finding a small opening in the net. Dr. Bracken waved wildly. "Don't let it get away, Erik! Shoot it if you have to."

Dr. Norlund raised a harpoon gun as the net rose slowly from the water. Kelsey stared in horror. He wasn't even going to tranquilize the animal: he meant to kill him. Pewter eyes stared up at her. Something wrenched at Kelsey's heart. She couldn't be a part of this, no matter how unscientific her feelings were.

She flung herself at Dr. Norlund just as he squeezed the trigger. His shot missed the mark, but the dart slashed across the silver skin on the seal's back. The seal screamed in pain.

"I won't let you do this. It's wrong. Wrong!" Before she could question her actions, before she could think about the horrified look Dr. Bracken gave her, Kelsey grabbed the line from the first mate's hand and let it fly.

The rope rocketed up through the pulley, the net hit the water with a splash. Sunlight glinted off his flippers, then the seal was gone.

What had she done?

She'd just made the biggest mistake of her professional career, that's what. She was ruined. But the thought that the seal was free and not facing Dr. Bracken's knife filled her with a fierce gladness.

Sagging against the rail, Kelsey took a deep breath, but it was no use. Overcome with nausea, she sank to the deck and promptly purged her stomach all over Dr. Norlund's feet.

Some time later, Kelsey sat with her back against the railing and nibbled on one of Mrs. Devon's roast lamb sandwiches. Despite the homemade grain of the bread, her mouth felt as gritty as sea salt. She wondered how long it would take to rid herself of the ocean tang. She closed her eyes and rested her head against the back of the seat the first mate had made for her out of several cushions when she'd insisted she couldn't tolerate being inside the cabin.

"What the hell were you thinking of, MacKenzie?" Dr. Bracken's voice didn't sound angry, just puzzled, but the way he addressed her didn't bode well for her future.

Still, she kept her eyes closed and pondered an answer. How could she explain to her mentor, her professor, one of the greatest marine biologists in the world, that she couldn't capture a specimen because the look in his eyes broke her heart?

She sighed and looked up at him. "I'm sorry, Dr. Bracken. Really. But I don't regret what I did."

He shrugged and sank down beside her. "I've dismissed people for less. Norlund was supposed to tranquilize the creature, but a dead specimen is better than no specimen."

"I know." She spread her hands. "I'll pack my things and leave as soon as I can arrange transportation."

Dr. Norlund snorted and leaned against the rail. "That's the first sensible words I've heard the girl utter."

Dr. Bracken waved a dismissive hand at him. "There are other issues to consider."

"Really, Dennis. Do you think there's any chance of that now?"

"Yes," he snapped. "Based on what just happened, I think it's a very real possibility."

Kelsey glanced back and forth between the men, wondering what on earth they were talking about. "I'm sorry. I'm not following."

Dr. Norlund harrumphed, as if that didn't surprise him at all, but Dr. Bracken considered her. "You've had a terrible experience here today, Kelsey. Let's just chalk up what happened to the shock and trauma of what you went through."

"He saved my life," she blurted, before she could stop herself.

"He, as in the seal?" Dr. Bracken handed her a plastic cup of hot cocoa and a scone studded with dried apricot.

"I know it sounds crazy. I'm not sure how I suddenly ended up taking a dive, but there I was, certain I was going to drown, when the seal swam up." She gestured. "From beneath me. Supported me and started swimming towards the boat." Her eyes filled with tears. She wasn't normally a weepy person, what was wrong with her? "I couldn't let you kill him," she choked.

Dr. Bracken patted her hand, but his attention seemed elsewhere. "Interesting. You couldn't let us kill him. Why would you assume it was a male?"

"Because... I don't know." She set down the empty cocoa cup and the half-eaten scone and wrapped her arms around her legs. "Does it matter?"

"Perhaps." He stared off towards where the inn grew from a tiny speck to a mound of gray rock. "I think, Kelsey, that we'll continue to need your services here after all."

Chapter Twenty

Dr. Bracken insisted she take the next day to rest after her ordeal at sea. Mrs. Devon clucked and fussed over her, insisting on drawing a hot bath for her and bringing a tray of supper to her room, but nothing calmed the restlessness. Kelsey stood at the window, the food untouched, and watched the pale moonlight chase the twilight shadows across the sea. How she wished Cade was back so that she could share the strange events of the afternoon with him.

Her short nightgown fluttered in the cool breeze. She smoothed down the soft cotton, letting her hand linger on her abdomen. Dr. Bracken's conversation floated back to her. "If you have a problem, I'd try to help." "It was obvious you and Cade were enjoying each other's company the night Dr. Norlund and I returned." She'd never been able to chart herself with the moon, but still....

Turning away from the window, she went to the desk and pulled out her personal calendar. An odd feeling settled in her stomach like a rock sinking to the bottom of a pond.

She was several weeks overdue. In fact, she hadn't had a period since arriving in Orkney, not that it was terribly unusual, but something was definitely out of kilter.

Could she possibly be pregnant? What in the world was she going to do if she was? She imagined herself confronting Cade.

I hate to trouble you about a little problem, Dr. Douglas, but it seems I'm pregnant and you're the most likely candidate for father.

She didn't want to see the anger, the rejection in those fascinating silver eyes. He'd think she was crazy.

Maybe she was. Perhaps that was why she couldn't remember the afternoon they'd taken the skiff out.

For the first time in her life, she wished she'd taken her father's advice and stayed several thousand miles away from Orkney.

When day fell into the strange mystical twilight, Meredith called the clan together. Eager faces watched him, waiting for his decision.

"The sea near Murdoch Castle poses great risk for all of you. Much as I don't want you to risk yourselves, Cade must be found. By us. If that witch hunter Bracken or Norlund should happen on him, he's doomed. Which means the rest of you are as well. Search the area. Stay in teams of two and report to me immediately if you see the slightest evidence regarding his whereabouts."

With much chatter among themselves, the family dispersed, leaving Meredith to sit on the porch of his humble cottage and consider the sea.

Of all his grandchildren, he loved Cade the most. The others knew it, surely, but had never shown the slightest bit of jealousy. Cade, of course, had always been the least compliant, the most stubbornly determined to do things his own way.

The way he was about the girl.

Why couldn't he have left her alone? Why did he have to go charging out to save her as if he were a white knight?

Bracken would most certainly not have let the girl die, even if he had no compunctions about using her as bait. And if she had died, what would be the loss? It would serve Bouschour right to lose a daughter when he'd cost Meredith a son.

He searched for Cade in his mind, but all that came to him was a blackness as vast as the sea under the grimlins and the shadowy twilight.

Deciding to take Dr. Bracken's advice, the next day Kelsey stayed out of the lab and roamed the beach. A couple of days rest might be all that she needed to be herself again. She couldn't really be carrying a child.

Could she?

She rolled the dilemma over and over in her mind and couldn't come up with an answer.

If she wasn't pregnant, then her body was certainly doing a marvelous imitation of it. Again this morning at breakfast, she'd had all she could do to down a piece of dry toast and a glass of milk. Even Mrs. Devon had clucked at her in concern and suggested any number of items intended to tempt her appetite, but which had the opposite effect of making her feel like she was going to lose the little bit she'd managed to choke down.

Her stomach fluttered. Kelsey sank to a rock and pressed her palm to her abdomen. Taking a deep breath, she waited. There it was again. A sensation as soft as a butterfly kiss whirred inside her. For a moment, her heart leaped with joy.

She carried his child. All the dreams had been reality. Closing her eyes, she relaxed and let the images wash through her. This time instead of the familiar headache that came when she tried to remember, she felt Cade's hands caress her skin, felt his tongue tease her in an intimate kiss, then felt the fullness of him inside her, moving slowly, stroking her to an ecstasy she'd never known before.

She wasn't crazy, she wasn't dreaming. She'd been his and carried the proof.

Gradually the happiness became tinged with the chill bite of the west wind. Summer would soon be over. What would she do then? She was unmarried, unattached, involved with the most peculiar, secretive man she'd ever met. And she was pregnant.

"Oh, Cade," she whispered. "What have we done?"

She stayed on the beach till long past luncheon, trying to

find a way out of her dilemma. She'd have to confront him. If he was the same man who'd made love to her so tenderly and been so concerned for her welfare, he deserved to know about the baby. If he was the man she thought he was, they could find a solution, together.

Her mind made up, Kelsey's heart felt lighter than it had in days. She strolled the beach, looking at the treasures washed up on the tide. Behind a rise of black rocks, a flattened object huddled. She walked closer, recognizing Cade's ever present backpack.

She picked up the soggy knapsack. If this was Cade's, then were was he?

Concern for him sharpened inside her like a knife. Dr. Bracken had said Cade had left to attend to some family matters. Kelsey had assumed he'd meant he was spending time with Meredith or that he'd gone to the mainland. But if he had, why would his backpack wash ashore?

Not knowing what else to do with it, Kelsey lugged the pack to the inn. Mrs. Devon or the housemaid, Gwendolyn would let her into Cade's room to leave it, then she could find her way to Meredith's cottage and assure herself that if Cade wasn't there, he at least was all right.

As she'd hoped, Cade's room was unlocked, so she didn't have to bother Mrs. Devon to let her in. Kelsey set the tote down and glanced around. Since he'd come to her in her room, she'd never had occasion to see how he lived, or what types of personal things he liked.

The room was peculiarly without any signs of habitation, or personality. Not even a hairbrush marred the Spartan appearance. Despite her reluctance to pry, Kelsey realized she needed to empty the pack and spread out the contents to dry, just in case the sea had seeped through the lining.

Sitting cross-legged on the floor, she unzipped the bag and pulled out the contents. A nylon jacket rested on top. Papers crackled inside the pocket.

She hesitated, then drew a folded packet out. Computer

print outs of articles. Cade's own articles. The Utilitarian
Value of Seal Whiskers by C. D. Douglas, Ph.D., Dalhousie
University Press. She thumbed through the article, then
another. Dr. Douglas' picture stared up at her.

Only it wasn't Cade.

Like a flood tide, the memories returned. Her suspicions
about Cade. Her furtive research. Then nothing. Why hadn't
she asked him about this?

Because somehow, he'd made her forget, then he'd stolen
her papers so she wouldn't have proof, even if she did
remember. Fingers trembling, she opened the pack to see
what other terrible secrets it held.

Her hands brushed something soft and furry. Startled, she
cried out and yanked her hand away.

She was being ridiculous, there was nothing to be afraid
of. Taking a deep breath, she pulled the sides further apart
and peered inside.

Silvery fur caught the light.

Unable to resist the lure, she drew the pelt out, slowly,
letting the soft fur trail against her bare arms. The pelt was
identical to the one Dr. Bracken had shown her. Could it
possibly be the same one?

That would mean Cade had stolen it from him, the way
he'd stolen the articles. What was he trying to hide?

Deciding she'd have to wait until she could confront him,
Kelsey started to put the pelt back when the hair on the back
of her neck prickled. She looked up, unable to stop the guilty
flush that stole up her neck when she saw Dr. Bracken
silhouetted in the doorway.

"Ah, Kelsey. Feeling better, I trust?"

"Yes, thank you." Noticing his gaze fixed on the pelt
trailing half in and half out of the backpack, she pulled it all
the way out. "I found this on the beach and decided I needed
to make sure nothing inside had gotten soaked."

He moved into the room and nodded in agreement. "A
wise decision. What do you have there?"

She gestured with the animal skin. "A pelt. It appears to be like the one you showed me the other night."

Dr. Bracken snatched the pelt from her and examined it carefully. "So it does."

She hesitated, then decided to be forthright about it. After all, she had nothing to conceal. "It's not yours, is it?"

"No, no. This one's slightly different. Look, there's an abraded area." He looked up, his pale eyes glowing. "See, Kelsey? I'm not mistaken about the seals. There could be dozens, maybe hundreds of these. We could have found them if…" his voice trailed off.

She refused to admit she'd done wrong by freeing the seal. "What would have been the point of killing him if what you really want is to find the entire colony?"

"Yes. Perhaps you're right." Dr. Bracken smoothed his hand down the pelt, lost in his own thoughts. For several minutes, he was silent. "It's just that I've waited so long, so many years. If we could just study them, find out what makes them what they are." His gaze sharpened on her and he gave her a long considering look. "Put it on."

"What?" She must have heard wrong. Why would he want her to wear the seal skin?

"Yes, that's it." He seemed to be talking to himself, but he cupped her elbow and pulled her to her feet, all the while speaking in a low persuasive tone.

"See how soft the pelt is, Kelsey. How it feels like velvet to your hands. What would it be like to wrap yourself in it? Maybe the skin itself holds the magic. You could be the one to unlock it."

Kelsey glanced in the mirror. Dr. Bracken's eyes glowed as if with fever. Not knowing what else to do, she stood quietly while he continued talking in riddles.

"Your mother, now. She might have had a chance, except for your father, but she was so delicate, so easily frightened. But you. You're much stronger than Annabelle."

Settling the pelt around her shoulders, he smoothed the

soft fur around her neck. Kelsey shivered as much from unease as the silky sensation. She closed her eyes to block out the zealous glow in Dr. Bracken's eyes. His hands smoothed the pelt up her neck. The head and snout settled over her face and for an instant she thought she wouldn't be able to draw a breath.

She opened her eyes. With her face partially obscured, the mirror assaulted her with a bizarre image of half-woman, half-seal, grotesque, but absolutely riveting. Her heartbeat seemed to freeze.

"The selkies. Now do you understand what this is all about?" Dr. Bracken's voice remained smooth and soothing, but his expression was fanatical. "You could have lived with them, Kelsey, if your father hadn't intervened. Now you carry the seed of one inside you." His hands rested on her shoulders, trapping her, forcing her to continue facing the parody in the mirror.

She shook her head, despair welling inside her. A scream strangled in her throat. "No!"

His grip tightened painfully on her shoulders. "Don't try to fool me or yourself, child. I recognize the signs. We just have to wait till your time is up. Do you wonder, as I do, which shape it has now? And what form it will be in when it's born?"

The scream escaped from her fear-choked throat. Kelsey wrenched away from his loathsome touch, his terrifying words. The seal skin still cloaking her shoulders, she escaped from the room, as panicked as if Dr. Bracken embodied all the mythological demons of hell.

She had to get away from him. From his ranting. From the fear that what he said might be true. She ran down the hall and pounded down the stairs. His amused chuckle echoed after her.

"It was your destiny, Kelsey. And now you can't undo what's been done, despite Meredith Douglas' tricks."

Chapter Twenty One

Her footsteps led her back to the beach. Still clutching the detested pelt in one hand, Kelsey scuffled along the tide line, walking blindly, wondering if, or when, she'd feel like she could face Dr. Bracken again.

She didn't dare leave the seal skin where he could get his hands on it. The man was sick. There could be no other explanation.

To think that he actually believed Cade was a selkie, not a human man. Certainly, Cade was hiding something, but that was… impossible. Her scientific mind refused to accept it.

She couldn't bring herself to consider all the oddities she'd experienced since arriving in Orkney, let alone just what exactly, made Cade as different as he seemed to be.

She stopped and let her fingers smooth through the pelt for the spot Dr. Bracken had said was abraded. There it was, a deep groove along what would be the right shoulder. The precise place where the seal had taken Dr. Norlund's dart yesterday.

With Cade still gone and not knowing who else to turn to, Kelsey found her footsteps winding along the beach, heading towards Meredith's cottage, on the other side of the peninsula from Murdoch Castle.

The wind held the chill of fall, reminding her that in this part of the world, summer was almost over. Kelsey shivered and rubbed the gooseflesh pebbling her arms.

What had Dr. Bracken meant about her living with the selkies, about her mother not being strong enough, her father interfering?

She'd have to dismiss all of it as deranged babbling. What

other explanation could there be?

Kelsey stumbled on a clump of seaweed and collapsed on her knees. The wind whipped her dark hair against her face, plastered her oxford shirt to her chilled skin. She forced herself up and continued. The cottage was much further than she had remembered from the day Cade had walked her back to the inn, but of course, they had taken a more direct route over the hills. The shore line curled inland and out again, sometimes embracing large craggy outcrops that forced her into climbing around them, or wading into the sea up to her knees.

At last, Meredith's cottage came into view. A thin curl of smoke drifted from the chimney, but otherwise the hut looked deserted. The seal skin clutched in one hand, she hauled herself up from the beach and made her way to the porch that looked as if it had been tacked on as an afterthought.

Despite how tired she was, for several moments, she considered going back to the inn, perhaps even going through the woods. Remembering the peculiar memory lapse she'd experienced after the last time she was here made her wonder if she was making the right decision in seeking Meredith.

Still, Cade was his grandson. Meredith wouldn't want anything to happen to him, even if he didn't care what happened to Kelsey.

And Dr. Bracken had certainly metamorphosed into something to be concerned about. She couldn't reconcile the wild-eyed fanatic she'd seen a short time ago with the professor she had known and respected for years. Eventually she'd have to return to the inn, but right now she dreaded it.

No sounds came from the cottage, although the wooden door stood ajar. Kelsey rapped on the panels and waited.

Several long minutes passed before Meredith stood in front of her. His gray hair a wild mess of tangles, face weary, he looked as if he'd aged a decade since she'd last seen him.

"Mr. Douglas—Meredith, are you all right?"

"What is it you want, to finish destroying my family because your father couldn't?"

Not knowing what he was talking about, she decided to get right to the point. "I'm worried about Cade. He hasn't been back to the inn for several days. I found his backpack on the beach. This was in it." She held up the pelt.

Meredith all but snatched it from her. "It won't do him any good now, the state he's in. Leave this place."

Kelsey heard a low moan emanate from a darkened corner of the room. Forgetting Meredith's angry words, forgetting the distance she and Cade had put between each other, she stepped past the old man and hurried into the hut. "He's here, isn't he?"

Meredith clutched the pelt. "You can't help him. No one can now."

Beneath a lump of blankets, Cade huddled, skin hot and ashen, eyes open, but unfocused. She knelt and automatically took his wrist in her hand. A thready pulse beat beneath her fingertips. "He's burning up. What have you tried to do?"

Meredith cradled the pelt in his hands. "Every remedy I know and a few I made up. Nothing seems to help."

"We've got to cool him down. Fetch some water and clean cloths." Yanking the blankets down, she began removing Cade's trousers and looked up to find Meredith staring at her.

"You're not a doctor."

"No, but I've spent plenty of sleepless nights doctoring sick critters. We've got to break this fever. Any idea what caused it?" She glanced up at Meredith, then gasped when his gaze directed her to the neatly stitched gash on Cade's right shoulder.

"How did he get this?" Hands trembling, she carefully examined the cut. Whomever had done the needlework had done an excellent job. If Cade survived, he wouldn't have much of a scar.

If he survived. She couldn't let herself think for a minute that he wouldn't. Of course, he'd survive. If the fever was from infection, they could get antibiotics.

Meredith shrugged. "You were there. Perhaps you should tell me."

"I was there…." Not knowing what he was talking about, she let her voice trail off. Meredith was mistaken. She hadn't seen Cade for several days, and this was a fresh wound. She lowered her head. It didn't matter what he was trying to hide or how he'd been hurt. The only thing that was important was his life.

"Please, Meredith. Help me. Together we can make a difference, I know we can."

"Very well. You fetch the water, I'll undress him."

"I don't know how to use the pump." Ignoring his attempt to shoo her away, Kelsey shook her head and peeled Cade's khaki twill slacks off. She didn't care if Meredith didn't think it was proper, she was going to take over, now.

Meredith considered her for several moments. "You've remembered, haven't you?"

"Yes. And I intend to discuss that with you later. Right now I'm only concerned with Cade."

A moment stretched towards an eternity. Cade's breathing rattled in the tiny cottage, drowning out the furious beat of her heart until finally Meredith nodded and went to the sink. He pumped out a basin of water and brought it to her along with a pile of clean white rags.

"Do you have any alcohol? To put in the water?"

He nodded and returned with an unlabeled bottle of clear spirits. Kelsey uncapped it, took a whiff that almost sent her reeling and dumped a large portion into the water.

Dipping a rag in the basin, she wrung it out and carefully began bathing Cade's hot face.

"I've done that already, a dozen times at least."

She didn't glance up. "Then we'll do it another dozen, then another or a hundred times, if that's what it takes." She smoothed the cloth his forehead, against his temples. Finally, he closed his eyes, and a little of her tension eased. Somehow that seemed more natural, as if he rested now instead of lying there with the look she'd seen too many times on dead creatures since she'd arrived in the islands.

Like the creatures she'd seen on the beach. The odd thought stayed with her as she went on to bathe his neck, his chest. Meredith hovered near, despite her suggestion he take a rest himself.

"Help me roll him onto his good side so I can do his back."

Without a word, Meredith complied, supporting Cade's weight while Kelsey dragged the cool rag down his back, then repeated the process several times before she let Meredith ease Cade down. She motioned to Cade's legs and arms. "He has a lot of scrapes. Did he get those at the same time he was wounded?"

Meredith nodded.

"How?"

Meredith studied her. "The nets, probably."

The rag slipped from her fingers and landed in the basin, making a splash that spattered water on her jeans and shirt and Meredith's gray sweater.

"Or it might have been the rocks when he came ashore."

She scooped the rag up and continued her ministrations. "Was he in some kind of boating accident?"

"You know as well as I do, it was no accident."

An image of yesterday's expedition flashed through her mind. The seal in the net, gazing sorrowfully at her with pewter-colored eyes. Her intense reaction. Had the whole island gone mad? "Perhaps you really don't mean to be speaking in riddles, but I think it would be a good idea if you told me exactly what you're talking about."

Meredith opened his mouth as if to speak when Cade thrashed wildly, knocking the basin of water to the floor. Kelsey took his hand in hers and squeezed gently.

"Cade, it's me. Kelsey. If you could tell us what happened, we could find a way to make you well."

"Kelsey." He groaned her name, and opened wide unseeing eyes, then closed them. "Can't tell her, can't let her know. Have to save her."

"Save me from what, Cade?" She kept her voice gentle. "Please tell me so we can help you."

Meredith set a fresh basin of water on the floor by her feet. "He shouldn't have been in the sea. But I suppose when he was wounded, instinct took over, and he came back to this island. The water's poison here."

"Do you know why?" Kelsey watched Cade drift away from them again. She released his hand and again picked up the cloth to bathe him with the fresh water.

"You're the scientist. You tell me." Meredith's voice was charged with bitterness. "Or is Bracken so focused on his personal quest he's lost interest in his research?"

Good question. She wondered the same thing herself. She latched on to Meredith's earlier statement. "Are you suggesting the water near this island is different than the others?"

"'Tis the other way round. You have to go to the islands on the other side of the North Sound to find a safe place where the very air doesn't seem to choke you."

Kelsey gently ran the cloth down Cade's chest. He shivered imperceptibly. Not wanting him to feel chilled, she covered his upper body with the thin sheet while she bathed his legs. "Who are the other islands safe for, Meredith?"

"The seals, Kelsey. Why do you suppose you haven't seen a one since you arrived? Why else did you think Bracken was so intent on his expedition? It's a pity he didn't wait until you were near our sanctuary before he pushed you overboard."

She paused, took a deep breath, then re-dipped the cloth and continued. "That's a pretty strong accusation. What on earth would make you think Dr. Bracken would try to drown me?"

Meredith sat quietly, clasped hands dangling between his knees. "You were bait, Kelsey. You have been ever since you arrived on this island."

"Where's your star pupil been today?" Dr. Norlund looked up from his notes as Dr. Bracken burst into the lab.

Bracken wrung his hands. "I told her to take the day off, then I found her in Cade's room. She left in a great hurry. I'd hoped she had come here."

"Why?" Norlund got up and went to where Bracken paced aimlessly around the small space. "What have you told her now? Have we wasted the summer waiting for 'results' only to have her rush out on the first ferry because of your impulsiveness?"

Bracken stopped and jammed his hands through thinning brown hair. "She found his pelt. We talked." He looked away, a look of shame shadowing his lined features. "I got a bit carried away, I'm afraid."

A murderous rage rose in Norlund, nearly choking him. He clenched his hands and took several deep breaths before responding. "You old fool! Did you at least get the pelt?"

"No." Bracken continued his pacing. "It's Cade's of course. The problem now is where she's gone with it." He snapped his fingers and spun around. "Meredith Douglas."

"The grandfather. Doesn't he have a cottage near here?"

Bracken nodded. "There is a road, for part of the way. I'll have Devon drive me, then I can hike in the rest of the way. See if she's there."

Norlund stopped his flight with a heavy hand on Bracken's sleeve. "Wrong again. We'll go. Summer is almost over, and there's no way I'll spend another winter on these islands that were tossed up from hell. I can't afford to watch you let things get beyond your control. Again."

Bracken's gaze darted nervously over Norlund's features. Beads of sweat popped out on his forehead. So the old fool at least had enough sense to be worried. Fortunately, he didn't know yet what he needed to be worrying about. Norlund suppressed a grin.

He just about had everyone right where he wanted them.

At Kelsey's urging, Meredith finally fixed a pallet for himself in a far corner of the cottage and lay down for some much needed rest. She continued to sit by Cade's side, sponging his heated skin, talking softly to him.

She continued to bathe him in cool water, although her back ached and she felt lightheaded from not eating. Kelsey leaned over his still form and prayed harder than she ever had in her life. This was her fault. If he hadn't been trying so hard to stay away from her he wouldn't have caught this strange fever. Even if it meant she had to leave his life forever, she'd gladly do so, if it meant he would be well.

She dipped a spoon in cool water and let the drops trickle over his mouth, hoping desperately he'd be able to take the needed fluid.

He licked his lips, slowly, then swallowed, carefully. Painfully. "Kelsey." Her name emerged in a croaky whisper.

She clutched his hand and brought it to her face. "I'm here. I won't leave you."

He turned towards the sound of her voice but didn't open his eyes. "Must not know. Can't bear... if she knows."

Tears formed, and she blinked hard to keep them under control. "It's all right, Cade. You can tell me anything. Later." She smoothed his hair back. His skin felt slightly cooler from the repeated sponge bathing, but she knew he was still gravely ill. "Sleep now. We can talk when you're well."

"Show her a new world. The sea. If she would. Let me. Change her. Swim around the islands. Tell her everything."

Kelsey's heart slowed and pounded out a painful rhythm. "What could you show me, Cade?"

His grip tightened painfully on her hand. "The seals. The silver ones. Father. Bracken. Wants so badly. Be one with me. If she'd let me." Everything she'd ever heard about selkies poured through her mind. All the folk tales she'd read. Dr. Bracken's bizarre assertions about the silver seals and the selkies. Mrs. Devon's statement that no one had ever found the silver seals and lived to tell about it. Now Cade was deathly ill and claiming he was a selkie. She let out a slow breath. He was delirious. He didn't know what he was saying.

Then all the strange events that had happened to her since she returned played through her mind. Cade appearing like Neptune from the sea. The interlude at the sea cave and her mysterious transport back to the inn. Swimming at the pond with the silver seal. Her peculiar memory lapse. Her rescue at sea by the same silver seal. The seal in the net, his eyes pleading with her.

Cade wounded in the same place the silver pelt was marked. One strange coincidence after another. The other explanation wasn't acceptable to her scientific mind. She squeezed his hand reassuringly and whispered soothingly. "It's okay. Don't worry. You must get well so I can tell you my secret."

His face twisted into a grimace and for a long time he was silent. Did he even know she had spoken to him?

After several agonizing moments, he finally, spoke. "Hate me. If she knew. Never touch her again. If I told her. Just like her mother and my father."

Chapter Twenty Two

Kelsey watched Cade drift into an uneasy sleep. His words pounded in her ears.

Just like with her mother and my father. She tried to piece together the scraps of information she had about her mother's death. Annabelle MacKenzie Bouschour had been an archaeologist, working to unearth the heritage of the islands, until her mysterious death when Kelsey was three. Her father had always been stubbornly close-mouthed about her mother's death. Dr. Bracken had said she might have been clinically depressed.

Did that mean Annabelle had taken her own life?

The thought twisted in her like a knife. Lost in contemplation, she didn't hear Meredith until he gently pried her fingers from Cade's and forced a mug of steaming broth into her hand.

"Here." His voice was gruff. "You can't abandon your own health or you'll not be of any help to him."

She inhaled the rich aroma and gave him a searching look. "Considering what happened to me the last time I had some of your soup, Meredith, do I dare drink this?"

He sat down opposite her. "You're right to be cautious, but I do apologize for the other incident. Drink up, girl. I mean you no harm. I never did."

Flecks of herbs floated in the creamy broth. She swallowed a mouthful, letting the soothing heat spread through her. She smiled at him over the rim of the mug. "Much better than the nettle soup. Thank you, Meredith."

He nodded stiffly as if embarrassed by her appreciation.

She considered him a moment before she asked the

question that had haunted her since the day her memory returned. "Why did you want me to forget Cade?"

"I lost my son to an ill-fated love affair. I won't let the same thing happen to my grandson."

He meant her mother and Cade's father, if Cade's delirious ramblings were to be believed, but Meredith's closed expression indicated he wouldn't discuss it further. Why was everyone so reluctant to discuss something that happened over twenty-five years ago?

Kelsey stood and stretched, easing the stiffness from her legs. She walked to the tiny window and peered out into the shimmery dusk. With the end of the summer approaching, the incessant daylight was finally giving way to daytime hours she was more accustomed to. Still, twilight stretched out and cast an unearthly light on the sea.

"Why are you so certain I'm not the right woman for him?"

Meredith picked up the pelt lying beside Cade and came to stand beside her. "He needs a mate of his own kind."

Kelsey opened her mouth to protest, but he held up a hand. "You've been told and you've seen inexplicable things with your own two eyes. Do you expect a change to take place in front of you before you believe?"

"If you're a shape shifter, why haven't you gone with the rest of your family? Why is Cade part of the research team? What is he searching for?"

Meredith ran a hand down the pelt. "Cade is looking for the cure for the sickness as well as for what was stolen from me twenty-five years ago."

"A pelt?"

Meredith nodded. "He's looking for clues as to where it might be hidden. I've begun to despair of ever finding it."

She reached out a tentative hand and sifted the soft fur through her fingers. "Dr. Bracken has it. At least he showed me one much the same as this."

At first, Meredith looked disbelieving, then practically

hopped up and down. "I was convinced your father was the thief, but he's never returned here to settle things."

She wondered what needed to be settled between her father and Cade's grandfather. How had her mother fit into all this? Surely Meredith had the answers she wanted about her mother's life, and her death. "I must know what happened to my mother. Cade said something strange about—"

Meredith cut her off. "Your mother regretted what she gave up, but what happened then is for your father to tell you. But I will say this: you think your love is strong enough, but many have tried to overcome the boundary that separates humans from shape shifters. All have failed."

She thought of the way she felt about Cade and the strong feelings she knew he held for her. "But—"

Meredith's expression hardened. "The love never lasts. The seal always longs for the freedom of the sea. The human longs for land and the human comforts it's familiar with." He shook his head. "Both end up miserable and the love vanishes like a wisp of smoke on the wind."

"I'm pregnant." Kelsey turned from the window and faced him. The news she'd wanted to share with Cade burst from her and she couldn't help the smile that spread across her face. Telling someone made it more real, somehow, and Kelsey felt certain Cade would want his grandfather to know.

Meredith staggered back as if she'd struck him. "No. You're mistaken."

"It's true." Even now she sensed the faint stirring inside her, like a fragile butterfly testing its wings. She closed her eyes and concentrated, placing her palm against her abdomen. The fluttering came again, an almost imperceptible sensation, and she might have imagined it, but there were other signs, the nausea, weight gain, the insatiable need for sleep.

"'Tis too soon. You wouldn't be able to tell unless—" His

sharp gaze darted over her as if trying to make a diagnosis. He took her arm and examined the tiny cluster of burst veins that had only recently appeared. He traced the spidery red mark with a roughened finger, then glancing over to where Cade slept, he looked her straight in the eyes. "The seed was planted the day you were at the sea cave."

"He told you about that?" An embarrassed blush stole into her cheeks.

"He didn't have to," Meredith snapped. "Your scent was all over him like a new skin, and he was so weak from spiriting you back to Murdoch Castle, I nearly despaired of making him well." He turned away and began pacing. "Yes, it would have to be the cave. What else could it mean?"

He wheeled suddenly and Kelsey jumped.

"Who else knows?"

"No one, although I think Dr. Bracken suspects." Or had hopes. He'd certainly been maintaining a peculiar interest in her health for the past several weeks.

"And you intend to go through with it?"

She nodded, wondering why he'd think she'd consider any other alternative.

"Even knowing what you do about us?"

She stared into eyes that held more secrets than she could imagine and didn't even need to think about the answer. "Yes. I love your grandson, Meredith, and I consider our baby a gift of that love."

"No matter what?"

"Yes." She spoke with fierce certainty. She couldn't destroy what they had created in love, no matter how uncertain she was of the outcome, or what Cade's feelings would be about it. She had to take the chance everything would work out.

A night bird called, drawing her attention outside. Two shadowy shapes moved across the heather towards the cottage. She squinted, trying to identify Meredith's callers.

"You have visitors. Were you expecting anyone?"

Meredith shook his head. The faceless figures continued their purposeful stride towards the cottage.

"It looks like Dr. Bracken. And that must be Dr. Norlund with him."

She turned, but Meredith had disappeared, taking the silver pelt with him.

Glancing over at Cade to be certain he was still sleeping, Kelsey met the two men at the door. She stepped out onto the porch and pulled the door shut. "Good evening, Dr. Bracken, Dr. Norlund."

"Kelsey, thank God." Dr. Bracken made as if to embrace her, but Meredith's allegation that he and Dr. Norlund had tried to drown her rang in her mind.

Kelsey moved out of his reach. "What brings you here?"

"I was worried about you. Can't have my star assistant wandering these hills or the shore in this murky light."

Especially when a woman's already been murdered, Kelsey wanted to retort but managed to keep silent. Even if Meredith was right about the boating accident, it didn't necessarily follow that someone had killed Lana.

Yet what other possible explanation could there be?

"Did you decide to talk to Meredith Douglas about your mother?" Dr. Bracken leaned closer and peered at her.

She could tell he didn't like the idea of that and wondered why. "Cade is very sick. I've been helping so Meredith could get some rest."

"What about you, Kelsey?" Dr. Bracken's expression became anxious. "You mustn't neglect your own health."

His constant carping about her well-being was starting to grate on her nerves.

"I've never felt better." Which was true and a lie all at the same time. "Let me tell Meredith you're here."

She stepped inside the cottage and found Meredith hovering over Cade. "Is the fever escalating again?" Kelsey knelt beside the cot and touched his forehead. Warm, but not as hot as he'd been before.

Meredith gripped her shoulder. "You must go back with Bracken."

"No." Not only did she not want to leave Cade, the thought of being with Bracken and Norlund made her distinctly uneasy. "If you're right, and they engineered that 'accident' on the boat, then it's not safe for me to be with them."

Meredith paced alongside the cot. "I don't believe he wanted to harm you, just force Cade to show himself." He stopped beside her, his eyes weary and pleading. "You may be his only hope to get well. If you could find a cause, then you can find a cure."

She knew he was right, but she needed to protect herself. "Any chance you still have some nettle soup we could offer to the good doctors?"

Meredith's face lit up. "Brilliant. They will forget, for a time anyway, this quest. That will allow all of you to concentrate on the research." He scurried to the kitchen area and began rattling pots, then lit a fire in an ancient stove.

Kelsey rejoined Dr. Bracken and Dr. Norlund on the porch. "Meredith has invited all of us to join him in a late supper."

Dr. Norlund nearly smiled. "Excellent. That hike over the hill has left me ravenous."

Dr. Bracken looked uncertain, but Kelsey motioned him to the rocking chair. "I'll bring out a few more chairs so we can have our meal out here and not disturb Cade. Besides, it would be a shame to waste such a lovely evening, don't you agree?"

The last vestiges of sunset streaked the sky in purples and painted the clouds crimson. A soft breeze rippled over the marsh grass, bringing the salty tang of the sea.

Dr. Bracken sat and grabbed her wrist as she passed him on her way inside. "Watch yourself with the old man. I'm not sure I trust him."

Kelsey stifled a laugh. How ironic. She leaned down and

dropped her voice to a whisper. "Don't worry. I'll go keep an eye on him."

Meredith was putting the finishing touches on a sturdy wicker tray crowded with soup mugs when she entered the cottage.

"I refilled yours with anemone chowder, Kelsey. It will be very fortifying for you. Let me serve the others. You bring out the barley bread."

Dr. Norlund enthusiastically accepted a mug of soup and inhaled deeply. "Ah, wonderful of you to be so hospitable, Meredith."

"I wouldn't have it any other way." Meredith handed a mug to Dr. Bracken, who accepted it with noticeably less interest.

"What is it you're having, Kelsey?" Dr. Bracken eyed her soup as the pungent spices of his own assailed his senses.

"Chowder. Spicy foods seem to upset my stomach lately."

Dr. Bracken exchanged a knowing look with Dr. Norlund. She had to turn away to hide her smile.

Both men drained their mugs, but only Dr. Norlund accepted Meredith's offer of a refill. Dr. Bracken was in the middle of eating a slice of bread when the soup overtook him. His head rolled against the back of the wicker rocker. Dr. Norlund leaned heavily into the post he'd propped himself against, then slid slowly to the porch floor. His arm dropped limply to his side. Eyes open, both men stared unseeing past Kelsey.

She suppressed a shudder. "Eerie. Are you sure they're going to be okay?"

Meredith nodded. "Believe me, Bracken and Norlund deserve worse."

She wondered why, but instinctively knew he wouldn't tell her, at least not yet. "What's in that stuff, anyway?"

He smiled at her. "Secret family recipe. Don't fret. They'll come around shortly. When they do, I think it best if you leave immediately."

Kelsey rose. "I'm going to tell Cade I'm leaving."

Inside, she knelt by his bedside and picked up his hand, then brushed his knuckles against her cheek. Tears burned behind her eyes, but she swallowed and willed herself not to cry. It wouldn't help him and would make it that much harder to leave.

"Cade," she whispered. "I have to go back to the lab, but I'll be back. I'll find a cure. I promise. Don't give up."

The rattle of his breathing echoed in the small cottage, and she feared he wouldn't be able to speak again.

Then his eyes drifted open, and her heart lurched with hope at the lucidity she saw. But the expression on his face was one of pain and despair. "There is no cure for being selkie. Go. Before you put yourself in any more danger."

Chapter Twenty Three

A short time later, Kelsey walked over the hill towards the dirt track that passed as a road, Dr. Bracken and Dr. Norlund trailing behind her. She stole a glance over her shoulder. Meredith's cottage sat near the shore, a dark hulk against the shimmering silver of the night sea. A small boat floated to the water's edge and someone emerged from the craft. It looked like a woman, but she didn't dare try to see for sure, afraid the other two scientists would notice her interest.

Dr. Bracken yawned hugely and blinked, squinting behind wire rim glasses like a sleepy-eyed turtle. "Excuse me. I don't know quite what's come over me. I can't remember ever feeling so groggy. I wish we'd asked Devon to come back for us."

"It's not that far." Kelsey stepped up her pace, anxious to put the traces of jealousy from her mind and concentrate on finding a cure for Cade's mysterious illness. Meredith had advised against going over the hill and around by the pond. She wondered what kind of secrets he was afraid Dr. Bracken and Dr. Norlund would stumble across, but took his advice and followed the longer route down the road.

The men lagged further and further behind. Impatient to get back to her work, Kelsey had to force herself to slow her pace. She really didn't want to wait for them, but knew she'd be able to work better if she was certain the two scientists were settled in their rooms for the night. Finally the pile of gray stone comprising the inn came into sight.

She practically ran up the stairs, leaving Bracken and Norlund to trudge the remainder of the way on their own. Switching on the desk lamp, she pulled out her research notes and pored over them. Something was different in the water surrounding this island than the one where she and Cade had spent the afternoon. If she had separate samples from the islands further out, she could conduct tests and perhaps find the problem.

She'd have to find a way to do that without Dr. Bracken suspecting what she was up to. Perhaps Meredith could use his resources to get her the samples she needed.

Meanwhile, the shellfish from this island could be studied in greater detail. Winkles like the ones she and Cade had collected would be a good way to start. Now that she had a better idea of what she was searching for, she could narrow the scope of her tests. In the morning, after the tide went out, she could gather more.

Kelsey waited until the sounds of Dr. Norlund moving around in his room next to hers ceased, then quietly slipped downstairs and out to the lab and went to work.

Two days passed during which Kelsey kept busy with research and testing in the lab. Meredith sent word by way of the Devons that Cade's condition hadn't worsened or improved, but one of his cousins was helping Meredith so that Kelsey could concentrate on her lab work. She worried about him constantly and strengthened her resolve to find a cure.

Late one afternoon, she threw down her pencil and rubbed her eyes. She was at an impasse. The testing on the winkles and other shellfish she'd collected on this island definitely showed an unusual bacterial growth, but without other specimens to test, she couldn't reach any conclusive results.

After dinner, she eluded Dr. Bracken, slipped away from the inn and headed for Meredith's. Taking the path through the thicket and around the pond, she arrived at the cottage as dusk settled over the heather and cloaked the hut in gray light.

Meredith sat rocking on the porch. "Good evening, Kelsey. What takes you away from your work?"

She leaned against the railing and regarded him. "How is Cade?"

"No worse, no better. We're doing what we can." His clipped tone reminded her of what she was expected to do.

She sat on the step and caught her breath. "I need to visit the island Cade took me to."

A dark look crossed his face so she hurried to explain. "I can test samples forever, but if I want answers, I need a basis for comparison." She leaned towards him, hoping he'd catch the sense of urgency. "I need specimens from the island where the seals have taken refuge."

Meredith's gnarled hands tightened on the arms of the rocker. Silence stretched, then at last he nodded. "We've asked you to trust us. 'Tis only fair we extend the same to you." He rose and headed for the door. "Very well. I'll have Eleanor take you when her brother comes to fetch her."

She followed him inside. A young woman sat beside Cade, carefully smoothing clean linens over him. Long, silvery blond hair tumbled past her hips. She brushed it back, revealing a face of such delicate perfection, Kelsey's heart twisted. She stifled the unfamiliar twinge of jealousy and extended her hand. "You must be Eleanor. I'm—"

"Kelsey." Eleanor straightened but didn't touch her. Instead she turned back to her tasks, her body language clearly telling Kelsey she'd better not touch her patient.

Ignoring her, Kelsey knelt by the bed and took Cade's hand. "How is he today?"

Cade moaned softly, and Eleanor frowned. "Much the same. I think your presence disturbs him. He must rest if he is to recover."

Kelsey started to protest, but Meredith intervened. "Eleanor, your brother is waiting. I need the two of you to take Kelsey to the seal island. Help her collect what she requires for her research and have Brodrik bring her back. I'll see you again in the morning?" He kissed her cheek and led her away.

"Of course." She motioned to Kelsey. "Come along then." Kelsey followed her to the shore to the waiting skiff and climbed in behind her. Brodrik nodded curtly, but didn't speak as he navigated the small craft away from the island. Cool air cut through Kelsey's sweater and tossed Eleanor's glorious hair around her face. The ride seemed interminable, the sea and sky immense, surrounding them. Kelsey watched the island become smaller and smaller as the boat cut a path through the choppy sea. The motion made her slightly queasy, but not wanting to earn more of Brodrik's and Eleanor's displeasure, she concentrated on keeping the feeling under control. At last the sandy island came into view. With the dark rock formations at each end like giant anchors, the island seemed to float mysteriously in the dusky light.

Eleanor pulled something from under the seat, stepped from the boat into knee-deep water and pulled the craft onto the sand while Brodrik cut the engine.

"Eleanor!" Brodrik's voice was sharp with warning.

Ignoring him, she tossed her hair back and gave Kelsey a defiant look. "I'll help you find what you need, so that he'll be well. But I want you to see the part of his life that you can never share."

Kelsey sat in the skiff and stared as Eleanor pulled a silver pelt from the bundle she held under her arm. Closing her eyes, she settled the fur carefully over her head and stretched her arms out as if she wished to embrace the sky and sea.

Like viewing something through a filter, Kelsey watched Eleanor's form begin to change, the straight lines of her arms and legs softening, shortening. Her face blurred. Kelsey blinked and in the short span of time the image shifted. She gasped with astonishment. In the place where a woman had stood, a seal rested, its magnificent coat shining silver. The seal gave her a haughty look, then arched its body and moved into the water, disappearing beneath the surface in a movement of speed and grace.

A splash behind her sprayed sea water into the skiff and spattered icy droplets over her. Another seal, this one's coat as dark as Brodrik's charcoal gray hair, slipped past.

Her mind whirling, Kelsey climbed from the boat, shone her pocket flashlight near the water's edge and began to search for winkles and other shellfish. She glanced uneasily over her shoulder, but saw no sign of the seals. Or rather Eleanor and Brodrik.

Even the sea birds were silent, and the surreal quiet added to the eerie quality of the night. Mrs. Devon's words returned. *No one has ever seen the silver seals. And lived to tell about them, that is.*

Cade's family needed her to find a cure for him. What would happen after she did? Or if she failed?

By the evening of the third day, Kelsey knew her reprieve from Dr. Bracken's strange quest had ended when she caught him eyeing her with the speculative look he usually reserved for a particularly fascinating piece of plant or marine life.

"Feeling better today, Kelsey?" He stopped by her desk and rested a hand on her shoulder.

She had to force herself not to flinch from his touch. Giving herself a few moments to gather her composure, she finished logging in her analysis of plankton before she laid her pen down. "I'm fine, Dr. Bracken."

His gaze flitted over her face. "No more queasiness, then?"

"Absolutely not." She gave him a one hundred watt smile and smoothed a hand over her stomach, glad her bulky sweater and lab coat hid the fact that a large safety pin hooked through the buttonhole of her pants, giving her extra room at the waistband. "My jeans fit better, too. All that walking must be what I needed to drop those extra couple of pounds."

"Oh." He looked positively crestfallen, and Kelsey would

have laughed if the situation weren't so serious. "Well, good for you, my dear. I haven't had any word on Cade. Have you been by Meredith's?"

"I'm sure Dr. Douglas would be back to work if he was over the flu." Kelsey ignored the question and bent over her microscope. "Mrs. Devon said there's a very tenacious stomach virus making the rounds in the village."

"Perhaps that's what was troubling you."

She returned his considering gaze, then turned her attention back to her work. "Maybe so." After several moments, he moved away, and she breathed a sigh of relief. She'd have a tough time accomplishing anything if he hovered over her, especially since she wasn't sure she wanted him to know just what direction her analysis was taking.

She studied the slide comparing the local mussels with the ones Eleanor and Brodrik had gathered the night before. A microscopic particle drifted past. Kelsey carefully increased the magnification and took another look.

There it was again. Something was different about the shellfish. Now all she had to do was isolate the organism and try to identify it. Maybe the answer was in reach after all. Her spirits lifted at the thought.

Kelsey waited until everyone had retired for the night and the inn was quiet before she started out for Meredith's. On her way, she passed the pond and thought about the picnic she and Cade shared and the glorious feeling of isolation they had enjoyed while Dr. Bracken and Dr. Norlund had been gone. Then relived every detail of her swim with the silver seal. How could she have ever thought she'd dreamed it?

Her thoughts traveled to the precious nights she and Cade had spent in her antique bed at the inn. Even if they could never be together again, she'd carry the memories forever. In more ways than one.

She smoothed a hand over her stomach. Despite the

difficulties she'd have to face, the idea of having Cade's baby thrilled her.

Dr. Bracken's ominous words rose to taunt her, but she shoved them away. Their baby would be fine and Cade would get well. He had to, no matter what she had to sacrifice to make it happen.

Meredith was sitting beside Cade when she arrived. She glanced around, glad to see that he was alone.

"If you're looking for Eleanor, she's gone. I don't dare let any of them be here too long, for fear another may fall ill."

Kelsey pulled up a chair beside him. Fear and jealousy made her throat tight and kept her from asking questions about the beautiful woman who harbored such animosity to Kelsey.

Meredith surprised her by patting her hand. "You've no need to think of Eleanor as your rival, child. She's my granddaughter. Cade's half-sister. In order to keep the line strong, we must be careful not to mate too closely."

She winced inwardly at the choice of words. It sounded so strange, so—inhuman. But how else could she expect a selkie to discuss propagation?

Meredith's eyes took on a faraway look. "Shayla was the one I had chosen for him, but it seems the gods had other plans."

She swallowed the lump in her throat. So Cade had been promised to someone else. "Who is she?"

Meredith sighed. "A headstrong female. Cade was here. She felt the need to follow. It cost her life."

Suddenly, Kelsey remembered her first night on the island. The dead seal on the beach, Cade appearing like an apparition from the shadowed light of the midnight sun and then disappearing just as abruptly, taking the seal with him. For she was sure now that was what had happened. The dead seal must have been Shayla.

"I was certain she was the one for him. I even thought perhaps they had...." His voice trailed off and his gaze sharpened on Kelsey. "I must ask you something. Forgive me for being so direct, but it's crucial that I know. Were you untouched?"

Her instinctive response was to retort that it was none of his business, but something about the pain etched around his eyes, the earnestness of the question, the seriousness of Cade's illness and the whole bizarre situation made her feel as if he deserved an answer.

Heat rose in her face, but she met Meredith's gaze. "Cade is the only one I have ever been with." She waited several tense moments for his reaction, but if she'd thought he would be glad, she was wrong. Despair clouded his eyes, then his shoulders drooped. Silence grew between them until she thought the cottage would burst with the tension. "I don't understand," she said finally. "How does that change anything?"

"Our clan has survived much, over the centuries. But this might well be our destruction."

Chapter Twenty Four

Kelsey was up the next morning and out of the inn before dawn and hiked to the craggy hill overlooking the inn. Sunrise glimmered behind her and reflected in puffy, white clouds hanging over a tranquil sea. Surrounding hills and the quiet inn below looked as it must have for centuries, imperturbable, steadfast. Able to withstand the ravages of time, tides and treachery.

Early in the summer, the hill had been carpeted with delicate white flowers, but the blooms had faded, leaving a wave of tall grasses. According to Meredith, the cliffs harbored rare shells containing an extract which could be the key to an antidote for Cade's strange illness. She made her way through waist high grass to the place where she had stood her first night on the island.

The wind kicked up, rippling through the grass, tossing Kelsey's hair around her face. Sea birds wheeled, squawking, overhead. Below her, waves charged the rocks in noisy challenge. The sea called out, luring her closer to the edge and she wondered....

"She died here, but you must remember that."

Skin prickling, hair standing out from her arms, Kelsey whirled at the sound of the voice that broke through the quiet morning. "Good day, Dr. Norlund. You're out early. Any chance you're going to tell me what you're talking about?" She crossed her arms against a sudden chill and calmed her racing heart.

He came to stand beside her, and she involuntarily took a step back from the precipice.

"Your mother, of course. That's really the reason why you

came to Orkney, not to assist in this dull project, or participate in Dr. Bracken's wild seal chase. You want to know all about your mother's death. Isn't that what you've been waiting to find out?" Her throat dry and scratchy, Kelsey swallowed a lump that felt like cotton. "Father said she drowned."

Hands on her shoulders, Norlund stood at the edge of the cliff and peered down, forcing Kelsey's gaze to the treacherous rocks below. "Oh, I doubt that. The fall probably killed her."

"What do you mean?" Kelsey had wondered if her mother had died the same strange way Lana had, but never for an instant had she thought she'd been the victim of a cruel accident. Or was there something else?

Norlund continued his grim musings. "Yes, she probably lost consciousness the moment she hit the rocks." He released her and gave her a macabre smile. "You were here, Kelsey. Don't you remember watching while your mother took her fatal leap?"

She backed away. He was lying. Norlund hadn't been here twenty-five years ago, so how could he know what had happened? "I was just a child, barely three."

"Think about it," he urged, his soothing voice at odds with the cruel expression on his face. He moved away from the cliff, half-circling her until he stood between her and the way back. "Not only was she caught in her adultery, but the poor woman must have been quite distraught to discover she carried one of those creatures inside her. Wouldn't you be?"

Instinctively, Kelsey crossed her hands over her abdomen. Norlund's lips twisted in a look of disgust.

"So Bracken was right. You are pregnant."

She backed up. "So what if I am? You've suspected for some time that Cade and I were having an affair."

"An intelligent woman takes precautions."

Goaded by the sneer on his face, she blurted out the first thing that came to mind. "Cade said…" Again his words flashed through her mind. *I can't give you a child, Kelsey. It's impossible.*

Norlund laughed. "I'll bet he told you he couldn't get you pregnant. Or more to the point, it wouldn't be human. You don't have to imagine how your mother must have felt, knowing that thing was flipping around inside, growing, feeding off her. You're living it. Isn't it marvelous how history repeats itself?"

"You don't know what you're saying. What about my father?"

Norlund jammed his hands in his pockets. "Yes, let's discuss the exalted William Bouschour for a moment. Suppose he really believed in the silver seals. Why would he abandon the search? Why would he refuse to return here? I think he must have realized your mother was weak in the mind. Better to get the child away before the same illness appeared."

A sick feeling grew in Kelsey. Could that be the reason her father wanted little to do with her over the years? Did he believe Annabelle had been insane? Was his reason for coming to Orkney only because he feared she'd follow the same fate as her mother?

So many things didn't make sense. "How does Dr. Bracken and Meredith fit into all of this?"

Norlund's expression hardened. "Bracken's losing it. And I intend to see that he's removed as director of the project."

And then Norlund would step in and take over. Which meant Kelsey would be fired and sent back to the States. Disgraced.

Norlund warmed to his subject. "The good professor will be lucky if he can find work with the circus. Meredith will die an old man. Cade won't last much longer. Then that will be the end of it."

So Norlund had no idea there were other selkies. "I intend to notify the foundation of what you and Dr. Bracken have been doing."

"Which is?"

"Diverting the research monies to fund his personal quest. Misuse of personnel and equipment. Sabotaging research efforts."

Anger flared in his eyes, and she knew she'd guessed correctly. Norlund, not Cade, had been the one who destroyed her careful research.

"You won't get the chance." His words slithered around her. Kelsey took another step back. "You carry one of them, and it's time for the race to die out. You were their only hope. And now it's too late." Norlund moved closer.

Fear skittered down her spine. He meant to kill her. Just as he had done to Lana. The certainty blazed through her. "You killed Lana."

A spark lit his gaze. "Such a waste. All those brains and ethics hidden in that extraordinary package."

"Does Dr. Bracken know?"

Norlund shrugged. "He may be obsessed, but he's not stupid. She wouldn't or couldn't interest Cade to satisfy Bracken's disgusting experiment. She was going to ruin things for us here." He spread his hands. "Accidents happen."

Kelsey's blood ran cold. All she was to her respected professor was a means to an end.

She remembered Dr. Bracken telling Dr. Norlund, *Any time now we'll know if the experiment took.* His constant pressure on her to "get along" with Cade, his fixation with her health. Obviously, he'd wanted her to get pregnant and had been watching for signs that she was.

She swallowed and glanced behind her. During their conversation, Norlund had maneuvered her onto the promontory jutting high above the sea while he blocked the only way back to the meadow. "What are you going to do?"

"Nothing. You, on the other hand, overwrought by memories of your mother's tragic death, are going to find out how it feels to free fall."

Kelsey edged forward, reluctant to get closer to Norlund, but needing every bit of solid ground beneath her she could claim.

"Think of your mother. How she held your hand and led you to the edge. How she needed you to go with her. She's been waiting all this time for you. You don't want to suffer for months, knowing that creature is growing inside you. Go now, before you have to experience the agony of giving birth to that thing. Let this be the end of it. No more of creatures who can't or won't make up their minds which world they want to live in."

"Never." She dug her heels in, searching for a way to get past him.

He towered over her like a mountain. "Doesn't matter to me if you jump or I push you. Either way, you'll be just as dead. Few people will mourn you and the ones who do will chalk it up to an unpleasant family history."

Her foot dislodged a rock and sent it clattering over the edge. A flock of puffins screeched up from the side of the cliff. Norlund looked away from her, momentarily distracted. Kelsey lunged to the side, hoping to get past him. The big man was quicker, tackling her by the ankle.

She hit the ground hard. Sharp rocks dug into her side. Using all the strength she possessed, she slammed her foot across the bridge of his nose. Norlund screamed and released her. Blood spurted from his face.

She scrambled back to avoid his fist swinging at her with deadly force. Sharp rocks dug into her knees, dirt crumbled beneath her. She was at the edge of the cliff. Her hands clutched rocks and grass, dug into the earth.

With a roar of pain, Norlund lunged. As he launched himself towards her, Kelsey flattened herself to the ground and dove beneath him. Norlund's foot caught on the rocks. He grunted and then was airborne, tumbling headfirst over the precipice towards the jagged rocks below.

Gasping for breath, Kelsey lay on the ground while the

world tilted and whirled above her. Gradually, she pulled herself up and got on her knees. She clutched her side. If anything had happened to her baby....

She sat on her haunches and contemplated what Norlund had said, the reality of what she knew and had seen. Cade rising from the sea. Eleanor changing from a lovely woman into a beautiful seal. She should be frightened about what it meant for the child she carried but instead found the possibility fascinating. Whether her child had special powers wouldn't make her love him or her any less.

When you loved someone, you accepted them for what they were. Wasn't that all she had ever wanted from her father? Her father. Her head ached with memories begging to be set free.

Memories of twenty-five years ago. Her mother, dark hair to her waist, standing at the edge of the cliff.

Come watch for Daddy, Kelsey. We can see his ship from here, if we look hard.

She'd ignored her, more interested in digging her chubby fingers into an abandoned birds nest than in looking for the father who rarely spared her a hug at the end of the day. Her mother, exasperated, had come back and taken her by the hand.

Stand with Mama. See how good the wind feels. Just a little bit closer.

She'd hung back, protesting. Her mother had wrapped her arms around her when something, no someone, had stopped her just as Kelsey's shoes dislodged bits of rock and dirt from the cliff. She squeezed her eyes shut, trying to remember, grasping for the memories that hovered just out of reach.

A man she didn't know had been there. He'd argued with her mother. Kelsey couldn't remember the words, no matter how hard she tried. The language was unknown but vaguely familiar. Someone else....

Her father. Suddenly, she saw her father, shoulder length

hair tied back, face dark with anger. She cowered by her mother's legs, afraid his rage was at her.

The pictures swam too quickly before her, like trying to see through the wind. Her mother's grip painful on Kelsey's shoulder. A man's angry shout. Her mother beside her, then in the next instant, gone. Blank air beneath her feet. Her father's hand clutching her tiny fingers. The pain as her leg slammed into the jagged face of the cliff. The screams she couldn't keep inside.

He'd saved her life.

The father whose love she'd always doubted had rescued her from the grasp of her mother, a woman clearly despairing and out of her mind. The other man on the hill that day must have been Cade's father, but no matter how hard she tried, she couldn't visualize what part he had played in the tragedy.

She wouldn't let despair drag her down the way her mother had. She sat on her heels, her breath coming in little gasps, as she slowly returned to the present.

She loved Cade. She loved his baby, no matter what. She wouldn't end its life, and she wouldn't throw her own away, either. Her mother had been frightened or misguided. Maybe both. Poor Annabelle.

Cautiously, she crept to the edge. Norlund lay face down, alone, crumpled on the sharp rocks, and she wondered why she'd been expecting to see two bodies crushed on the boulders. Had Cade's father died here with her mother?

Waves darted in around Norlund's lifeless form, throwing spray high and carrying the smell of salt. He was beyond help, now. She'd have to notify the constable. There would have to be an investigation. She glanced at the crumbling rock beneath her and sucked in a breath.

Below her, just out of reach, the shells she'd hoped to find protruded from the surface of the cliff. Just as Meredith had told her, they peppered the black rock with a soft shine of white. Lying flat on her stomach, she edged forward, attempting to scrape at the embedded shells with the flat blade she carried in her pocket.

She edged back carefully, then stuffed the samples in a plastic bag. By this time tomorrow, she'd know if she'd found an antidote for Cade's illness. She had to return to the inn and confront Dr. Bracken, but she'd better wait until the constable arrived. She tried to find sorrow for Dr. Norlund's senseless death, but with his ominous words still ringing in her ears, she could find only an overwhelming relief.

A billow of white caught her attention, dragging her gaze towards the sea. A large schooner crested the horizon, sails luffing against the sky, its jib the blue-gray of the Scottish sea. She didn't need to see the flags to recognize the Mystic Maiden. Anticipation and happiness welled inside her.

Her father had arrived at last.

Chapter Twenty Five

"Kelsey!" Urgent voices carried across the meadow. She stood and shaded her eyes. Dr. Bracken, with Mr. and Mrs. Devon in tow, hurried towards her through the tall grass.

Gordon Devon held a shotgun under one arm. "You all right, Miss?"

She nodded. How much did the Devons know about what had been going on at their inn? Obviously enough to make Gordon think he needed to be armed when they looked for her.

"Thank God, you're all right. When I didn't see you up here any longer, I feared the worst." Dr. Bracken made as if to embrace her, but she shrugged away from him.

"I'm fine, but Dr. Norlund is dead." Kelsey rubbed her arms against a sudden chill. "He was trying to push me over the ledge and fell."

Mrs. Devon gasped. Gordon's eyebrows shot up. Dr. Bracken was solicitude personified. "You don't know how sorry I am, Kelsey. I've feared for some time he was losing his grip."

"Funny, that's what he said about you," she retorted.

He gave her a sad look and sighed. Refusing to be swayed by the good things she knew about him over the reality of the past few months, she crossed her arms and stood far from the promontory when Dr. Bracken and Gordon Devon went to the edge and peered over.

Mrs. Devon circled Kelsey's shoulders with her arm. Kelsey let the housekeeper lead her away. "Poor child. How frightened you must be. There's been some strange goings on here the past year, starting with that other young miss dying." She shook her head. "Don't know what it's all going to come to."

Although Mrs. Devon seemed determined to escort her to the inn, Kelsey insisted on going to the dock instead. The constable, having been alerted by the Devons, arrived by skiff at the same time her father's ship sailed up. Kelsey left Mrs. Devon's somewhat smothering attention and ran across the lawn to the pier.

She waved wildly and was rewarded by an enthusiastic wave uncharacteristic of her very reserved father.

"Kelsey!" He bounded from the boat before the first mate had the lines tied. He strode down the dock to stand before her. "Why didn't you come to Barcelona like I told you to?"

Secure in her memories, she didn't jump to the defensive as she usually did. Instead, she looked up into his lined face, saw the anger borne of concern, the crows feet that had deepened over the intervening year, and the thinning gray hair. He'd aged since she last saw him, and for the first time she thought about the realities of his life. Living on the Mystic Maiden for most of the year, he traveled from place to place and project to project, never staying anywhere long enough to cultivate friends, or put down roots, or have a family.

She was all he had.

She glanced past him to where his crew watched. He'd sailed from Spain at who knew what cost, because he cared about what happened to her, but he might never be able to tell her so.

It didn't matter anymore. For years she'd been waiting for him to accept her for who she was and in all that time, she'd never questioned her own lack of acceptance of his life, his choices.

"Hi, Dad. I'm really glad to see you." Acting on an impulse borne of love and new understanding, she threw her arms around him. He smelled of sea air and wintergreen, and when she closed her eyes, it was as if she'd come home after years of drifting.

His arms went around her, awkwardly at first, as if he were embracing a cactus. Then he squeezed her tightly, and his voice became gruff. "Works both ways, Kelsey. But I'm only here to insist that you leave this place." He released her, and she stepped back, whisking away a tear, not at all surprised a suspicious moisture gleamed in his eyes.

She shook her head. "I can't. I'm too close to finding the answer. And besides—"

"Excuse me, Miss MacKenzie." From behind her, the constable cleared his throat. "I need to ask you some questions."

She turned, and the stocky, florid faced man bobbed his head and extended his hand to her father. "Constable Farlay, sir. Such an honor to have you here, Dr. Bouschour. I'm sorry to interrupt, but I must speak with this young lady."

"What's going on?" Her father scowled at the man, as if no one should dare intrude.

Kelsey interrupted. "Dr. Norlund fell from the cliff. I think he's dead. I'll go answer questions and meet you inside as soon as I finish."

Remembering the packet of shells, she pulled the plastic bag from her pocket and handed it to her father. She'd have to trust him on this one and maybe putting him face to face with Cade's grandfather would resolve years of bitterness and be the best thing for all concerned. "This needs to go to Meredith Douglas. Immediately. He'll know what to do with it. He lives in the crofters cottage around the other side of the peninsula."

Bouschour weighed the packet in his hand, scowled, then started to speak. She laid her hand on his arm.

"Please, Dad. His grandson is terribly sick."

His gaze traveled over her face. His expression tightened at what he must have seen there, but he sighed and nodded. "Very well. If it is important to you."

"Thanks." She stood on tiptoe and brushed a kiss on his cheek then followed the constable to the inn.

While the constable's assistants removed Dr. Norlund's body from the rocks, Kelsey told the constable her suspicions about Dr. Bracken's involvement with Norlund and her near drowning. They searched the hill, then the grounds for Dr. Bracken, and finally found him in the lab.

He sat amidst a heap of papers and books, his head in his hands, graying hair standing in spiky tufts as if he'd repeatedly run his hands through it.

He looked up at Kelsey, his face full of despair. "It's gone. Everything. The pelt, my notes. All the proof I've documented over the past twenty-five years. Gone."

The constable flipped open a small notebook and took a seat opposite the scientist. "And what is it ye be missing, Doctor?"

"I've searched his room. He must have destroyed it all."

Eyes wild, he gestured at Kelsey. "She's seen it. She knows. Tell him, Kelsey."

The constable looked expectantly at her. She shrugged. "I fear Dr. Norlund's death has addled him. I don't know what he's talking about."

"The selkies." Jumping up, he caught Kelsey by the elbows and nearly lifted her off her feet. "Tell him you've seen one. Touched one. Tell him your secret."

She gasped in shock and twisted in his grip. "Dr. Bracken!"

"I would never have harmed you, Kelsey. You know that. I didn't have any part in Lana's death, either. That was all Norlund's doing." He shook her. "Tell him!"

Farlay pried Dr. Bracken away from her and twisted his arm behind his back. "Be a good chap and keep your hands off this young lady." He looked over at Kelsey. "You say he tried to drown you, miss?"

Kelsey nodded.

"Attempted murder. Probably accessory to murder as well

from the sounds of it." The constable clamped a handcuff on Bracken's left wrist, then the right.

"Quite off his nut, I'd say. Any idea what he's babbling about?"

She shook her head. "Just before he fell, Dr. Norlund confessed to killing Lana Reynolds. I don't have any proof Dr. Bracken had any involvement in that, although he probably knew more than he told you at the time."

Dr. Bracken looked bewildered. "I already told you I wouldn't have hurt Lana anymore than I would harm you, Kelsey."

She rubbed the tender flesh where his fingers had bit into her upper arms. "You pushed me off the boat."

"No!" He shook his head.

"Then you let Dr. Norlund do it."

"I meant you no harm!"

"I could have drowned."

"He wouldn't have let you. Don't you see? We just needed you to bring him out. Please. Tell Farley about the silver seals. The selkies. Tell him you know how to find them."

She watched as the constable led Bracken from the lab. "Where are you taking him?"

"The mainland. Don't have a lock-up on this island." He looked at Bracken as if he were a rotting fish. "Never needed one before. I'll be in touch about the inquest."

Kelsey nodded. "I'm not going anywhere." Orkney might not be home, but neither was the Mystic Maiden or wherever her father was headed next. She intended to stay in the islands as long as there was a chance Cade needed her even if he only needed her until he'd be well enough to leave her behind forever.

Meredith's ears rang with the echoes of bygone footsteps. Something was going to happen today. His nerve endings raced with it. He jumped up from the chair beside Cade's bed and hurried to the window. The tall mast of a schooner disappeared beyond the peninsula Bouschour. The thieving shark was back.

Cade moved restlessly and moaned. "Kelsey."

Meredith returned to his side. Sliding his arm behind Cade's shoulders, he raised him and held a cup of water to his mouth. "You must stop tormenting yourself so. Drink up and be well."

Cade opened his eyes and stared into his grandfather's face. "She's in danger. Why did you send her away?"

"I did no such thing. We need her skill as a scientist, not a nursemaid."

Cade sank weakly back against the pillows. "My fault she's in trouble."

"Her father is here now. Worry about yourself, instead."

"If anything happens to her...." His voice trailed off.

Meredith studied his grandson. Trouble. He didn't know the half of it. "Tell me something. I must know. When you took her at the cave, was she your first?"

His words were as faint as the scuffle of hermit crabs across sand. "First woman. Only woman."

Meredith gestured impatiently. "Yes, yes. That part I understood. But as your other self. What about Shayla?"

A grimace crossed Cade's face. "Never found the need."

Meredith sank back into his chair. Interesting. If Kelsey did truly carry Cade's progeny, it must be not only because of who her mother was, but because they crossed the line of innocence together. Which meant they were bound.

But would either of them be able to accept what was now their fate?

Lost in contemplation, he merely looked up in surprise when he sensed the change in the air around him. Bouschour. Any minute now. Here.

He went to the porch and watched William's long stride devour the ground stretching from the sea. Bouschour halted at the bottom step.

Meredith remained at eye level with him. "Did you come to return what you stole?"

"I have nothing of yours. Except this." He extended his hand.

Meredith refused to accept it. "You are not welcome here."

"Take it." Bouschour continued to thrust something at him and finally pressed a plastic packet into Meredith's hand. "It's from Kelsey."

Meredith turned the package over. Shimmering white shells from the cliff. How had she managed to find them?

Bouschour turned to leave. "I hope your grandson will soon be well."

"Have you told her, William? Will you ever?"

Bouschour turned to face him, dark eyes snapping. "Tell her what, old man? That her mother was deranged? Thought she was in love with a selkie? So she killed herself and tried to take her only child with her?"

Meredith shook his head. "Annabelle was a victim of forces beyond her control. I simply wondered if you'd ever found the courage to tell Kelsey how much she means to you. So much that you gave up the woman you loved to save her."

"No child needs that kind of baggage."

"She's not a child, William. Open your eyes and look at what's on the land around you for once in your life."

"What about you? Have you decided to stop blaming me for the death of your son and the loss of whatever it is you think I stole from you?"

Meredith rubbed a hand over his face. "Graham chose his own way. It does no good to blame anyone else. As for the other…." He sensed Kelsey approaching over the heather, a small pack on her back. She waved and increased her pace the last hundred yards, arriving breathless at the cottage.

"Is he any better?"

Meredith shook his head. A look of pain crossed her face. Nodding a greeting to her father, she hurried inside. Meredith followed. She dropped the pack inside the door and hurried to the bedside.

Meredith watched her, hair as dark as a moonless night, eyes the color of the sea he lived for, caring evident in the tense line of her body as she knelt by the bed and took Cade's hand. She did love him and Meredith suspected that what he'd mistaken for simple lust on Cade's part was in reality a love as deep as hers. Perhaps there was hope for them.

If they could make Cade well. If.

"Come child. There's much to be done, and I need your help."

Hours later, Kelsey sat at the battered table and rested her head on her arms. Meredith administered the last of the potion she'd helped him concoct. Cade protested and grimaced, but drank. Her father sat in a straight chair and studied her.

"What kind of witchery have you become involved in, daughter?"

She raised her head and smiled. "Herbal medicine, Dad. People have been using it for centuries. It's making a comeback, even in the States." When he didn't respond, she continued. "I discovered toxins in the red algae growing in the islands in the western and southern portions of Orkney. The islands east of the North Sound don't have the algae growth, thus no toxins, therefore no sick and dying seals. It's a type of distemper."

Her father raised a brow. "So what does all this have to do with young Douglas?"

From the corner of her eye, she saw Meredith slightly shake his head. So her father didn't believe in the selkies, despite the impact it had on his own life. She regrouped her thoughts. "Apparently, Cade's immune system reacted in much the same way, which, based on the research I've done in Baltimore, isn't unusual."

Her father spread his hands. "Perhaps, but humans don't cavort in the sea here."

"They do if they're trying to save someone's life." At his shocked look, she hurried to explain. "Dr. Norlund pushed me overboard several days ago when we were on an expedition. Cade saved my life."

"What? Bracken knew? And didn't turn Norlund in?" He gestured furiously. "It doesn't matter. You and I are leaving this place of madness immediately."

She shook her head. "Norlund's dead. Bracken's been arrested. I still have work to do here."

Her father stared at her. "You can't be serious. What can be left to accomplish? The Foundation will have no choice but to shut down the project."

She sat up straighter. "Not if I can convince them to let me continue."

"You?" He arched a brow. "But you're—"

"Not a little girl, anymore, Dad. I'm perfectly capable of running the project here and unless the Foundation decides otherwise, I'm not leaving Orkney."

He stood, plainly not ready to give up the argument. "You're exhausted, not thinking clearly. Come. We'll go back to the inn and discuss this in the morning."

Realizing he was right, she'd had a rough day and desperately needed a good night's sleep, Kelsey went to say goodbye to Cade. She brushed a silky lock of hair from his forehead and bent to leave a kiss.

Rising, she met Meredith's gaze. "I'll be back in the morning. The backpack is Cade's, but there's something inside I'm sure you'll want to put away."

Meredith nodded and touched her lightly on the abdomen. He lowered his voice to a whisper. "Have no fear, child. Even though one may possess gifts from their father, everything will be as you wish it."

Relief washed through her. He was trying to tell her she

didn't have to fear for her unborn baby. She squeezed Meredith's hand. "Thank you."

After their footsteps died away, Meredith left Cade's side and retrieved the backpack from where Kelsey had set it near the door. Hands trembling with weariness and anticipation, he struggled with the zipper, then took a deep breath. He drew out a silvery pelt, the fur rich, exotic and his. Closing his eyes, he rubbed his cheek against the softness and let contentment wrap him. So Bracken had been the culprit. He could let go of his anger at William Bouschour. Because after twenty-five long years, he could go home at last.

Chapter Twenty Six

Her father insisted on accompanying her to Kirkwall for the inquest, then on to London for a meeting with the Foundation. Afterwards, he took her to dinner at the city's best Chinese restaurant.

Raising his wineglass, he tapped it with hers and smiled. "Congratulations, Dr. MacKenzie. May you be most successful as the new director of the Orkney project."

"Thanks, Dad." She smiled and took a tiny sip of wine, not wanting to spoil his celebration, yet not ready to tell him the results of the doctor's visit she'd also had in London while he'd renewed acquaintances at the university. Instinctively, she let her palm curve around her stomach and smiled, gazing into the glow of the candle and seeing Cade.

"When is the baby due?" he asked quietly, his voice cutting through her wistful daydreams.

She whipped her gaze up to meet his, but relaxed slightly from the love she saw shining in his eyes. Still, she stammered, too taken aback to even think about denying it. "How did you know?"

"You have a glow about you. A way of touching your stomach when you think no one will notice. A tenderness in your eyes. Your mother had that same look."

This was her chance to ask him. Probably the best opportunity she'd ever have and the only one for some time since he was leaving again as soon as he accompanied her back to Orkney. "Tell me about her." Kelsey reached for her water goblet and took a sip.

William rested his arms on the table and stared over her head. A few weeks ago, his failure to meet her eyes would have made her nervous, but she let him take his time, knowing he would tell her in his own way. His smile grew soft and contemplative and sent a flutter of sorrow through her. He had loved her mother, it was obvious in the sad acceptance in his expression. "She was beautiful, like you. Dark hair to her waist. Eyes the color of the sea. A brilliant archeologist, very driven." He drank some of his wine and was silent for several moments before he continued.

"Your mother was disowned by her family when she ran away with me thirty years ago. She wasn't even as old as you, but our interests were similar. I thought we could be happy together, and for a while we were, but it didn't last.

"She decided she had to return to Orkney, just for a visit, even though her own family was no longer here. Then she wouldn't leave until she'd unearthed all she needed to prove the source of the legends the islands are so famous for. Or so she said. I had much work to do myself and it's never mattered what I called home, so we settled into the cottage near the inn, and I took to the sea." William sat back in his chair.

"She calmed down for a time after you were born, but soon she was back into her digs, unearthing all manner of strange artifacts and even stranger tales.

"I was offered the chance of a lifetime—a well funded project in the Great Barrier Reef. Dennis Bracken and I sailed to Australia and were gone for nearly a year."

"I don't remember," Kelsey said softly.

His eyes filled with anguish. "You didn't remember me, either, when we finally came back. As for your mother—" He looked away but forced himself to continue.

"She was pregnant, far enough along to be showing beneath her full dresses, her belly round as a ripe melon, her head bursting with stories of shape shifters and silver seals."

Kelsey swallowed as a gentle memory of her mother singing her a Scottish lullaby came to mind. Although her mother's voice rang sweet and clear in Kelsey's mind, the words blurred into the strange dialect she heard only in her deepest dreams and didn't understand. "Then you never believed Bracken's theory about there being an undiscovered breed of silver seals."

Doubt flashed briefly across his face before his eyes narrowed. "Preposterous. How could an entire species live in an inhabited area and yet not a soul has ever seen one? But she believed. Somewhere between the time she took Graham Douglas as a lover and the days preceding my return, she became convinced that her lover wasn't a fisherman, but some sort of creature who could turn itself into a seal."

"What happened?"

"Night after night, I'd wake up to find her out in the chill air, rocking on the porch, staring out to sea. If I went into the village, I'd come home to find her at the cliffs. One day, she took you with her."

The memories she'd recaptured the day Norlund fell came swarming back, stealing her breath, making her heart race. Her mother standing at the precipice, a man who looked much like Cade pleading with her. The little girl she'd been trying to wriggle her fingers from her mother's death grip. *Let go, Mommy. You hurt me.*

Kelsey took a deep breath, gazed into the candle flame and continued her father's story. "You followed her up there and met Graham Douglas for the first time. You argued with him, then with her. Mother wrapped her arm around my shoulders. She said it wasn't any use being with either one of you, both of you loved the sea more than you loved her. That she'd made a choice when she married you and couldn't go back."

The scene replayed like a slow motion video, Graham lunging towards Annabelle, the ground crumbling beneath Kelsey's feet, her father's hand reaching out and wrapping around her tiny fingers. Her leg slamming into the jagged cliff. Two bodies crumbled on the rocks, her father pulling her to safety. She stared without seeing into the flame. "He tried to save mother. You saved me."

He spread his hands. "She was not herself when I returned from Australia. I blamed myself for leaving her alone so long."

The realization came swiftly, like a spring tide that washed over her, flooding out her own doubts. Her mother had despaired of Graham's love, not over the unknown fate of the baby she'd carried, like Dr. Norlund had tried to tell Kelsey. Even Annabelle hadn't been afraid of having a selkie child. Somehow the thought proved enormously relieving.

She looked up at her father. "It's not your fault. She could have chosen to go with you, and didn't. She could have gone with Graham, but didn't. She may have been asking you to force her to make a choice. I don't believe she meant to fall."

He sighed. "Perhaps not. I think I could have forgiven her if only she would have given me the chance." Silence stretched between them again, but it was a bonding, comforting quiet. "Do you love young Douglas?"

Kelsey nodded, unable to stop the smile that sprang to her lips.

"And he's going to do the right thing by you?"

She lowered her eyes. As if she had any idea what the "right thing" was in this instance. Perhaps the best thing, the safest thing for Cade and his family would be for her to board the Mystic Maiden and go with her father to Spain. Impossible. She couldn't leave Orkney after she'd finally found the place where she belonged. "Now don't get any ideas of dragging him to the altar with a harpoon," she teased. "We'll work things out once he's well."

The waiter arrived with the bill and three fortune cookies. Kelsey selected one and waited for her father to open his.

He grinned. "New horizons await you."

"That must mean your project in Spain is about to end." She cracked hers open and tugged the tiny strip of paper out. "Accept love in all its faces." Meeting her father's loving gaze and thinking of how much she loved Cade and the child she carried, she knew she already had.

Several days later, shortly after landing in Orkney, Kelsey went to Meredith's to see how Cade was faring. Everything about this island beckoned to her, drawing her in like the home she'd never had. The soft scents of grass, the tang of peat fires, the saltiness of the sea air embraced her.

As she climbed the last ridge, the cottage came into sight, the thatched roof stark against the blue-gray backdrop of endless sea. Dread gripped her stomach. No welcoming wisp of smoke curled from the chimney. No one sat in the rocker on the porch.

Her heart as leaden as the sky surrounding her like an overturned bowl, she walked up the steps and rapped at the door, although with the emptiness pounding in her ears, she knew no one would answer.

After several minutes that felt longer than her whole life, she tried the latch, found it unlocked and stepped inside. The cot Cade had used was neatly made, the blankets folded at the foot. The floor was swept, the pots clean.

He must be well, then. Meredith would have left word if Cade's condition had worsened. Which could only mean one thing: now that Meredith had his pelt back, both of them had returned to the sea. To someplace where she could never find him.

She'd never see him again.

Loneliness battering her soul, she sank to the cot and gathered up the folded blanket. Cade's scent of musk and sea air still clung to the soft wool. She buried her face in it and let the sorrow engulf her, sobbing tears wrenched from deep within.

Why did it have to end? Why was life so cruel to bring her together with the one man who made her complete, only to tear her from his side? She pictured him with Eleanor and Brodrik and the other cousins enjoying the sea, sharing a life she couldn't even fully imagine. Did he think of her and wish for a different ending?

A long time later, exhausted from weeping, and feeling as empty as the cottage, she put the blanket back, took a steadying breath and with one last lingering look, walked away. He wasn't coming back here. She knew it with the same certainty she had that the waves would continue to reach the shore.

On the gentle shores of Seal Island, Cade doubled over, pain stabbing deeply into his chest. Eleanor dropped the sheaf of sea grasses she held and rushed to his side.

"Meredith, come quickly!"

By the time Grandfather reached him, Cade, clutching his side, had managed to sit. Closing his eyes, he leaned his head back against the stone wall of the cottage they were rebuilding. What the devil was the matter with him? Ever since they had arrived here, he'd been getting stronger every day. Today he'd been certain that the time to leave and find Kelsey was nearly here.

Meredith hovered over him. "What is it?" Leaning down, he brushed Cade's hair back, and laid roughened fingers against his forehead. "No fever. Eleanor, fetch some water."

Blast it, anyway. He was tired of being treated like a sick pup. Cade caught at Meredith's hand. "I'm fine. I just need to catch my breath."

"You need to lie down, that's what you need. Why you insist on wearing yourself down this way," Meredith's voice trailed off.

Grandfather didn't understand the driving need he had to finish the cottage and make it a home. He had to have a place, on the long shot that he could convince Kelsey to come back with him. "Something is wrong with Kelsey. She is ill, or hurting. I can feel it."

Meredith snorted and seemed to relax. "Hardly. The girl's

a little too healthy, if you ask me."

Something strange in his grandfather's voice made Cade open his eyes and lurch to his feet. He gripped Meredith's shoulder. "What is it? Did she tell you she was leaving Orkney? Has she been ill, too?"

A strange gleam in his eyes, Meredith tsked and shook his head. "Nothing that won't ease in about six more months."

Frustrated to the limits of his endurance, Cade wanted to shake the older man. "Tell me!"

Meredith spread his hands. "I didn't want to make you go rushing off when you're still too weak to make the change. And I'm going to insist you stay out of the water near that island. Understood?"

He'd promise anything, if only Grandfather would get to the point. "Agreed. Now tell me."

"It would appear your elders have been misinformed about the situation, probably because we didn't realize the implications of her heritage."

Cade shook his head in an attempt to clear it and make sense of what his grandfather was saying. "I don't understand."

Meredith shrugged. "Neither did I at first. This has never happened in our history—a selkie woman marrying a man, raising a human child. I didn't want to believe your father's insistence that Annabelle was another like us, from a different clan, of course. I thought he was merely trying to justify his obsession with her."

"Are you telling me that Kelsey's mother was a selkie?"

"Yes."

"And Kelsey?" He hardly dared hope for what he wanted most.

"Kelsey is pregnant." Meredith's eyes shone with a pride that belied the gruffness in his voice.

For a moment, a thrill of possessiveness raced through Cade. Then he slumped back against the stones. He'd given her no reason to think he cared for her. In fact, he'd done everything to push her away. How could he expect her to want him now? "How does she feel about this?"

"Like you'd expect: possessive, tenaciously maternal. Stunned. If you want a better answer than that you'll have to ask her."

Wary, Cade looked at his grandfather. He had hoped to eventually reconcile Grandfather to the idea of Kelsey living among them. Or he planned to abandon his life here and make things work in her world. Could it be possible to have the best of both worlds? "Then I have your blessing to go to her?"

Meredith waved his hand impatiently. "As if you wouldn't go whether I wanted you to or not. But yes. Since she's half-selkie, there is a way, if your love is true. But you must know your love to be as pure as the mist rising from the sea, and as enduring as the ancient circle of stones. If you and Kelsey believe all these things with every particle of your being, with every breath you draw, then here is what you must do."

For two days, Kelsey busied herself in the lab, making lists of supplies needed, going over notes and reports with her father and seeking his opinion or listening to his corroboration of her own. The Foundation wanted her to remain through the winter to finish the tests she'd started. Then in the spring, a new team of scientists would be formed with her as director.

"I'm proud of you, Kelsey," William said on the evening of the second day. "You've accomplished a great deal under extraordinarily bad circumstances. Are you certain you'd rather plant yourself here instead of on the Mystic Maiden? It will be a long, cold winter."

Especially without Cade, but at least she had the baby to be waiting and planning for. She patted her gently rounding stomach. "At this point, wallowing on the high seas is not a viable option. But I wonder if you know how much I appreciate the offer."

He bent and kissed her on the forehead. "Get word to me when you hear something from Douglas."

She nodded, wondering if she ever would, knowing that if she didn't she still didn't regret her time with him, nor did she regret the small life she carried inside. No matter what happened, hers and Cade's child would be living proof of how much she'd loved and been loved.

Her father left Orkney the next day with a promise to return for Christmas. This time she knew he'd keep it.

The afternoon of his departure brought the reality of her self-imposed isolation on her. Even Mrs. Devon's special blend of honey and spiced tea didn't ward off the lonely chill seeping through her. Unable to bear another evening of sitting in the great room, staring out at the silvery expanse of sea, she took her sweater and a blanket and left the inn, hiking up the hill to the thicket where Cade had taken her on a picnic in what now seemed like a lifetime ago.

Sunlight faded quickly in the autumn sky without the lingering twilight she'd become accustomed to. Unwilling to break the spell of other worldliness that always encompassed her at the pond and return to the inn, Kelsey spread out the blanket, then wrapped her flashlight in her sweater and made a pillow near the standing stones. She lay on her back. Stars winked in the darkening sky, but she stayed, lost in the memories of swimming in the pond with the silver seal. If only....

Droplets of water splattered her from above and Kelsey bolted up.

Cade stood over her, backpack in one hand, his fingers dripping with pond water. "Still wishing on stars, are you?"

Her heart slammed into her side, but she forced herself not to fling herself into his arms. "And why not? Do you know of a better way to ask for the impossible?"

He settled beside her, a small distance between them that

seemed as endless as the stretch of ocean from her world to his. "Tell me what you wish, and I'll see what I can do."

She wanted him—couldn't he see that? First, they had to talk about what she'd seen, what she now knew. About his family, him, the baby. "I'm glad to see you're feeling better. You looked like hell the last time I saw you."

He grimaced. "I feel like I've been there and back, but do you know what the worst part was?" He stretched out alongside her and coaxed her to lie beside him.

"Tell me."

His fingers traced the shape of her face, brushed a wisp of her hair back. "Waking up and finding you gone."

"Then why didn't you wait for me to come back?"

"Grandfather was anxious to rejoin the rest of the family and felt that I needed more time to recuperate, away from here. We're rebuilding the cottages on Seal Island."

Kelsey considered that and wondered if that meant he would be living with his family now. "Just who is the rest of the family I keep hearing about?"

He brushed her lips with the tips of his fingers and grinned when she nipped at the pad of his thumb. "Well, you've met Eleanor and Brodrik. They're my half-sister and brother. A few aunts, uncles, a few cousins, Meredith. About thirty of us, all related by blood or marriage."

Marriage. Kelsey swallowed. She wondered what constituted that in his world. Meredith's reaction to her pregnancy had indicated that the sea cave where she and Cade made love the first time was a special place. Perhaps in the eyes of his people they were already as good as married. The thought gave her a flutter of pleasure. "And they all can—they're all—"

"Selkies." He bent and whispered a kiss against her lips. "Does that scare you?"

She wanted to kiss away the anxiety she saw on his face. "No. It's just—mind-boggling. I watched Eleanor change. It was like watching a rosebud bloom under time-lapse photography."

He watched her carefully, searching her eyes. "How did that make you feel?"

"A little scared. Awed." She hesitated. "Jealous."

His brows shot up. "Jealous? Of Eleanor? Why?"

"She looked so graceful, so at one with her surroundings. It made me wish I could change. All my life I've been so clumsy. I've always admired the seals for their grace and speed."

He rolled onto his back as if he hadn't considered that a possibility and was silent.

Sensing her opportunity, she decided to dive right in. "I have something to tell you, but before I do, I want you to know I'm not expecting or making any demands of you."

"You're pregnant."

She frowned, disappointed at not being able to tell him herself. "Meredith told you."

"Grandfather has told everyone in the family. He's so proud, you'd think it was his child, not great-grandchild." Cade laughed and turned towards her, touching her abdomen reverently, then placing his ear against the slight curve of her belly.

She sifted her fingers through his hair. "It's too soon to tell anything that way. I can barely feel any movement myself."

He cupped his palm over her stomach and gazed up at her. "But you're quite sure?"

"Yes. I saw a doctor while I was in London."

"What do you think we should do?"

Get married, find a vine-covered cottage to live in, she wanted to say. *Live happily ever after.* "I already told you I wasn't expecting anything from you."

He scowled, reminding her of the fierce intensity he showed her when they first met at the beginning of the summer. "Is that your way of saying you want me out of your life?"

How could he think that after what they'd been through? Unless it was what he wanted. "It's just that—I understand there's a part of your life I can't share."

"Can't? Or won't?"

She wondered how he could even ask, but decided his need for reassurance must run as deep as her own. She knew too well what it was like to be different and long for acceptance. Well, someone had to be the first to say it. She cradled his face in her hands. "I love you, Cade. And I want to be with you."

He covered her hands with his. "Once you commit, there is no turning back. Your mother learned that the hard way."

"What are you saying?" She clung to him, knowing what he was going to tell her before he spoke the words.

"Your mother was a selkie. A different clan than mine, and she gave up her family to marry your father. But she regretted it as soon as they returned to the islands."

"Did my father know?" She whispered, as if that somehow could ease the hurt William had felt over Annabelle's deception.

He trailed a gentle finger down her cheek. "No, I don't think he ever realized she spoke the truth and not some madness."

"Then that means—" She waited from him to continue, her heart beating a furious rhythm.

"You can be one. But once you choose, it's forever." He reached into his backpack and pulled out his silver pelt, then draped it over her lap.

Kelsey ran her fingers through the luxurious fur. To live in the sea, to swim with a grace she'd never have on land. How she'd envied Eleanor and Brodrik and all the seals she'd worked with over the years.

Watching her, he let his fingers hover over hers, then caressed her skin as she stroked the fur. "We live very simply. We have to, in order to avoid detection. You wouldn't be able to see your father."

"I don't see him much now." Still, the thought gave her a pang of sadness. At last she and her father had managed to come to an understanding, a mutual acceptance. To think of never being able to talk with him, see him, hug him, filled her with melancholy. But if seeing her father was what she must sacrifice in order to be with Cade, she would do it. She would never love anyone else the way she loved Cade. She knew it with every part of her being.

Still watching her carefully, he continued his hypnotic caress. "We would have to arrange it so that he wouldn't come looking for you."

His words wrenched her heart. "He doesn't believe in selkies. Or silver seals."

"He believes what he must, in order to continue. But, Kelsey. If he decided to search for you in Orkney, it would cost the existence of my entire family."

She thought of his acceptance of her pregnancy, his concern for her. How he'd saved her from her mother's fate. Tears stung her eyes, but she nodded and her voice was shaky. "How many times must I prove I would do anything for you?"

He cupped the back of her head and pulled her down for a gentle kiss. "One more time, Kelsey. You have to trust me completely."

"I do," she breathed. "Oh, Cade, you know I do."

His mouth coaxed, drawing her inevitable response. Her tongue mated with his, teasing and withdrawing, letting him delve deeply. He squeezed her waist, then his hand trailed down her hip. She eased down beside him, lost in his kiss, his caresses and before she realized what he was doing, he'd unbuttoned her oxford shirt and was sliding it down her arms. Kelsey shivered, as much from the velvet of his lips on her throat as from the cool air brushing her skin.

He removed her jeans, then placed her lacy bra and

panties on top of the stack of clothes before he began slowly unbuttoning his own shirt, then jeans. His clothes joined hers in a haphazard pile, then he stretched out alongside her and ran his hands down her back, rocking her against him. She moaned, and his mouth sought her breast while his fingers worked magic, coaxing and caressing until her skin ignited and she shuddered, hovering on the brink of completion.

"For me, there is only you." His gaze locked with hers, hot and intense as he entered her, cupping her buttocks and pulling her tightly against him as he moved with delicious languor. "If you truly want to change, then come with me. Don't hold back and don't take your eyes from mine. Let me share my magic and make it yours. I love you, Kelsey."

Kelsey gripped his shoulders, unsure what he meant, already lost in the heady upward spiral of her climax. He drew the silver pelt over them and thrust into her, over and over, drawing out the action, savoring her response, waiting for the moment of complete trust.

"I love you." The words tore from her throat as she gave up control, gave of herself, and shattered around him. Release roared through her, spreading to the tips of her fingers and toes, rushing across her skin like a heat wave.

She fell into his gaze, tumbling into a silvery pool from which there was no escape, and the world shifted around her. Terrified, but thrilled, Kelsey felt herself begin to change simultaneous with Cade's transition, as if she watched in a wavery mirror. Her bones softened, her body lengthened, stretched. Marsh grass whispered, a small fish swished deep in the pond, the earth smelled damp and rich as she became aware of a thousand sounds she'd never heard before, a hundred scents she'd never noticed.

At last the ground stopped shaking and her own trembling ceased. She stared into Cade's pewter gaze and knew she had become what he was.

Cade bunted her nose with his and she tried to laugh, but the sound emerged foreign and squeaky. He spoke to her in her mind, then withdrew and moved to the edge of the small lake.

When he slid into the pond, she followed. A hundred new sensations bombarded her senses: water caressing her skin like cool satin, weightlessness, moving beside Cade like a skater gliding over ice, the feeling of not needing a breath. Rich scents of mud, fish and ancient rocks surrounded her.

His instincts became hers, and she knew how to dive deeper, when to break the surface for a breath, how to propel herself with a gentle swish.

Cade rolled through the water like a torpedo and she imitated the motion, bumping into him, earning a significant look and his pursuit as she swam away, and he gave chase. Moonlight filtered down like liquid silk, coating him with silver. He was so beautiful.

And he wanted her. Kelsey's heart beat faster. There was no mistaking the elemental purpose in his friendly play. She let his thoughts speak to her, soothe her and deliberately turned her back, letting him coast alongside her. She nestled against him, at ease in the world she'd made hers, and they glided through the water together, souls joined for eternity.

EPILOGUE

A chill March wind drifted through the windows of the cottage and lifted the eyelet curtains, bringing the salty scent of sea, marsh grass and the faintest promise of spring.

Kelsey cuddled her baby daughter closer, gently caressing Tiera's perfectly formed fingers and toes. She was absolutely beautiful. Sighing with contentment, she tucked a soft blanket around the nursing infant. The sensation of the rosebud mouth at her breast stabbed into her womb in a rush of pain and pleasure. Closing her eyes, she rested her head against the bedstead and breathed evenly, letting the contraction ebb away.

The cottage door burst open, flooding the room with pale sunshine. Cade hurried to her side. "Are you all right?"

She smiled up at him and touched his cheek. "The midwife said it's not terribly unusual to have after pains with a first baby. It will pass."

He turned his head and pressed a kiss into her palm before turning his attention to the baby. Reverently, he brushed the dainty hand with his fingertip, letting the tiny fingers curl around his. "I brought you a visitor."

"You do good work, daughter."

The gruff voice in the doorway made Kelsey jerk upright so suddenly Tiera lost her grip on Kelsey's breast and wasted no time letting out a loud wail.

"Dad!" Kelsey eased back down and resettled the baby. "What—how—"

Cade pulled a chair up to the bed and motioned for William to sit, then perched on the edge of the bed. "You have a very distinctive style of writing, particularly to a father who's saved every research article you've published since your master's thesis. Your father was threatening to turn all of Orkney inside out searching for you. Meredith and I thought it best if he could see you for himself."

Since her "disappearance" from Orkney last fall, Kelsey had continued her research and through Meredith's mysterious connections, had published several pieces in various scientific and oceanography newsletters. Her father kept her research articles? She tried to picture him pasting each one carefully in a scrapbook like a beloved child's school papers, but the image didn't fit with the picture of her father she'd held in her mind all her life. Still the thought filled her with pleasure.

New lines of worry had creased William's deeply tanned skin. "Why didn't you send word, Kelsey?"

She reached out and gripped his hand. "I'm sorry. As you can see, we live very simply here. No phone, no mail." She let go of him and swept the room with a gesture, taking in the plain but sturdy wooden furniture, the braided rugs, the simple curtains she had sewn for the two room cottage she and Cade had made into a home. "I didn't think you'd understand my decision to stay here rather than returning to Baltimore."

He was silent for several minutes as if considering her surroundings, her healthy glow. "Who am I to say? I've spent most of my life on a boat, and it's your decision to make."

She let out the breath she didn't realize she'd been holding. At long last he realized her right to choose what she wanted for her life.

He handed her a package. "I brought something for the little one."

"Thanks, Dad." With Cade's assistance, Kelsey pulled off the pink bow and tugged pink and white paper and tissue from a plush toy. Synthetic silver fur shimmered from a rare burst of sunlight illuminating the room. Black eyes shone above delicate whiskers and a black nose. "It's a seal. A silver seal."

"Yes, well." For the first time in her life, her father actually looked embarrassed. A faint flush crept up his neck into his weathered face. "I thought she should have one. We can't have little Tiera growing up to chase after creatures that don't exist now, can we? I brought something for you as well."

Rising, he went to the door and brought in a dress-size box. "I've been saving this all these years, wanting you to have it, but not knowing how I'd ever explain it to you."

Puzzled, she motioned for him to set the box on the bed. Cradling Tiera in the crook of her arm, she tugged a worn string from the box and lifted the lid. Beneath layers of oilcloth lay a silvery-gray pelt. Kelsey pressed a fist to her mouth to stop a sudden burst of love and tenderness as Cade drew the soft fur across her lap.

"Your mother's." William's smile was shaky, his eyes bright with unshed tears. "She never told me, you know. And I was too blind to understand why this was so important to her until it was too late."

Cade took her hand and nodded so slightly, she might have imagined the gesture but for the pressure of his fingers on hers. He knew. Her father knew what Cade and Meredith and the others were. He'd always known.

No wonder he didn't want to study the seals in the North Sea. As a conservationist and humanitarian he had turned his back on what could have been the most exciting discovery of his career and this century in order to protect the selkies from people like Dr. Bracken.

To think that all the answers she'd ever needed in her life had been kept in an old dress box hidden away in some dark place. She let out a pent-up breath. "Where are you headed next?"

Her father leaned forward and touched the baby's head where she rested against Kelsey's shoulder. He let his hand linger before raising his eyes to met Kelsey's gaze. "Hawaii. We're continuing the series on the monk seals and that's the next most logical place."

"I'm going to miss you. I have missed you these past months." A lump rose in her throat, threatening a fresh burst of emotions.

He tapped her cheek with gentle fingers and smiled. "You'll be fine, Kelsey. You always have been. Now are you going to let me hold my grandchild before I leave for the other side of the world?"

She nodded, tucked the blanket around a satisfied and sleeping Tiera and handed the pink bundle to her father. He was right. She would be fine. Everything she'd ever wanted was right here in this tiny room, in this small cottage, on the most magical islands on earth.

Her father gently rocked the baby, a look of wonder and amazement on his face. When he smiled at her, she knew her happiness was complete.

She shared his awe. For love, she'd given up everything only to have it returned a hundred times over. At last, she knew exactly where she belonged.

Cade squeezed her hand, and she met his gaze, cherishing the words he spoke that only she could hear. "I love you, too," she silently told him. "Now and always."